# FIRST STEP

"You had no kisses stolen in gardens in your London Season?" Mark Camden inquired lightly.

Juliette wrapped her arms around herself in a mock shiver. "No indeed, for it was still quite cold then."

"Nor in any dark hallways or convenient antechambers?" Mark pressed on.

"Mine was a very brief Season, sir." She looked up at him from under fluttering lashes.

"I'm sure you regret your lost opportunities," he said.

Abruptly Juliette became completely serious. "No, never. I think a girl's first kiss is a very special event."

He turned to her. In the torchlit shadows of the formal gardens she saw his black eyes go even darker as they looked into her own. His hands came up and gently rubbed her arms below the puffed sleeves of her muslin gown. Juliette's heart began to pound as she poised to take her first step in her campaign of conquest—no matter where it might lead. . . .

# My Lord Ghost

*by*

*June Calvin*

A SIGNET BOOK

SIGNET
Published by the Penguin Group
Penguin Books USA Inc., 375 Hudson Street,
New York, New York 10014, U.S.A.
Penguin Books Ltd, 27 Wrights Lane,
London W8 5TZ, England
Penguin Books Australia Ltd, Ringwood,
Victoria, Australia
Penguin Books Canada Ltd, 10 Alcorn Avenue,
Toronto, Ontario, Canada M4V 3B2
Penguin Books (N.Z.) Ltd, 182–190 Wairau Road,
Auckland 10, New Zealand

Penguin Books Ltd, Registered Offices:
Harmondsworth, Middlesex, England

First published by Signet, an imprint of Dutton Signet,
a division of Penguin Books USA Inc.

First Printing, October, 1996
10 9 8 7 6 5 4 3 2

To my son, Craig Compton Calvin, who made this book possible by convincing me that "the willing suspension of disbelief" applies to writers as well as readers. For that—and for reminding me of ball lightning—thanks, Craig!

# Prologue

They tell a tale fair old
  Of the first Lord Hammerswold:

A worthy bride he spurned;
  For the wrong woman he yearned.

The wicked wench he wed
  Impoverished him, then fled.

His life too soon did end,
  His fortunes ne'er to mend.

Now the ghost of Hammerswold
  Returns to say full bold

Which bride the heir should seek
  If health and wealth he'd keep.

The Countess of Hammerswold reread the bit of doggerel on the front of the letter she was writing to her older grandson with a faint smile. "That old ballad isn't much as poetry goes, but it gets the point across."

"Actually, NiNi, I think it was the attack Jared had this summer that got the point across." The earl brushed a loving hand across his wife's creased forehead, smoothing a stray hair away as he had been doing for the last fifty-five years.

"It wouldn't be so desperate a case if Mark would marry, but after that disappointment with Patricia Markham two years ago . . ." The countess sighed in remembrance of her younger grandson's heartache.

"Jared says he's determined to wed as the ghost advises," the earl reassured her. "Where better to seek that advice than Hammerswold on All Hallow's Eve?"

"And what better way to give both him and our ghost a choice, than to invite several young ladies to spend a month with us?" The countess's brow smoothed. Her eyes crinkled with joy. "I will fill Hammerswold with eligible females—young women of good family and unblemished character. Blondes, of course, for it must be someone who catches Jared's eye."

"If you can get them to come, with Jared's reputation." It was the earl's turn to look worried.

"Oh, they'll come, for a chance to be a countess one day. The question is, will the ghost come? He hasn't seen fit to appear at any of our gatherings arranged for this purpose, for father or for son." There was a faint quaver to her voice as Lady Regina Camden, Countess of Hammerswold, contemplated her older grandson's long-prolonged bachelor state.

"Don't worry, love. The ghost will appear this time, now that Jared is serious about choosing a wife. Our family's apparition has never been one to waste his appearances."

Regina smiled. "That's true. Oh, I do so hope . . . I want to hold our great-grandson in my arms before I die." It was one of her rare acknowledgements of increasing fragility.

"You will, love." The earl sat on the bed beside his beloved wife and gathered her in his arms. *There will be a ghost this year*, he swore to himself, *one way or another!*

# Chapter One

"Oh, my! It quite looks as if it *should* be haunted," the Honorable Adelaide Beasley gasped as she peered out the carriage window at Hammerswold.

Juliette Berceau leaned across the seat to join her cousin at the window. "It is certainly gloomy enough to satisfy the most Gothic of tastes," she agreed as she caught sight of the massive castle. Though only the oldest portion of the structure was said to hail back to the time of William the Conqueror, additions and renovations from Tudor times until the present had been made in imitation of the style of that ancient keep.

"According to the guidebook, three of the four massive curtain walls still stand, forming part of the park enclosure while enhancing the grandeur of the castle. The west walls were destroyed by Cromwell's armies, and formal gardens stepping down to the abbey were planted in their place," Miss Susan Campbell informed them, looking up from the *Patterson's British Itinerary,* her constant companion on any trip.

"Only just think, Julie! Ghosts!" Adelaide allowed herself a delicious shiver. "I declare, I don't know if I want to join this gathering after all! I think Mama was wrong to send us all by ourselves to a castle that is known to be haunted." She hugged herself apprehensively.

"By yourselves!" Miss Campbell, their erstwhile governess, now acting as their companion and chaperone, grumbled her objection. "I believe I have been insulted!

Your mother knows I will take care of you, and after all, it is a notoriously benevolent ghost, Addie."

Adelaide eased back against the cushions. "Ye-ess, I suppose. But much as I would like to be a countess someday, I don't know if I have the courage to face a ghost, be he ever so kindly disposed, to do so."

Next to Miss Campbell, the maid the two girls would share crossed herself and muttered in her native French. A nervous woman in her mid-forties, Marie was never a comfortable traveler. She was particularly unhappy to be journeying to meet a ghost.

Juliette smiled indulgently at her pretty blonde cousin. Though no featherbrain, Adelaide was inclined to be a good deal more superstitious and gullible than Juliette, who was determined to keep the younger girl from being imposed upon. "However deliciously haunted the castle looks, and however naughtily the viscount and his friends may try to frighten us, depend upon it, Addie, there is no such thing as a ghost. I only hope—"

But her hopes were forgotten as Juliette's eyes alighted on the enormous ruin that a further turn in the road revealed to them. Vast columns arched toward blue skies. Weathered walls long ago deserted by roof or window braced themselves against the elements.

"Oh-h-h," she breathed out in a mixture of awe and reverence. "The Abbey of St. Mildryth. It's . . . it's stunning!"

Though Adelaide leaned forward again, she wrinkled her dainty nose. "It just looks like an enormous pile of rocks to me. But only fancy its being so close to the castle."

Amusement lifted Juliette's eyebrows. "That's because the castle was originally built on the abbey's lands, to protect its holdings. How ironic that ultimately it was the owner of the castle who pillaged the abbey. The Camdens have used it as a quarry for centuries." She sighed. "Such a waste. Only think what it must have been once, to still be so magnificent today."

Adelaide's eyes lit up at a sight much more likely to capture her interest than any ruin. "A party of riders. They must be coming to greet us. They're so handsome! Such fine horses! Oh, Julie, we mustn't be hanging out the coach like country bumpkins!" She abruptly resumed her seat, jostling her cousin in the process, but not before Juliette had also had a chance to appreciate the sight of the line of horses flowing across the autumn-kissed fields and over the stone fences like a large, colorful, sinuous snake.

"That must be the Beasley chit. That's the last of them, then." Jared Camden, Viscount Faverill, motioned toward the coach they could see toiling up the winding road to Hammerswold. "I hope she is not as plump as that last one. Gad! Grandmama should at least give the family ghost a more palatable set of choices." His florid face heavy with disdain, Jared shifted his bulk in the saddle.

"You are hard to please, Jared. Each of those young ladies is in her own way a piece of blonde perfection. And aren't there *two* more expected? Else why did NiNi insist on my being here?" Mark Camden's irritation at being called from his pressing duties at Faverill Springs to spend a month with Jared and his rackety friends was evident in his voice as he squinted into the afternoon sun.

"Y-a-s-s," Jared drawled in a bored tone as he turned back briefly to glance at the distant carriage. "Miss Beasley and her cousin. No dowry and scarcely more than passable in looks, I hear!"

"There you are out," Jared's friend Victor Makepeace asserted. "Miss Beasley is a diamond of the first water! I say, let us ride down and give them a royal welcome." Suiting action to words, he put his spurs to his horse and was followed by Jared's pack of friends as he galloped eagerly across the field.

"Meant the cousin," Jared grumbled. "Miss Beasley has a generous dowry." He reluctantly spurred his horse after the others, leaving Mark to follow them disapprovingly with his eyes. They'd been in the field for hours; the horses were lathered and had no business being put to another se-

ries of stone fences. He whistled back the equally exhausted gundogs before they could follow the riders.

*So NiNi invited a plain, poor cousin*, he thought. His curiosity was aroused. Was that for his benefit, to include one
young woman who wouldn't feel she was wasting her time
if she had to partner him at dinner or dancing?

But no, likely the poorer the girl, the more determined
she would be to snare a rich husband. Mark grinned at his
own self-pitying thoughts. It wasn't as if he lacked for feminine attention. Second in line for the title, he would be of
little interest to these marriageable young ladies, but a
handsome, virile man was always in favor with married
women seeking an escort and, perhaps, a lover once their
husbands began to slight their marital duties.

Such companionship had been enough once. But by the
age of twenty-five he had grown increasingly dissatisfied
with existing on the margins of women's lives. He had
begun to yearn for one who would make him her whole
concern. He felt in himself the capacity to be a faithful husband to a faithful wife. Two years ago he had made up his
mind to wed. However, his chosen bride, Patricia Markham, had shown him how difficult it would be to find a
woman who would be contented with what he could offer
her—genteel poverty at the fringes of society.

Observing the riders attain their destination without
spilling anyone at the fences, he let out a breath he hadn't
realized he was holding, and turned his horse's head toward
the stable.

"Look at the state of those horses," Miss Campbell
grumbled.

"Those young men are very careless with their cattle,"
Juliette agreed.

Adelaide, however, found no fault with the parade of so-
cially prominent, high-spirited young men who surrounded
their carriage and escorted them the rest of the way to
Hammerswold. Mr. Makepeace claimed the position by her
window, to her obvious delight. He had been a favorite

dancing partner during their brief sojourn in London this spring. He was not so wealthy as Viscount Faverill, and his expectation was for a mere barony, but he was attractive and amusing. Juliette knew Addie wouldn't turn down the chance to be the future Countess of Hammerswold, but if the ghost bestowed his approval on another young woman, she thought Addie might regard Mr. Makepeace as a tolerable second choice.

As for Juliette, she smiled until her jaw ached, rather than let herself be put out of countenance by the poorly disguised disappointment of the man who rode on her side of the carriage.

It was Faverill himself. She was surprised to find a corpulent, florid-faced man, considerably older than she had expected. His blond hair was thinning, and his hazel eyes were bloodshot. His full mouth hinted as much at petulance as sensuality. The viscount was superficially attentive to her, but his eyes constantly darted past her to Adelaide.

Not that she particularly wanted the viscount's attentions. Faverill's reputation as a glutton, a rake, and a wastrel was such that she did not hope to catch his eye. In fact, she had been more than a little shocked when her Aunt Lydia and Uncle Ronald, Lord and Lady Paxton, had insisted the girls accept the invitation to spend a month in his company at Hammerswold.

"But Aunt, the man is barely received in society in London," she had protested. "Surely you cannot want him as a husband for Addie."

"It is not that he is not received, my dear, for mark my word, with his title and fortune in the offing, he would be welcomed in most drawing rooms and assemblies. He merely does not wish to attend. And mine is no purely selfish concern. After all, the ghost might choose you. You are just such a person as he is known to favor—morally upright, full of good common sense, and with an even temperament."

"Gracious, Aunt Lydia, I hope I am too full of common sense to want such as Viscount Faverill as a husband."

"But don't you see? The ghost always chooses a wife who can reform the heir and make of him a good earl. Now, either you or Adelaide would answer, I expect, and I owe it to you both to give you the chance."

Uncle Ronald harrumphed from the depths of his overstuffed chair. "Can't pass up a chance like that, my girl!"

"You can't reform a man who doesn't want reforming," Juliette responded pertly, biting back a smile and the temptation to glance pointedly at his swollen, gouty leg that was propped on a stool in front of him. Lord Paxton simply could not resist rich foods or generous helpings of port after his meals.

He caught the flash of amusement and shook his finger at her. "Naughty minx. Serve you right to have to take that young monster on!" Then, in a more serious tone, he admonished her, "Now mind, I mean one of you to nab him if you can, so you be on your best behavior, do you understand?"

Now, observing the viscount's disinterest, Juliette thought, *"If Viscount Faverill has anything to say in the selection of his wife, I need have no fear of having to take him on. He is as unimpressed with me as I am with him."*

The carriage drew to a halt in front of the massive central entrance of Hammerswold, which featured a huge covered carriageway where the drawbridge and portico had once been. The moat, of course, had long since been filled in. Taking in the magnificence of the place, Juliette experienced a flash of disappointment that Faverill wasn't an enchanting man who was instantly enamored of her.

Viscount Faverill left her to fend for herself while he hastened to be the one who helped Adelaide down from the carriage. Juliette motioned Miss Campbell to precede her out the other side, and let a footman assist her down, as all of the beaux had gathered around Adelaide. Marie followed her out, pale as the ghost she feared to see. For pity at her distress, Juliette sent her upstairs to rest, while she herself directed the unloading of their baggage and followed it up the steps. As she climbed the impressive carved marble central stairway, she paused to admire the intricate tile floor in the huge entryway. From here she could see that the pattern was the Hammerswold arms, laid out in meticulous detail in colorful Italian tile.

Adelaide, surrounded by beaux, stayed below to meet the other guests.

Susan would not let Juliette unpack. "You must not assume the work of a menial, my dear, or others will treat you as one. Marie will recover after a brief rest and attend to it." The former governess, taking her cue from the family, had never treated Juliette as a poor relation, and wouldn't permit Julie to behave as one.

"I like to be useful," Juliette insisted. But Susan's admonitory scowl made her lift her hands in surrender. "I'll just refresh myself a bit and go exploring, then."

"Shouldn't you rest awhile? I know I am quite done in."

"I am never done in, dear Susan. I am just so tired of sitting I may never do so again. I think I will try to find the long gallery and view the famous Hammerswold art collection." Juliette stepped to a pier glass and examined herself front and back, smoothing her sensible traveling robe of forest-green twill over her neat, well-proportioned figure, and quickly tucking a few stray curls back into her thick chignon.

She took the opportunity to reassure herself that she was not an antidote, in spite of the viscount's barely disguised disdain this afternoon. No, she was well enough looking with her rich brown hair and golden-brown eyes. It was only that around the frothy pink-and-white beauty of her cousin she showed to disadvantage. The cousins were both of average height, but Addie's slenderness made her seem delicate and willowy, whereas Juliette's fuller figure gave an impression of sturdiness. Where Addie's heart-shaped face hinted accurately at a sweet, pliable disposition, Juliette's square jaw and firm chin with equal accuracy made her look self-possessed and determined.

*So, we are different types*, Juliette acknowledged to herself. *Not all gentlemen are drawn to dainty pastel females.*

She strongly resembled her mother, and her father had fallen madly in love with her at first sight. He had also appreciated his wife's ability to stand up to the rigors of following the drum or making a home in a humble cottage. Juliette lifted her chin proudly at the thought of how like her mother she was.

"Do you think you should go by yourself?" There was just the slightest apprehension in Miss Campbell's voice.

"You aren't going to start, are you? There is no such thing as a ghost, but if there were, I am sure he wouldn't emerge in broad daylight. Get some rest, dearest. I'll return in good time to dress for dinner."

A friendly maid directed Juliette to the floor two stories above where she stepped eagerly into the bright but diffused light of two impressive stained glass windows, one on each end of a gallery so long and wide it seemed to her that one could have curricle races in it. Overhead a magnificent glass dome surrounded with elaborate plasterwork and painted cherubs brought even more light into the vast room.

Along the walls, artfully arranged, were paintings of every era, most of them family portraits. A full-length portrait of the viscount by Thomas Lawrence was the first to greet the eyes upon topping the stairs. The walls were punctuated at intervals by ornate alcoves, occupied by marble statuary. Again, some of this bounty was ancient, as cracked and discolored surfaces testified, and some was as modern as Sir Richard Westmacott.

Wishing she had a guidebook or a knowledgeable person to identify the various works and their subjects, Juliette began a slow, thoughtful perusal of the banquet of art spread before her.

Thus occupied, she strolled for some time before a faint sound, as of cloth rubbing against a hard surface, caught her attention. She stopped, listening. Was that breathing she heard? Shallow, carefully controlled breathing? A little shiver of alarm ran through her.

What nonsense! She tossed her head. *I'm letting Ade-*

*laide and Marie's sensibilities affect my own.* She returned to her perusal, slowing making her way toward the west end of the gallery.

Suddenly an unmistakable sound startled her like a gun-shot in the silent room. A cough! Masked, but nevertheless a distinct cough.

"Is someone here?" Juliette stepped away from the paint-ing she had been examining and looked toward the other side of the statuary niche a few feet in front of her. "I hear you and know you are there, so please show yourself."

There was no answer, but she felt sure her eyes could make out the dim outline of a man's figure in the shadows behind the statue. She felt a prickling at the back of her neck and along her arms.

"If you think to frighten me into believing you are the ghost, you are fair and far out, for I don't believe in them, and if you don't step out here, I am going to come in and drag you out!"

The erratic tempo of her heart told her she was not quite as brave as this speech indicated. But her bravado was not put to the test. Slowly a shape detached itself from the shadows and stepped forward.

# Chapter Two

In spite of her brave words, Juliette stepped back, her heart in her throat. But it was no ghostly apparition that emerged from the shadows behind the large statue of Apollo, but an elderly gentleman, modishly attired in a blue morning coat, richly embroidered red and gold waistcoat, and buff trousers. He was very nearly bald, with just a fringe of white hair around a gleaming pink scalp. His whiskers and bushy eyebrows were also pure white. He was so slender he looked as if a breath of air would blow him over.

This harmless-looking gentleman gave her an elaborate bow. "My dear young lady, please forgive me for alarming you. I am sure you will scarcely credit it, but my purpose in hiding myself from you was to avoid doing just that."

Juliette returned the bow with a polite curtsey, but her face must have reflected her perplexity at this excuse.

"You see, I was wishful of communing in quiet with my ancestors." He gestured widely to encompass the vast gallery, "and in so doing fell into Morpheus's clutches."

"You were sleeping behind the statue?"

"No, child. I was sleeping on the banquette there," he explained, pointing to the bench beneath the east window.

"I awoke to see you quietly pacing the other end of the room, and feared if I made myself known at that point, I might unduly alarm you. So I stole my way down here to Apollo, hoping to escape to the stairway while you were engrossed at the other end. Unfortunately—"

"I was heading this way!" Juliette laughed. "Well, no harm done. But I expect for propriety's sake I must go."

The elderly dandy chuckled. "You flatter me, my dear. I am long past being regarded as a threat to a young lady's virtue. Would you like me to act as your guide to the family portraits?" He offered her his arm.

As Juliette's enjoyment of the famed Hammerswold collection had been seriously curtailed by a lack of information, she willingly agreed to this program. She expected him to introduce himself, but he began lecturing upon the pictures immediately as she accepted his proffered arm.

Together they slowly walked the gallery as he regaled her with tales of the lives of the people portrayed on the walls, by artists from Holbein to Gainsborough to Lawrence. He was an informative raconteur. Juliette felt that she was receiving an illustrated review of English history.

When they had almost completed the circuit of the gallery, Juliette realized one important bit of this family's history had not yet been mentioned. "But where is the portrait of the first Lord Hammerswold? The one whose ghost is said to advise the heirs in their selection of a suitable bride?"

Her guide winked knowingly at her. "Ah, that one! You *would* be interested in it, wouldn't you, lovely lady? Perhaps you hope he will put in a good word for you?"

Juliette hastened to disabuse him of this notion. "No, indeed, sir, I assure you that is not so."

Surprised, the old gentleman drew a little away from her. "And why not?"

Juliette hesitated. This man was a member of the Camden family. She had no wish to offend him or them by giving her unvarnished opinion of the heir.

"I am ineligible, you see. My dowry is so small as to be counted as none at all, and I'm no beauty. We are here on behalf of my cousin, Adelaide, who is everything a gentleman could wish for in a wife."

"The ghost is not necessarily partial to beauties." The elderly man seemed disdainful of her objections.

"There is more to Adelaide than beauty. She is intelligent, good-tempered, amusing, and knowledgeable about how to run a great house."

"Your loyalty is commendable, but still, there is no doubt you yourself would make a fine countess."

Juliette chuckled. "That we shall never know, for the viscount, you see, *is* partial to beauties. Adelaide has already caught his eye. I, on the other hand, am invisible to him. And in truth, I do not think Viscount Faverill and I would suit."

"Ah, I see." The elderly gentleman balanced back and forth on the balls of his feet, considering her.

"You still haven't pointed out the ghost's portrait."

"It is so very difficult to get one to sit, you know."

Juliette laughed. "Yes, I expect so. Then there is no portrait of the first Lord Hammerswold?"

"Actually there is, but it is hung elsewhere."

"I see." Juliette studied her companion. He was looking very serious and a little sad. "Have I offended you, sir? Because if so, I beg—"

"Not in the least."

The sound of a loud gong startled Juliette to an awareness of the time. "Gracious! The dinner bell. Only look how late it has gotten, and I am not dressed."

"I relinquish you with regret," he said. "You are a charming companion."

Juliette politely curtsied in acknowledgement of the compliment. "It will be a brief parting. I expect we'll meet again for dinner." She looked expectantly at him, and then at the stairs, thinking he would escort her down.

"Would you mind very much if I do not accompany you? I wish to spend a few more moments here." Again a sad expression caused his white whiskers to droop.

Juliette nodded and turned away. He had said he wanted to commune with his ancestors. That look of sadness . . . Perhaps he sought privacy in which to find comfort for some bereavement by visiting the portrait of a dear departed loved one?

If so, he was doomed to disappointment. A booming voice announced more visitors to the gallery. It belonged to the viscount, just turning onto the landing from the flight of stairs below. On his arm was a classically beautiful blonde woman, leaning so heavily against him that her full bosom pressed against his arm. Her pink sprigged-muslin dress was alarmingly low cut.

"What, you here, Miss Berceau? Who's that with you? We heard voices." Faverill frowned up at her as he ascended the stairs.

Who, indeed? Juliette suddenly realized she had never learned her companion's name. Embarrassed by her inability to answer his question, she silently awaited the pair moving up the steps. Behind them, on the arm of an astonishingly handsome dark-haired man, was an older woman who resembled the blonde so much she must surely be her mother.

Juliette looked around, expecting her companion would step forward. He was nowhere in sight. "I . . . have been talking to . . . a gentleman. He's here somewhere." Juliette was rarely unsure of herself, but she was unnerved by the man's disappearance.

"Gentleman? What gentleman? I see no one!" The viscount gained the floor beside her and looked around.

"Why . . . he never gave me his name, but I am sure he is a member of your family. He knows so much about your history. Oh, where has he gotten to?" She turned about, bewildered and embarrassed.

"Jared, perhaps you will introduce me to this young lady?" The handsome man smiled at her, black eyes alive with interest.

Faverill introduced Juliette to his cousin Mark Camden. "And this is Mrs. Patchfield and her daughter Sylvia."

Juliette said all that was proper, all the time wondering where her mysterious gentleman could have gone. *He must be somewhat eccentric, to keep hiding like this,* she thought.

Mark Camden, after bowing courteously to her, looked up and down the gallery. "I do not see anyone either."

"Perhaps Miss Berceau has seen the ghost already, and stolen a march on us all." The blonde accompanied this suggestion with a tinkling laugh, but Juliette saw that her eyes were narrowed. Oddly enough, it seemed to be jealousy rather than ridicule that ruled her emotions. Even harder and more calculating was the look on her mother's face.

Juliette doubted that Miss Patchfield had intended to transfer all of the viscount's attentions away from herself, but that is what happened. Faverill sprang forward and took Juliette's hands in his own. "Is it true? Have you seen him? You must have done, for there is no one here. Only think, Mark, he's appeared already. What did he say to you? Did he say anything about me? He must have, else why did he appear to you? We must tell NiNi and grandfather at once!"

Juliette kept trying to slow this river of words with a denial, but she couldn't get a word in edgewise until Mr. Camden interrupted his cousin.

"What an enterprising young woman," Mr. Camden observed, his expression cold. "You're already seeing ghosts, and not in the castle a day."

"By no means! I have just spent the last hour touring your art gallery with a very lively and entertaining elderly gentleman. I leaned on his arm—he is flesh and blood! I cannot imagine where he has gotten to, but I expect you and Lord Faverill know him quite well."

Mr. Camden studied her intently while Faverill eagerly interrogated her. "What does this man look like?"

"Oh, bother." Juliette strode toward the alcove that held the Apollo. "Please come out of there and explain yourself, sir. You are making me look quite—" She stopped in astonishment when she was close enough to see that there was no one hiding behind the large statue.

She spun on her heel, determined to search every alcove on the floor, and ran straight into Mr. Camden's arms.

"Oof! Excuse me!" The man was solid muscle. She was thrown off balance and found herself supported by his arm.

"My fault for following so close. You had me convinced there was someone in there." He set her away gently.

"He's hiding somewhere, just as he was when I arrived, though he doesn't seem shy." Juliette moved to the next statue.

"Tallyho! We'll run him to ground," Faverill boomed, heading for the other end of the gallery. The two other ladies joined in the search. Soon the four of them had examined every nook and cranny of the large room.

"See anything, Jer?" Mr. Camden called to his cousin.

"Nothing. I checked all the hiding places."

"I know he's here!" Juliette stamped her foot with exasperation.

"Suppose you tell us what this gentleman looked like?" Mr. Camden had followed her, and stopped her by grasping her elbow as she sought to squeeze herself behind a rather shocking version of Venus. He was looking grim.

Juliette drew herself up and lifted her chin. "Certainly. He is a dapper gentleman of, I should say, seventy years or thereabouts, with a fringe of white hair on his head. His moustache and bushy eyebrows are also white. His eyes are brown, not quite so dark as yours. He is short, little taller than I, and very slender, almost fragile looking, yet he has a wiry strength."

Mr. Camden's countenance became only marginally less severe at this description, but Faverill was excited. "Do you hear, Mark. The old boy's put in an appearance already! He's going to do the thing this year. Exactly what did he say to you?" The viscount's eyes were alive with interest as he looked at her, in startling contrast to his bored expression as he rode by her side on the way up the drive to the castle earlier in the afternoon.

"If you mean to convince me I have seen the ghost, sir, I can tell you that I won't be so easily fooled!"

"I thought you meant to convince *us* of this, Miss Berceau," sneered Miss Patchfield.

Mr. Camden was watching her closely. His expression suggested that he shared the blonde's suspicions.

"Certainly not! I have no interest in . . . that is . . ." Juliette longed to tell the puffed-up viscount that she wouldn't wed him if he were a royal duke, but after all, the man was her host, nor did she wish Adelaide to suffer because her cousin had insulted the heir. "This was no ghost! He was as real as you and I."

"Never mind that. What did he say to you?" Faverill insisted. He made her repeat everything she could remember of their brief conversation, excepting his descriptions of the gallery's contents. Not wanting a shred more of Faverill's attention than she was already receiving, she also omitted the discussion of her and Adelaide's eligibility as the viscount's wife. Faverill seemed disappointed by what he heard. Still, when she was finished, he turned to Mark with an excited air.

"Well, cuz? He hasn't chosen yet, but he's prowling about, nursing the ground, so to speak. We must go and tell NiNi the news."

"NiNi?" Sylvia Patchfield tittered. "What a ridiculous name. Who is this NiNi?"

"My grandmother. 'Tis her pet name since childhood," the viscount explained. "Come, Miss Berceau." He took Juliette's arm and began towing her toward the stairs.

Mr. Camden positioned himself to block his cousin. "Grandmother will be very glad to hear Uncle Ramsey has returned from Italy."

"Uncle Ramsey? Ram Camden?" Mrs. Patchfield looked considerably startled. "I heard that he had left England forever, after the, ah, unfortunate incident."

Faverill nodded his head in agreement. "Uncle Ramsey! Not bloody likely. Been gone these fifteen years. Grandfather drove him off! Means to die in Italy."

"But Miss Berceau's description is of a living person," Mark Camden countered. "Ghosts are generally not so substantial, nor so colorful. They are usually quite gray, I'm told. Come, Jer, think! Don't you remember how much Uncle Ramsey resembled the portrait of the first earl?"

"Well, there you are, then!" Relieved to have the mystery solved, Juliette edged her way toward the stairs. "I must go and change for dinner." She was glad to note that the cold look in Mr. Camden's eyes had softened to a friendly twinkle. Still, she was off balance and wished nothing more than to escape. She completely forgot to wonder about the whereabouts of her mystery guide.

"No rush," Jared boomed out. "We are still on town hours. Come, let me introduce you to my grandmother. She'll be most eager to hear what you've told us, whether it is Uncle Ram or the ghost you've seen."

"But Lord Faverill, Miss Berceau must wish to make herself look more presentable. She must have stepped straight from her journey to the picture gallery." Mrs. Patchfield lifted a handkerchief to her nose, as if to imply that Juliette needed a bath.

"Besides, you promised you'd show us your famous gallery before dinner." Sylvia fastened herself once again to Jared's arm and fluttered long eyelashes at him.

Faverill looked helplessly down at her, obviously torn between his interest in his grandparent's reactions to Juliette's mystery guide and his fascination with Miss Patchfield's liberally displayed charms.

Juliette used the diversion to escape, and fled to their suite of rooms feeling a bit as if she had landed among bedlamites. Imagine the viscount believing a perfectly ordinary man was a ghost! And the Patchfield ladies so jealous of their prey, the viscount, that their very eyes seemed as if they might do a rival an injury.

Mr. Camden, of course, was no bedlamite. Now *there* was a gentleman who was awake on all suits. *And such a strong man.* Juliette felt a strange shiver run through her, a sensation she had never felt before, at the memory of his hard body against hers. Then another memory made her shudder: the cold look in his eyes for a while during their search. He had thought she was pretending to have seen the ghost, trying to dupe his cousin.

*I am glad I was* not *trying to deceive anyone*, she thought. *For he would be sure to find out such a scheme, and I wouldn't like to have a man like Mark Camden angry at me!*

# Chapter Three

Mark stood as far from the large fireplace as he could, avoiding what he regarded as excessive warmth on this mild October night. They were entertaining their guests in the Prince of Wales room, a recently redecorated drawing room so named because Jared had insisted on incorporating the Oriental style that the Prince, now Regent, had brought into fashion. Red and black predominated in the color scheme, and leering dragons peered at the humans from various places around the room—from statues perched atop the mantelpiece to paintings on the ceiling and cabinets. Even the furniture sprouted menacing-looking claws.

He was on the watch for Miss Berceau. She had left the gallery before he could ask her not to mention her unusual afternoon encounter in his grandmother's hearing. He hoped to convince her, as he had his cousin and the Patchfields, that Uncle Ramsey might have some reason for not presenting himself instantly to their grandfather and grandmother.

Recollecting that conversation, Mark shook his head wryly at Jared's stubbornness. He had not been entirely convinced the mysterious visitor to the gallery was his great-uncle, in spite of Miss Patchfield's lending her voice to Mark's persuasions. He earnestly wanted to believe that the ghost had made an appearance. Mark had been forced to show him where the slight film of dust behind the Apollo showed signs of footprints, to convince him of the corporeality of Miss Berceau's mysterious guide.

Even then, Jared argued the point. "Hang it all, Mark, a

ghost that can do the things ours has done in the past, could surely disturb a bit of dirt! And then didn't he just disappear into thin air?"

Miss Patchfield, who for all her sultry beauty was no birdwit, threw her influence toward Mark's interpretation. "Doubtless your uncle, like yourselves, knows some secret passageway from the gallery that permitted him to evade us."

At that Jared stared blankly.

Mark, better informed as to the workings of the household, laughed. "Of course! He must have used the servant's stairs, Miss Patchfield. There is a door hidden in the wall panel beside the public stairs."

"Oh, Mr. Camden, no need to be so circumspect. I won't tell. A castle without secret passageways and priest's holes would be quite a disappointment."

"Then you must, alas, be disappointed." He bowed to her ironically. "The Hammerswolds, being ardent persecutors of followers of the old religion, had no need of hiding places for its adherents."

Jared winked at Miss Patchfield suggestively. "I've always regretted the lack of such delightfully Gothic appurtenances. Only just think if now I had a secret entry into the bedrooms of certain lovely—"

Mark cleared his throat warningly. "Ladies present, Jared."

"Oh! Beg pardon. Out of practice!" Jared didn't look very chagrined, nor did Sylvia Patchfield look terribly shocked, though her mother's face had begun to turn an alarming shade of puce.

"I hope I can rely upon you, Mrs. Patchfield, Miss Patchfield, to say nothing about my uncle's appearance," Mark had requested. "My grandparents will be upset and perplexed that he has arrived without notifying them. I'd like to give him a chance to present himself appropriately, instead of being dragged out of hiding." The ladies had graciously acceded to Mark's request.

Now Mark waited to secure Miss Berceau's promise of

silence. He wondered if she'd told her relatives about seeing Uncle Ramsey. Very likely she had been brimming with eagerness to share the whole unusual incident. He shook his head at the thought of so many women keeping a secret. NiNi had yearned for Uncle Ramsey and the earl to be reconciled for years, but something like this would infuriate his grandfather. *I can hear him roaring, "Just the sort of thing that makebate would do,"* Mark mused.

The butler opened the door to the drawing room and Juliette appeared with a red-haired older woman and a dainty, extremely pretty blonde. Mark set his sherry on a round lacquered table as he hastened toward them.

He greeted Juliette cordially and then asked to be presented to her aunt and cousin.

"My aunt was not able to attend us, sir. May I present our dear friend and companion, Miss Susan Campbell. And this, of course, is Miss Adelaide Beasley."

As she watched Adelaide flutter her eyelashes at the viscount's handsome cousin, Juliette noted Mark's polished manners and impeccable attire. He seemed the quintessential gentleman. She wondered how to account for his complexion, which was dark and weathered, like a man who spent a good deal of time in the sun. It was not difficult to believe a gentleman might have such muscular legs, for they all spent substantial amounts of time on horseback, but how had he come by those wide shoulders, that deep chest that strained against the confines of the snugly tailored evening jacket?

She was not surprised at Adelaide's flirtatious manner, for Mr. Camden had as taking a countenance as any gentleman she could ever remember meeting, in spite of his unfashionably dark skin. Instead of the crisp curls he had sported this afternoon, his dark brown hair had been brushed and pomaded into deep waves. His straight, narrow nose was of aristocratic length, though no rival for Wellington's. His mouth was full, and when he smiled he revealed even, healthy white teeth.

And those eyes! Blacker than midnight and fringed with

long, thick lashes under high-arched, heavy, dark brows. This afternoon she had seen those eyes become cold with suspicion, but tonight they seemed invitingly warm. She was so lost in contemplating his attractiveness that she did not realize he had addressed her until he repeated his question.

"I asked if you enjoyed your brief tour of the long gallery with all of its family portraits?" Mark could not figure out how properly to get Miss Berceau *tête-à-tête* to ask for her silence, so he decided to test the waters. If she had told these two women what she had seen, they surely would reveal it by their reaction to his question.

Juliette noticed the wary yet hopeful look in Mr. Camden's eyes. *Hmmmm. Family secrets,* she thought. *I am glad I decided to say nothing to Adelaide and Susan.* She had not wanted to alarm Adelaide, not to mention Marie, who was already near panic.

"I enjoyed it very much, sir, though I am looking forward to a time when I can view the collection with a knowledgeable family member who can identify them for me."

"And this time you will wait for me to go with you." Adelaide asserted eagerly.

"I would be delighted to do so tomorrow, ladies, at your convenience." Mark beamed at Juliette, satisfied that, for whatever reason, Miss Berceau had not told the others what had happened. He began to introduce them to the other guests. It seemed that for now he had a little time to root out Uncle Ramsey and find out what he was up to.

As he did the pretty for Miss Berceau and her cousin, Mark reflected that, unlike as the two young women were, they were both very attractive. He was particularly drawn to the brunette. Dowerless she might be, but she was far from the plain Jane that Jared had led him to expect. Remembering the feel of her firm, well-formed feminine body in his arms this afternoon in the long gallery, Mark decided he was no longer sorry to have been included on his grandmother's guest list.

Juliette found none among the houseguests with whom she expected to achieve any degree of friendship. Like Adelaide, the other young women were all blonde—apparently Lord Faverill favored blondes. The young men were all just the sort she would have expected to be Faverill's cronies.

Except for Miss Patchfield, who seemed to her to be underbred, even somewhat of a mushroom, they were all of the best families. All of the young girls were most eager to engage the viscount's attention, which made for a pushing atmosphere that disgusted Juliette. And all seemed instantly aware of her status as poor relation. They gave her about the same degree of attention they gave Miss Campbell, which is to say, none.

Within ten minutes, Juliette was whispering in Susan's ear, "It is going to be a *very* long three weeks."

Susan hid a well-mannered chuckle behind her gloved hand. "Now, Juliette, if those young ladies continue to make such a cake of themselves around Faverill, you will have an opportunity to attach one of the other gentlemen. This is your chance to nab an eligible *parti*." She discreetly gestured toward the bored young men who watched the bevy of blondes flirt with Viscount Faverill.

Juliette gave her friend a repressive glare. "With the exception of Mr. Camden they are all of them far too much like the viscount to be of the least interest to me."

"Ah, Mr. Camden. *What* an exception." Miss Campbell sighed and patted her red hair, smoothing the tight braids unnecessarily.

It was Juliette's turn to giggle. "I have never heard you praise a gentleman of the *ton* before!" Susan Campbell harbored certain republican and egalitarian notions, and had little respect for the idle rich, though she successfully hid this fact from most of the world.

"Mr. Camden is an exception in more ways than you can guess!" Susan gave Juliette her wise, inscrutable look, and indicated they should remove themselves a little from the company. They sat in a *tête-à-tête* while Juliette listened eagerly to Susan's fund of information, learned from Mrs. Hopewell, the housekeeper, while Juliette was exploring the gallery.

"Mark Camden is the son of the earl's youngest son. Like his father before him, Mark acts as the earl's agent, managing all of his property. I've heard it said that his wise and careful management has greatly increased the earl's wealth. And Mrs. Hopewell says he has accomplished that while still treating servant and tenant alike in a fair manner."

Juliette turned thoughtful eyes toward Mr. Camden, who was quietly talking with the mother of one of the young ladies. "Then his dark complexion is probably not the result merely of years of riding to hounds, but of inspecting his grandfather's lands," she observed. Like Susan, she approved of gentlemen who had more on their minds than the cut of their coat or the bloodlines of their cattle. It occurred to her that though Mr. Camden was half a dozen years younger than his cousin, he was a man, while the viscount was merely an overgrown boy.

"Unfortunately, he is sure to be seeking a rich bride, for Mrs. Hopewell told me the earl's fortune is largely entailed. So it will not do to set your cap at him," Susan warned Juliette.

The butler's voice rose over the low babble of conversation, announcing the Earl and Countess of Hammerswold. Although Juliette had been aware that their hostess was crippled as the result of a long-ago carriage accident, she had not been quite prepared for the sight of her being carried into the drawing room in a special chair that resembled a throne on wheels.

The chair was carried to a place of prominence in the center of the main grouping of chairs and sofas, near the fireplace. Here it was set down and rolled smoothly into place. The two burly footmen who had carried it bowed to her and left the room as her husband adjusted the shawl around her shoulders.

The countess was dressed fashionably in a high-waisted

blue satin gown with blonde lace trim. She wore an ornate turban on her head from which floated several colorful feathers. Her hazel eyes crinkled at the corners, and a smile played across her lips as she fondly greeted her two grandsons and then, one by one, graciously met her guests. Her hand shook a little as she offered it to her visitors. In spite of the pleasant expression on her face, Juliette received the impression that she was both fragile and in pain.

By her side the elderly but robust-looking earl had drawn up a chair, and sat tall and straight in it as he watched the countess, concern and love glowing in his eyes. Juliette saw in his features and in his fringe of white hair echoes of the man she had met in the long gallery this afternoon. She also saw echoes of Mark Camden's features; the family resemblance was much more remarkable than that between the viscount and his grandparents.

As if reading her thoughts, Susan whispered in her ear, "I hear the viscount greatly resembles his mother."

Juliette nodded. She could see the resemblance herself, having met silly, vain Lady Faverill during their brief month in London during the season.

The countess kindly inquired about Lady Paxton. "I understand you had to leave town before the season was well begun, because she was ill."

Adelaide giggled and blushed a little. "My mother's mysterious malady turns out to be a baby on the way."

Lady Hammerswold was fascinated. "Imagine! Increasing at her age. Well, I doubt not the baby will keep her young!" The countess looked as if she envied Aunt Lydia.

Adelaide pulled Juliette forward and tucked her arm around her waist. "And this is Juliette Berceau. My mother wrote you about her. We are cousins, you know. Though she is as dear to me as a sister."

Both earl and countess smiled at her disingenuous expression of family affection. "I am very glad that you could join us, Miss Berceau," the earl assured her.

Juliette realized that the countess was studying her keenly, her eyes suddenly seeming almost to look into her very bones. She held out a thin hand and gripped Juliette's firmly. "I knew your parents, Miss Berceau," she said. "Your father was such a brave soldier. And your mother was brave, too, in her own way. Later we must have a quiet coze about her."

Juliette's face flushed, half in embarrassment and half in pleasure. Her mother's runaway marriage to an impecunious French count doubtless still had the power to scandalize, yet the countess had called her brave. She yearned to learn whatever this woman could tell her of the mother she had lost at the age of twelve and the father who had died at Waterloo scarcely two years later. "I will look forward to that, ma'am," she murmured.

The earl, too, looked at her intently. "You have the look of your grandmother."

"One of your flirts," the countess drawled, giving him a mock-reproving look.

The earl shrugged and winked at Juliette. "A lovely, lively lady she was."

Dinner was announced then, to the relief of Juliette and her party, who were *not* on town hours. Their rumbling stomachs had begun to trouble them even before they came downstairs.

The footmen claimed the duchess, and carried her chair into the long, elegant dining room, where they set it at her place. The earl hovered over her a moment or two to be sure she was comfortable before going to the head of the table.

The rest of them filed in according to rank, which meant that Mark Camden brought up the rear with Juliette and Miss Campbell on his arms. He didn't seem in the least put out by this. In fact, he was quite charming to Susan, which endeared him to Juliette. She had tremendous affection and respect for her former governess, and couldn't bear to see her slighted.

Mr. Camden turned out to be her dinner partner on one side. Mr. Algernon Fotheringay of the Hampshire Fotheringays sat on the other. He was a charming but somewhat rakish sort who looked Juliette over very carefully, his eyes resting long and often on her bosom.

It made her wonder if she should have worn the fashionably low-cut ivory satin dinner gown that had been created for her all-too-brief London season. Perhaps she should have worn a fichu? She glanced around the table to reassure herself that the other young ladies were dressed in the first stare of London fashion.

At first Mr. Fotheringay was inclined to flirt with her, but as the meal progressed, it became clear that his primary interest was in the different wine served with each course. He invited her to take wine with him several times, and she did, though merely sipping while he drank deeply. Long before the dessert course arrived, he was disguised and had ceased to regard her at all, in favor of humming under his breath. The words he occasionally mumbled to the tune convinced Juliette that she did not wish to inquire too closely as to the lyrics.

Mr. Camden's attention was claimed by his other dinner partner, the older woman he had talked to at some length in the drawing room. Lady Stephens-Hill was still very attractive, even though she had a seventeen-year-old daughter, Caroline, whom she hoped to marry to the viscount. She seemed to be setting Mark up for her flirt.

When he attempted to speak to Juliette as politeness demanded, Lady Stephens-Hill insistently drew his attention back to herself. As Mr. Fotheringay became increasingly inebriated, this left Juliette more time and leisure than she wished for in which to study the rest of the large party ranged around the tables.

There were the five lovely young blondes and their mothers, Adelaide, herself and Susan, Faverill's five friends, and the Camden family. No attempt had been made to make up the numbers with male guests. Juliette wondered if the other girls were fatherless. Faverill and his friends were such as might give a careful father pause, it seemed to her, once again mentally castigating her uncle for having insisted they come to Hammerswold. Doubtless the other fathers, like Lord Paxton, had not wished to leave their own estates at this time of year.

As she studied the company, Juliette's spirits fell. Susan, across the table, was being ignored on both sides. Adelaide was looking shocked at something Thomas Parton, Lord Tremayne, was saying to her. The earl was pontificating about politics to a very bored-looking Miss Patchfield. The countess was being shockingly ignored by both her dinner partners, who were instead peering down the décolletage of the ladies beside them. And Faverill, whose marriage this happy party was supposed to hasten, was looking neither to right nor left but shoveling in food and drink as if he had been on a prison ship for a fortnight. It wasn't difficult to see why his figure had begun to rival the Prince Regent's, corsets and all.

She thought, *So much exalted gentility at this table, and so little real civility!*

Juliette was unaware that a sigh had escaped her until she heard Mr. Camden's deep voice. "Not the most promising material for a house party, are we, Miss Berceau?"

# Chapter Four

Juliette's heart speeded up at the rich baritone of Mr. Camden's voice in her ear, and the feel of his warm breath on her cheek. She drew a swift composing breath before replying in her most practical voice, "I've seen better-matched company, to be sure, though matters could be improved somewhat by different seating arrangements."

Mr. Camden responded defensively. "If the arrangements are defective, you must blame me. My grandmother has been unwell, so I took over that responsibility, with suggestions from Jared and my grandfather."

"I meant no criticism, Mr. Camden. Sometimes it takes time to see how people interact, to know just how best to arrange them." Juliette's regret at having given offense was obvious in her voice and her eyes.

Mark Camden relaxed. "Oh, I see. Well, then, Miss Berceau, suppose you tell me what you would do to bring this collection of rattles and rakes up to snuff!" He lifted his eyebrows in challenge.

Juliette looked around the table consideringly. "Well, for one thing, I would place Miss Campbell at your grandfather's side, for she would love to hear his opinion on politics. Though if she grew to trust him enough to return the favor, she might shock him considerably, being very democratical in her tendencies.

"I am sure my grandfather would greatly appreciate such a dinner partner. That is well enough—go on!"

"Then I would arrange for Elizabeth Harpwood to be one of Lord Faverill's dinner partners." Their eyes swung to the plump young woman on the earl's other side. She was giving all of her attention to her plover's eggs. "Miss Harpwood is almost as good a trencherman—or trencherwoman, I should say—as your cousin, so she would not be upset that he ignored her to eat and drink. Doubtless would applaud it as a sensible way to approach an elaborate meal."

The black eyes began to sparkle. "And on Jared's other side?"

"Miss Patchfield, of course."

"Ah, yes. Sylvia does seem to have attracted his attention."

"So she might be able to coax a little conversation out of him where Gilda Whitten cannot."

Mark chuckled, eyes snapping with amusement. "So far, so good. But what would you do about my grandmother? Surely you don't think any of Faverill's friends will pay her an iota of attention with lovely young women on their other sides."

"No, I doubt any of them are up to such civility. But since there are so many more women than men, I would put two of the most compatible mothers on either side of the countess, instead of Sir Beauford Montrose and James Betterton, who are so studiously ignoring her. They would find a great deal to talk about, and their daughters could then sit on either side of the young gentlemen and charm them from their wineglasses."

"And where would you place ourselves?"

"As I am unconscionably selfish, I would place myself at your grandfather's other side. I too enjoy a lively political discussion, you see."

Juliette tilted her head to one side, making a great production of studying Mr. Camden thoughtfully. "As for you, why, I haven't quite decided yet. I would place you near whichever ladies needed you most, I expect. Perhaps between Millicent Davies, who is so very shy, and Miss Campbell."

Mark lifted his glass in salute to her. "Your plan is far superior to the one in effect tonight. In fact, I will see that your suggestions are followed tomorrow evening. By the way, I appreciate your keeping the appearance of our family ghost in the gallery quiet. He may yet name you as his choice, but I feel it *is* a bit premature—"

The twinkle in his eye meant Mr. Camden was probably quizzing her, but Juliette bristled at the import of his words. "You know that was no ghost this afternoon. Nor do I aspire to be the ghost's choice, I assure you."

"What? Not wish to be a countess. Pshaw!" Mark wagged his head at her. Not for a minute did he believe such a declaration.

"Not I. Certainly not if it entailed marrying Jared Camden." Juliette spoke in a more acidic voice than was perfectly polite.

"Perhaps I should be offended by your rejecting my cousin so emphatically." Mark tried to crush the odd little shoot of hope that was springing up in his mind. Was it possible there was a woman who would not automatically succumb to his cousin's title and prospective wealth?

"I hope you are not. No offense was meant." Juliette blushed. "It is just that I . . . that is . . ."

"Or perhaps . . ." Mark's brow crinkled. "Perhaps you have your eye on one of these other eligibles!" There was no reason why she should not, so Mark didn't quite understand his own anger at the notion.

If it would not have been a social solecism of the worst sort, Juliette would have thrown down her napkin and left the table. As it was, she drew in her breath and held it, to prevent her anger from escaping her.

"I am not on the catch for a husband, Mr. Camden!" She kept her voice low, to avoid attracting attention.

"If you are not, you are the only young woman here who isn't. Nor would I object in the least if you were. It is, after all, what every young woman seeks to do." Mark said what was only the truth, yet as he spoke he felt a guilty sense of hypocrisy steal over him. The fact was, he had grown very resentful about women's matrimonial ambitions since his unfortunate experience with Patricia.

"Your kindness is greatly appreciated," Juliette snapped, irritated at his insinuations. Giving him just the hint of her shoulder, Juliette turned her attention to the delicate meringue à la crème that had just been placed before her, sparing only the briefest glance at Fotheringay as she lifted her fork to her lips.

She was startled to find that the inebriate was staring at her, eyes bulging a little. "You saw the ghost?" He whispered harshly, obviously dreading her affirmative. "I heard Mark say you'd seen the ghost!"

"No, no, Mr. Fotheringay. It was his idea of a joke."

"Ahhhh." Fotheringay relaxed against the back of his chair. "Saw one meself, once, you know. Big ugly thing it was, with snakes in its hair and long fangs. Came right out of the wall and tried to gobble me up."

Juliette put her fork down abruptly. "Really, Mr. Fotheringay—"

"Really. And then the whole room filled with snakes." Fotheringay reached for his wineglass but spilled most of it on the way to his lips.

Appalled, Juliette couldn't think what to say. She was pleased when the countess began trying to attract their attention by ringing a little bell by her plate. She had never been happier to have a conversation interrupted.

When the hubbub of voices had subsided, the countess invited the ladies to join her in the drawing room.

"And gentlemen, don't spend too long over your port, for tonight I plan to tell you ghost stories." The countess's eyes twinkled with benevolent good humor, but beside her Juliette heard Fotheringay give a horrified moan.

"Winton, Mark, you'll see the gentlemen join us soon?"

At the affirmative response from her husband and younger grandson, the countess signalled and the footmen who had borne her into the room lifted her up and carried her out again. All of the ladies rose and trailed out after her.

No sooner had they arrived in the drawing room than the countess motioned Juliette to the chair nearest her, the one the earl had sat in earlier. Studying her with those shrewd hazel eyes, the countess murmured, "I wonder if you are as impulsive and romantical as your dear mother was?"

"I believe not, Lady Hammerswold. In fact, my relatives often complain that I am tiresomely practical!"

The countess smiled. "It is a good way to be; don't let them tell you otherwise. You take after your grandmother in more than merely looks, then." She spent a pleasant half hour regaling Juliette with stories of relatives whom, because they had turned their backs on her mother, she had never had the privilege of knowing. At the end of that time the drawing-room doors opened and the men entered.

Jared and his friends all looked and acted a little well to go. Their voices were loud, their steps unsteady. The earl and Mark Camden, however, both appeared quite in control. Juliette rose and relinquished her seat to the earl, taking a position on a backless sofa next to Susan. Adelaide joined them briefly, but two of the other young girls pulled her up and bade her join them in a giggling group closer to the countess and, incidentally, the viscount.

With the exception of Mark, the men ranged themselves around the room in various slumping postures. Juliette heard half-whispered growls of irritation at such tame fare as sitting in a drawing room listening to ghost stories. Mr. Fotheringay, the worst for wear of the group, did not look so casual as the others. He cast Juliette a strained look and took a seat as close to the fire as it was possible to sit without actually placing his chair in the grate.

Mark took up a standing position as far from the fireplace as he could get, much where he had been when they had first entered the drawing room. The look he gave to his grandmother was one of indulgent interest. *Does he believe in the ghost?* Juliette wondered, *or does he just love his grandmother and so humor her in her beliefs?*

"The story of the ghost of Hammerswold begins in 1539, when Ramsey Camden, Baron Fortmain, having established his loyalty to King Henry the Eighth, was made an earl and rewarded with a grant of land which included the newly suppressed St. Mildryth's Abbey. He took his title from this estate, called Hammerswold, which means Hammer's kingdom. It was named after a previous owner who had earned the sobriquet 'The Hammer' for the brutal, efficient way he had reduced the English's resistance to the Conqueror.

"The new Earl of Hammerswold was as yet unmarried when he was granted his lands and title. He agreed to be affianced to the daughter of a baron whose lands marched with his, who had recently died. The daughter's name was Matilda.

"The first Lord Hammerswold was well-enough pleased with his prospective bride at first, for she was personable and an extremely capable manager who had kept her father's affairs in good order while he had been intriguing at court.

"But then Lord Hammerswold met a beautiful woman of the court, one whose morals were suspect. She was spoiled and notoriously extravagant, but skilled in the art of dalliance. Before he quite knew what had happened, Lord Hammerswold had married this lady, Solange, instead of keeping his word to the king to marry Matilda."

All of the young girls' faces were turned to the countess in apparent rapture at this history lesson, but Juliette noticed that Miss Patchfield was with difficulty suppressing a yawn, and Miss Millicent Davies's features had a distinctly glazed look. Apparently the countess noticed it too, for she hastened the conclusion of her story.

"I expect the rest of it you know. Solange led the first earl a miserable life, wasting his money and indulging herself in infidelity. Ultimately she left him. His health failed, and he died leaving behind an infant son to carry on the line. Ironically, the son's guardians were Matilda and her new husband. They raised the boy well, yet when he was of an age to marry, he showed a tendency to choose an inappropriate bride as his father had done before him.

"It was on the eve of the second earl's betrothal to a beautiful, brainless adventuress that the Ghost of Hammerswold first appeared. He announced that his mission was to advise his heir as to which bride to select. If his advice was followed, the marriage would be happy and fruitful, and the earl would live a healthy life and die peacefully of old age.

"The second earl had rejected Matilda's excellent advice, which he thought a bit self-serving, to marry her own daughter. But he accepted the hint from his father's spirit, and just as predicted, the couple were happy, prosperous, and long-lived.

"So has it been ever since. The ghost appears when the heir is on the verge of chosing a bride, and makes it clear which bride should be selected. If the ghost's advice is followed, the marriage and the earldom prosper. If it is ignored, disaster follows. The prediction has thus far never failed, in over three centuries of marriages."

The countess folded her hands on her lap. "And that, as you all know, is why we are gathered here. My grandson, Viscount Faverill, has announced his intention of selecting a bride. Since the ghost has shown a partiality for appearing here at Hammerswold, we decided to invite you here to celebrate All Hallow's Eve with us. It was on that evening, fifty-six years ago, that the ghost appeared to me. Naturally, we hope that the ghost will advise Jared to marry one of his delightful guests."

The countess stopped. Interest had picked up as she brought the story to its modern conclusion. Adelaide leaned forward. "But my lady, I thought the ghost's advice was for the heir. Why did he appear to you?"

"An excellent question." The earl entered the conversation. "I was not so unwise as to fail to notice Regina's numerous qualifications that made her a suitable countess, not least of which was that I adored her. She, however, was not entirely sure she wished to be wed to such a wild young man as I had been to that point. My progenitor helped to convince her that with her love and support I could be redeemed." He leaned forward to pat his countess's trembling hand. "I am eternally grateful for his success."

Soft coos of admiration greeted this charming declaration. Miss Patchfield interrupted to ask, "How does the ghost manifest itself, ma'am?"

"The ghost has appeared in very different ways over the generations. In 1720—"

Mark Camden stepped forward suddenly. He did not like the avid look on Miss Patchfield's face, echoed almost precisely on her mother's countenance. Certain aspects of their behavior this afternoon had troubled him as well. Also, while he now regarded it as a very remote possibility that Miss Berceau had made up that encounter in the gallery, hoping to give the impression that she was communing with the ghost, he did not like to take a chance. He bent low and whispered into his grandmother's ear. She looked at him in surprise and started to say something, when Mr. Fotheringay spoke up.

"Y'r too late, Sh-shilvia. Ghost's already been seen. The palm goes to Miss Berceau. Already seen the monster, she has."

"I most certainly have not." Juliette tried to keep her voice from sounding hysterical. Of all the things for that drunken lout to listen to and remember!

"Has too. Wha'shmore, he'sh picked her for your bride, Jer. Heard all about it at dinner!" Fotheringay waved his hand confidently in Juliette's direction.

Everyone turned toward her, and Juliette was overwhelmed by the intensity of the emotions revealed by their faces, from astonishment, to jealous fury, to joy.

The countess found her voice first. Lifting her arms to Juliette in invitation, she cried, "Oh, at last! I am so thrilled. And I am sure the ghost has made just the right choice once again!"

# Chapter Five

Juliette now knew what a deer at bay felt when the hounds closed in. Most alarming of all was Viscount Faverill, who rose and bounded across the room. He dragged her to her feet, gripping her arms hard. "This afternoon you insisted you hadn't seen the ghost. Why?"

The earl, right behind his heir, growled, "You deny seeing the ghost, yet Mark told Fotheringay you have! Why?"

She cast her eyes around looking for Mr. Camden, who had crossed the room and was standing by his grandmother's chair, fists clenched. His eyes seemed to demand, "You've made this public. Why?"

She wrenched herself from the viscount's hurtful grip and approached the countess's chair. "Please, Lady Hammerswold, all of you, listen to me. I did *not* see a ghost. Mr. Fotheringay misunderstood a joking comment Mr. Camden made to me as we dined. You have but to ask Mr. Camden. He will tell you so."

The countess's face fell. "Oh, I see." She turned to look at Fotheringay, who was slumped down in his chair so far he was in imminent danger of falling out of it. "Whatever did you say, Mark, that could have given him that impression?"

Mark's fists had relaxed. A quirk to his mouth, he replied, "Miss Berceau was giving me some hints as to how to arrange the seating for dinner tomorrow. She has some excellent ideas; I am sure you will want to discuss them with her later."

Lady Hammerswold lifted puzzled eyes to her younger

grandson. "How could that have given Mr. Fotheringay the impression she had seen a ghost?"

Mark laughed, and Juliette was relieved to see that the laugh was genuine. His eyes as he turned them to her were once more warm with approval. "It was intended as a joke. I said that her scheme was so wise, the ghost might well name her as his choice. Fotheringay must have heard only part of the remark."

The earl looked between Mark and Mr. Fotheringay consideringly, but held his peace.

"He does seem to be a bit, ah, out of touch," the countess said, smiling at her inebriated guest.

"Seen ghosts myself," Fotheringay muttered. "Nasty creatures, ghosts."

Mark leaned down and half-dragged the drunken young man out of the chair. "Yes, I don't doubt any ghosts you've seen in this state were nasty ones. Think it's time you bid the ladies good night, Algernon."

As Mark escorted their mumbling guest from the room, the others took their seats again, chattering among themselves. The earl bent and whispered in Juliette's ear, "I would appreciate a word with you in the library after the countess retires." She nodded and resumed her seat. It was clear that the earl had not quite believed Mark's explanation of Mr. Fotheringay's remarks.

Sylvia Patchfield repeated the question that had gotten lost in the excitement. "Please, Lady Hammerswold, won't you tell us some stories about your ghost—how he actually appeared, what he did?"

The countess drew in a deep breath. "Perhaps I should save that for another evening. You young people will doubtless want to dance, and I know I am looking forward to a good game of whist."

Juliette did not join the dancers. She was far too fond of dancing to enjoy playing the role of wallflower, which she inevitably must do, especially with two of the men absent. Mr. Camden might have danced with her a time or two, but now both he and Fotheringay were absent, which meant the well-dowered blondes would absorb all available escorts. Instead, she obliged the earl with a game of chess. She had given him a good fight before tipping her king just as Mr. Camden walked up.

"She plays well enough to make one work for it," was the earl's recommendation as he stood to surrender his seat to Mark, who shook his head and held out his gloved hand to Juliette instead.

"I'm hoping you will honor me with a dance, Miss Berceau."

She lifted her chin proudly. "You needn't feel obliged to entertain me, sir. I am content to play chess or cards, or even to gossip." She nodded to where Susan and two of the mothers had their heads together in whispered conversation.

"As am I, on occasion, but just now I am eager for a dance, and you would be obliging me to be my partner."

He looked quite sincere, so Juliette dropped her prideful stance. "In that case, sir, I would be delighted."

Later the young people rejoined their elders for tea and some delicious spice cakes. Jared passed a flask around among his cronies surreptitiously but not so cleverly that anyone missed observing this fortification of their tea. Before the ladies had finished their refreshments, the viscount and his friends had withdrawn to the card tables for some serious play.

The countess watched them with a worried eye. To judge from her expression, she too had heard the rumor that Faverill was inclined to play deep. Mark leaned over and whispered in her ear, and she patted his hand, smiling.

Juliette thought approvingly, *Mr. Camden is so responsible. Clearly he intends to keep an eye on Faverill and his rackety friends.*

After tea, the countess declared her intention to seek her bed, and the other women, seeing that all hope of masculine attention was ended, rose to go also.

Juliette hung back on the pretense of asking the earl about a chess move, and then went with him to the library after the other women had disappeared. Miss Campbell accompanied them, making it crystal clear that she was here to chaperone Juliette as well as Adelaide, and would do so vigilantly. They had barely seated themselves before Mark entered, closely followed by the viscount.

Mark made it easy on her by urging her to tell the earl just what had happened that afternoon in the picture gallery. He and Jared added what they knew to the account. By the end, the earl's jaw was set in a furious grimace.

"That makebate brother of mine! To show up here and hide himself away, frightening our guests! Tomorrow, Mark, we are going to search every corner of the castle, root him out, and send him back to Italy."

Mark thrust his hand through his hair. "I don't think that would be right, sir. NiNi would be deeply grieved if she ever learned that he had been here and had not called in on her."

"Miss Berceau seems a reliable sort. You wouldn't tell anyone, would you, my dear?"

"Not if you thought best, but—"

"Miss Patchfield might," Mark inserted.

"Or her mother," Jared agreed. "You know you can't rely on a bunch of women to keep a secret."

Mark, observing the fulminating indignation on Juliette's features at this insult to her sex, hastened to add, "Or the servants. Someone must have seen him, and soon enough the news will have traveled through Mrs. Hopewell to NiNi."

"Hmmmm." The earl tapped his lips with his forefinger. "Well, I suppose we shall see what he has to say for himself first."

"Of course, it could have been the ghost." Faverill looked hopeful.

The earl stroked his jaw thoughtfully. "Likely not. Miss Berceau describes him in such vivid colors—brown eyes, shining white hair, scarlet waistcoat. The ghost is usually—" He turned suddenly narrowed eyes on Juliette. "Tell me,

Miss Berceau, how is it that you are so very sure it was *not* our amiable ancestral spirit you met up with?"

"I leaned on his arm as we walked. He was flesh and blood, sir."

"Mayn't a ghost appear to be flesh and blood?"

Juliette shook her head.

"Have you ever seen a ghost?" the earl persisted.

"Certainly not!"

"Then how can you be so sure what a ghost is like?" he looked as triumphant as when he had put her king in check earlier in the evening.

Juliette replied slowly, aware that she might be giving offense. "Because, sir, I do not believe in ghosts."

"What!" The earl and Jared spoke in simultaneous notes of indignation. Mark's eyes began to sparkle with humor again.

"Then to what do you attribute the various appearances to my ancestors? Both Grandfather and NiNi have seen him twice. How do you explain that, Miss Berceau?" Faverill queried indignantly.

"Not having heard all of the details, I am not sure how to evaluate these stories."

"Insulting baggage. You're as good as saying my grandparents are liars." Jared's fair face took on a mottled appearance.

"Certainly I am not! There are many possible explanations for what are called ghosts."

"Name one," he challenged her.

"Um . . ." *Worse and worse!* Most of Juliette's own personal speculations about ghost sightings would not be flattering. She believed sightings such as Mr. Fotheringay's, for example, stemmed from a bottle. "I think oftentimes people see what they want to see. Some sightings are surely pranks. Or perhaps someone who had something to gain from the appearance of a ghost had a hand in the matter." She darted a look at the earl.

"A perfect rationalist!" Mark exclaimed. "You would likely find a nonsupernatural explanation for every one of our hauntings through the ages!" Again Mark seemed more amused than angered. His back to his grandfather, he did not see the startled, guilty look on Lord Hammerswold's face that confirmed Juliette's suspicions.

Still, she could not allow Mark to think her so closed minded. "Not really. Though I do believe that most such experiences can be explained rationally, I do not mean to imply that I have no belief in the supernatural. But the idea of lost souls, doomed to wander between heaven and earth forever, no matter how beneficial their mission, is very offensive to my notions of Christian doctrine. After all, our Savior said—"

"A bleating theologian," Jared interjected in a tone of utter disgust. "Well, for your information, Miss Berceau, this family apparition has unerringly foretold the fate of one after the other of my ancestors. So don't prate to me of theology. After all, the Bible says 'There are more things twixt heaven and earth than are dreamt of in your philosophy!'"

Mark chuckled. " 'Fraid that's not the Bible, Jared. That's the Bard."

"Who?"

The earl's shoulders began to shake. "Your tutors ought to be horsewhipped! He means that quote is from Shakespeare."

Juliette interrupted before Faverill could express his indignation at his relatives' ridicule. "Whoever said it, I agree with it. I mean, I do believe in supernatural phenomena, such as angels, for instance. Perhaps what you have been calling a family ghost is really an angel. That means 'messenger from God,' you know."

Mark's eyebrows lifted in surprise. The earl's countenance cleared. "Now that's an excellent interpretation—"

But Jared's expression became, if possible, even more furious. "Not only a theologian but a bluestocking! Well, lost spirit or angel, the Hammerswold ghost does appear, and he is going to appear this year, to point out my bride to me. And I can assure you that he's wise enough not to sin-

gle out a bluestocking theologian for Jared Camden, so if
this is some deep game you are playing, Miss Berceau, in
which you first pretend to be talking to the ghost, and then
modestly deny it, to make me think you are the one, I assure you that you have wasted your efforts!"

The viscount stood and stalked angrily from the room,
leaving Juliette feeling sullied by his accusation. *Very likely
Mr. Camden, too, thinks I am a scheming female,* she
thought, remembering his grim face during their search of
the gallery. Juliette was too proud to accept such accusations with equanimity. She rose stiffly. "If you will excuse
me, my lord, Mr. Camden?" Susan rose too, and stood beside her, an angry expression on her face.

"Please don't take offense, Miss Berceau. My grandson
is not exactly a deep thinker." The earl lifted an imploring
hand to her.

Mark plowed his hand through his hair, breaking the
waves into springlike curls. "Nor much enamored of those
who are. And I am afraid his manners are utterly de-
plorable. Please accept my apology and my assurance that I
do not suspect you of any plotting."

"Nor do I," the earl inserted earnestly. "I am a fair judge
of character, Miss Berceau, and I do not believe you capable of underhanded dealings."

Much mollified, Juliette nodded her head in acceptance
of these apologies and turned to leave the room. Mark
swiftly crossed to her and took her hand, detaining her. In a
low voice, inaudible to his grandfather or Susan, he said,
"Furthermore, if it is any comfort to you at all, Miss
Berceau, I find female bluestocking theologians very intriguing."

Juliette did find it comforting, so much so that she
couldn't articulate a response. Her mouth fell slightly open,
her eyes widened, filled with the sight of Mark Camden
standing so close to her. Her nostrils flared at the spicy,
pleasantly musky male scent of him. One curl had tumbled
onto his forehead, and she felt her palms tingle with the
urge to smooth it back into place.

Smiling, he took her hand and raised it to his lips. "I bid you pleasant dreams, Miss Berceau."

Suddenly shy before this appealing man who clearly understood the effect he had on her, Juliette withdrew her hand slowly before curtseying respectfully to the earl, who had come to stand beside her. Then, taking Susan's arm, she left the room in something of a daze.

Adelaide greeted her cousin and chaperone at the door to their sitting room, hands on hips. "Where on earth have you two been?" she demanded. Marie stood behind her looking as anxious as Addie.

Knowing how uncomfortable even the slightest fib made Juliette, Susan spoke up. "The earl wished to show Juliette a fine carved-ivory chess set. Naturally I stayed behind with her."

"Oh!" Adelaide looked from one to the other suspiciously. Juliette's scruples didn't extend to contradicting Susan in her white lie, so Adelaide's brow cleared as she accepted the explanation.

"You have made quite a conquest of the earl, Julie," Addie teased. "If the ghost has similar tastes to Lord Hammerswold's, you will someday be his favorite."

"Nonsense. You know I haven't the slightest interest in being Faverill's bride."

"Well, so you said, but I thought you might have changed your mind after seeing this magnificent castle. And it isn't even their principal seat. Faverill Springs is said to be one of the finest examples of Palladian architecture in northern England."

Juliette chuckled. "Since when did you become interested in architecture, oh cousin who pronounced the ruins of St. Mildryth 'a pile of old rocks'?"

Adelaide had the grace to look sheepish. "Mr. Makepeace was explaining to me some of the architectural features of castles. He is very interested in architecture. You wouldn't think it, but he has quite a serious side."

"Mr. Makepeace, hmmmm? You danced with him more

than once in London, I believe?" Julie grinned at Adelaide. "And here I thought you came hoping to capture Faverill."

"And so I do," Adelaide declared, full lower lip stuck out pugnaciously. "To be sure, he is hardly a gallant or even likeable gentleman, but to be the Countess of Hammerswold is a great thing. Vastly above being a mere baroness, which is all that Mr. Makepeace could offer me."

Juliette frowned. "You still feel that way after meeting the viscount? I confess, my own doubts as to the wisdom of such a match for you, indeed for any gently bred female, have been increased tenfold. Did you not mark how roughly he grabbed my arm when Mr. Fotheringay started that ridiculous tale of my having seen the ghost? I am tempted to write your father and represent Faverill to him in such a way as he cannot fail to understand. He'd have us home in a trice, I am convinced, did he but suspect—"

"No! You mustn't. If you do I shall be very angry!" Adelaide was so dainty and childlike in appearance that people often thought her incapable of anger, but Juliette knew her better. Her cousin's shoulders were raised, her delicate pointed chin thrust forward, and her fists rested pugnaciously on her hips.

"You really, seriously would consider marrying that man, Addie?"

"Yes!"

Juliette looked at Susan for guidance, but the chaperone merely rolled her eyes.

"Ah, well. Then I shall say nothing—to Uncle Ronald— as yet. But I hope to convince *you* of your folly!" Juliette accepted her cousin's thankful embrace guiltily, for she wasn't entirely sure it was on Adelaide's part that she was agreeing to stay at Hammerswold. Mr. Camden's snapping black eyes were very much on her mind.

# Chapter Six

Mark, too, soon faced a puzzled relative. When he reached his suite, a footman was waiting for him with a summons from his grandmother. The instant he stepped into her bedroom, she raised herself as high as she could on her pillows and demanded to know why he had whispered in her ear not to discuss the Ghost of Hammerswold's manifestations.

"Just what game are you up to, Mark?"

"I am not up to a game, Grandmother, but I have reservations about some of your pretty young guests. I think at least one of them may have decided to give our ghost a little help in identifying his choice."

His grandmother scowled. "Now, what has given you such an idea? You surely do not suspect the estimable Miss Berceau, merely because of that idiot Fotheringay?"

Mark hesitated. His opinion of Juliette had improved after spending some time in her company. He truly no longer suspected her of dishonest dealings. He liked her intelligence and her forthright manner as much as he did her golden-brown eyes and fine figure. But he recognized that his judgement might be obscured by the powerful attraction he felt to her. *It wouldn't be the first time a woman has hidden her true nature from me*, he reminded himself.

He also had suspicions about Miss Patchfield, who had been so quick to suspect a hoax of Juliette. Was that because she herself had in mind some scheme of that nature?

But there was no way to discuss these concerns without telling his grandmother about the mysterious visitor in the gallery. He hoped to keep her from being hurt or disappointed if Uncle Ramsey failed to make himself known.

"Let's just say I have one of those intuitions you are always claiming. Nothing I can really put my finger on."

"Perhaps our ghost is warning you. Such scheming has been known to occur before."

He looked at her in surprise. "I didn't know that."

"Indeed, yes! But the perpetrator did not get away with it! At least, not in the way he thought." Her look was mischievous. He wanted to ask her to explain herself, but the longer this conversation continued, the more likely she would worm the basis for his suspicions out of him.

"I only wish to see that none imposes upon Jared."

"They might well fool Jared, or me, or even you, Mark, but no one is going to impose on the Ghost of Hammerswold!" The countess's voice was firm. "Still, I expect you are correct. We must be careful, for Jared is not overburdened with intelligence, and yet has the tenacity of a bulldog. Once convinced that a young lady was the ghost's choice, he might be difficult to persuade that she was an imposter."

"Just so!" Mark grinned as he bent to press a kiss on his grandmother's soft cheek. "You keep your knowledge of the ghost's behavior to yourself, and I'll keep my eyes opened for any less-than-authentic hauntings."

She grasped his hand as he straightened. "You do believe in the Hammerswold ghost, don't you, Mark? You aren't just humoring an old lady?"

"NiNi, I've never known a less fantastical person than you. If you say you saw a ghost, as far as I am concerned, there is a ghost."

Juliette and Adelaide had been provided with a handsome suite of rooms. The two bedrooms had a dressing room between them, and shared a large, beautifully decorated sitting room. Susan was to sleep with Adelaide, who still clung to the childish need for a nighttime companion.

As Juliette had been sleeping by herself quite happily

since before she could talk, Marie might have been expected to use the small bed in the dressing room, but the nervous maid kept putting off retiring. She interrupted Juliette's reading several times to see if she had called out, or needed anything. Finally Juliette took pity on her and directed her to pull out the trundle bed.

"Though there's no such thing as a ghost," she admonished the frightened maid, even as she allowed her to prepare to spend the night in her room.

"But yes. I haf seen zhem! Such an old castle, it has *beacoup de revenants*." Marie, unlike many so-called French maids, was indeed a native Frenchwoman, and tended to revert to her native tongue when upset.

"Many ghosts? You have seen them?" Despite herself, Juliette felt a shiver across the nape of her neck. "Nonsense. Now, no more such tales, or I will send you back in to sleep by yourself."

Marie subsided, grumbling a little under her breath. Juliette decided against reading after all, and blew out her candles. The only light in the room was from a sliver of moon in the night sky outside their balcony. It created an eerie atmosphere as it glimmered along the ormolu that liberally decorated the furnishings and ornate molded plasterwork of the ceilings.

Juliette grimaced as she heard Marie's breathing deepen. *Wonderful. She manages to set me on edge, and then goes right to sleep.*

Since sleep wouldn't come, Juliette reviewed the day's events, lingering especially on Faverill's handsome cousin. Mr. Camden had seemed wary and cold to her for a while this afternoon, but this evening he had been charming and attentive. Even in the dark she could feel a blush stealing to her cheeks at the way he had looked at her in the earl's library as he assured her that he found her interesting.

Delightful as this memory was to savor, another one had been tickling at the edge of her awareness for a long time, trying to get in. The man in the gallery—who was he? Why had he hidden from the Camdens, and—there was the elusive thought—where had he gone? Also, why had none of the Camdens ever so much as brought the subject up, much less accounted for his disappearance?

Juliette felt the skin creep along her arms and the base of her neck. Had it indeed been an apparition, a *revenant*, that she spent so long with in the gallery? Could a ghost so charmingly tell her all of the Camden's history, without her once suspecting? But she had felt his arm, strong with a wiry strength that belied his many years. She had walked closely enough to him to catch the scent of some expensive cologne. Did ghosts wear cologne?

*No, because there are no ghosts!* Aggravated with herself for the very thought, much less the chills of alarm running up and down her spine, Juliette tossed on her pillows. Then where had the genial old gentleman gone?

Just at that moment a loud crack and a series of small pops resounded through the room. Juliette's eyes automatically turned to the fireplace, though in the next instant she realized that the sound had not been made by a log breaking. In this unseasonably warm weather she had felt no need of a fire, indeed had opened her balcony doors to the night air, over Marie's protests.

She sat up and looked around, her heart pounding. She decided the sound had come from the wall between her bedroom and the suite next door, occupied by the Whittens.

The chills were back as Juliette slid quietly out of the bed and approached the wall. It was a rococo mixture of ornate plasterwork and carved wood. With a shock she realized that some of the carved work included small grill-like inlays, where flower petals and leaves needed filling in, for example. As she studied it, a muffled creak sounded just in front of her.

Suddenly she knew where the mystery man in the gallery had gone. *Secret passageways! Hollow walls behind which spies could move about!* The Camdens had acted so perplexed about her behavior, Mark Camden even feigning suspicion of her. Yet never once had they speculated on *how* the "uncle" had left the gallery. Why?

*Because they knew!* Juliette's furiously working mind saw with sudden clarity that the Hammerswold castle, amalgamation of many architectural styles and periods as it was, must surely have a system of hidden passageways, perhaps even a priest's hole or two.

Was it a plot between Mark Camden and Viscount Faverill? Was even the earl in on it? They must plan to play some great jokes on the hapless young women. Was there some unsavory, lustful spying planned? Suddenly aware of her undress, Juliette looked down at her muslin night rail. Was someone spying on her even now?

Fury at the thought of the masculine mockery and cynicism that would lie behind such behavior suddenly gripped Juliette.

*This is one female you won't tease or terrorize,* she thought. She moved as quietly as possible through the darkness toward the water pitcher on the stand by her bed. A glassful in the snout of that pig viscount might cool his ardor for such shenanigans! Keeping her body between the paneling and the pitcher, she poured, and then, hiding the glass behind her, approached the paneling again.

"Take this, you sneaking snake of an excuse for a man." she yelled, dashing the liquid into the center of the flower she thought would make the most convenient peephole. It splashed back on her, causing her to flinch at the cold.

At that instant Marie began to scream. "The ghost, saints preserve us, *le bon Dieu nous sauvons.*"

So focused was Juliette on her revenge upon the pranksters behind the wall that she was at first stunned and bewildered by Marie's screams. She was too late in her attempts to quiet her servant. Susan and Adelaide rushed in from the other room, demanding to know what had happened.

In fractured English and fluent French, Marie explained that she had seen the ghost hovering over Juliette at the wall. "Mademoiselle, she saw it too. She tried to protect us by throwing water on it, *pauvre chère—c'est impossible!*" Adelaide gave a loud shriek at this news.

Juliette tried to explain, but a knock at the door warned them that their activities had awakened others. Soon the room was full of milling females. Miss Davies, upon hearing that Marie had seen the ghost, promptly swooned. Carolyn Stephens-Hill screamed hysterically.

"It seems the ghost is singling you out already, Miss Berceau, or at least you would have us think it so." Sylvia Patchwood's cold, insinuating voice cut through the noise.

Juliette turned. "Once again, this was no ghost! Only a nervous maid, and—"

"And what?" Behind the cluster of females around them stood Mr. Camden, tall, dark, and forbidding-looking. "And a pretense of ignorance by a scheming baggage? I begin to think my cousin had the right of it."

So much for his apology of a few hours earlier. Juliette felt deeply hurt by this renewed suspicion.

"Don't speak to Miss Berceau that way!" The viscount shoved his way through the noisy knot of women to take Juliette by the hand. "I'm sure you've had a shock. Meeting a ghost, even a kind one, must be alarming."

*It wanted only this,* Juliette thought, gritting her teeth against the words of loathing she wished to lash out at him. Oily with solicitation for the woman he had resoundingly rejected as a "bluestocking theologian" a few hours earlier, Faverill offered her consolation and protection from his cousin's wrath. As he spoke to her, he led her from the room.

"Come tell NiNi, my dear. She can set your mind at ease. Did the old boy say anything to you? Why are you wet, by the way?" The spark of genuine interest in the viscount's eyes warned Juliette that in the brighter light of the wall sconces in the hall, she was quite indecent. Her night rail was splattered with the water that she had meant for the prankster's face. It clung transparently and suggestively across her bosom and down her waist.

"Ohhh! I cannot be seen like this. Let me go, please!" Faverill did not seem inclined to do so, and a definite leer spread over his features as she struggled.

"Of course Miss Berceau must fetch her robe first, Jared." A strong, dark hand clamped itself around the viscount's wrist. "Please join us in my grandmother's sitting room in five minutes, Miss Berceau, and bring that maid, too!" Mark spoke in a tone that brooked no opposition. Faverill released her arm, and Juliette scampered to get some clothes to cover herself. She heard Mark urging the other guests to return to their beds.

Her cousin and their companion insisted on accompanying her to the countess's sitting room. Marie wanted only to pack their bags immediately and depart the castle forever.

Juliette slipped into a severe, high-necked morning dress, the primmest and most proper in her wardrobe. Previously it had seen service while calling on certain of her mother's relatives who had never quite forgiven her for having a French father. Fully dressed, she felt better armored for a confrontation with the Camdens, particularly the arrogant, suspicious Mark Camden.

The countess received them in state, seated in a comfortable overstuffed chair, dressed in a magnificent brocade nightgown that allowed equally opulent blonde lace from her night rail to ruffle around her neck and wrists. She looked alert in spite of having had her rest interrupted.

The earl, seated by her side, took charge of the proceedings quite as if he were wearing his magistrate's robes and sitting upon the bench. When several people started talking at once, including Juliette, whose discomposure had given way to deep anger, he held up a silencing hand.

"One at a time. I will hear from the maid first."

Marie gulped down the last of a long series of hysterical hiccoughs, and came forward to curtsey.

"Tell me exactly what you saw and heard, my dear."

"Il y a . . . um . . . there was ze noise. Pop! Pop! Then a creak, like a foot on a board."

It was the first time Juliette knew that her maid had heard the noise. "I thought you were asleep," she interjected, but the earl motioned her to be silent.

"Then Miss Juliette got up and started looking along the

wall. She was feeling, too, with her fingers. *Pauvre petit chou*. She knows nothing of ze *revenant*. No use to try to feel them unless they want to be felt." Marie wagged her head knowingly.

"Then mademoiselle turned away. I couldn't see what she was doing so I sat up. That is when I saw it." Marie's shoulders began to shake again.

The earl stood and caught up the maid's hands. "Now, now, my dear. Courage. Tell us what you saw."

"T'was *un revenant. Gris. D'une grande dame avec la robe de l'autre temps . . .*" Her hands made a wide circle as she indicated the lady ghost's dress.

"A gray lady in an old-fashioned dress. Go on."

"*C'est tout*. That is all. Mademoiselle, she throw water just as I begin to scream, and ze spirit, it fade away."

Several people spoke at once. Juliette heard Viscount Faverill mutter a curse at learning that the ghost was female. "Not the old boy, then, damn his eyes."

The countess gasped, "Lady Isobella." The earl sighed, "I was afraid of that," and Mr. Camden, who had unexpectedly appeared at her side, muttered in her ear, "Very subtle, Miss Berceau. You don't want to marry my cousin, you spoke with a real man in the gallery, and your maid saw a female ghost. Very subtle indeed. When the time comes for you to inform us that old Hammerswold has spoken to you, we'll all believe it the more for your having refused to exploit these other occurrences."

"Not subtle, sir, because not true." Juliette rounded on him, fists clenched in fury. "Nor is your behavior and that of the viscount subtle. Wasn't there enough sport to be had on the estate that you men must find a way to make a May Game of your female visitors? It must be a very amusing, terrorizing young girls and their servants!"

"Explain yourself, Miss!" The earl looked back and forth between Juliette and Mark.

But Juliette stepped around him and addressed the countess. "This evening, Lady Hammerswold, I allowed myself to be party to a deception, for which I humbly beg your pardon."

"Ah, she plans to make a clean breast of it." A slight defrosting of Mr. Camden's tone did not in the least soothe Juliette.

"Your grandsons, ma'am, asked me not to mention it to you, and your husband, when he found out about it, agreed. I hope and believe he is not involved in this despicable plot."

The countess was deeply perplexed. "Please go on, Miss Berceau. Everyone seems to be accused of something dire, but I cannot make out what."

She proceeded to tell the countess of the older man who had guided her in the gallery.

"Ramsey! Come home at last!" At first the countess looked delighted, but then her face fell. "But where is he? Why does he not come to see me?"

"I cannot know for sure that it is Ramsey, ma'am, as I have only *their* word for it." Juliette's tone of voice left no doubt the value she placed on the Camden men's word.

"At any rate, whoever it was, his disappearance was left a mystery. It wasn't explained; all three men seemed to take it for granted. With so much happening, I really didn't give it much thought until I went to bed.

"Then I began to wonder how he managed to disappear. Just as I was puzzling over it, I heard the noise that Marie described. I realized there must be hidden passageways, perhaps priest holes and the like, as in so many other old houses. It is obvious that these passageways connect to hollow walls between the bedrooms. I got up to inspect the wall near the sound, and found decorative work that could easily hide a peephole."

Susan drew in an indignant breath. Adelaide squeaked, "Peepholes?"

"I was furious." Here Juliette turned to face Mark Camden. "Outraged. Who stood on the other side, peeping into my bedroom? You, Mr. Camden? Faverill? One of the other jolly young men?"

Both Mr. Camden and the viscount were wearing convincing looks of astonishment, but Juliette was not impressed. *Doubtless they are surprised that I have discovered their disgusting game!*

"I decided I might be able to, ah, dampen their enthusiasm for haunting."

"Hence the water!" A glimmer of amusement lightened Mark's features.

"It is not funny, sir. It is despicable! And anyone who is a party to it is also despicable! Marie is quite right. We are going to pack our bags and be gone tomorrow!"

# Chapter Seven

Juliette tried to turn and march out of the room, but was prevented by a firm grasp on her elbow. She twisted around in an unsuccessful attempt to be free from Mr. Camden's grip.

"One moment, young lady!" He was half-laughing as he effortlessly detained her.

"Let her go," Susan protested. "The child is quite right. I am sure that Lord and Lady Paxton would not want their daughter and niece staying in a household where such vulgar spying was going on."

"Nor would I want such a thing going on in my house!" The countess's voice quavered.

Mark's expression sobered immediately at the sight of his grandmother's distress. "But it isn't true. There are no passageways. The bedrooms are completely free of peepholes."

"Absolutely no truth to it, Miss Berceau." The earl's brow was wrinkled with concern. "There are no secret passageways. Our ancestors were part and parcel of the suppression of the monasteries and abbeys. Far from hiding priests, they were more likely to hunt them down and turn them in. There was no need of peepholes and priest's holes. Please believe us."

Juliette turned back, considering the people who surrounded her. The countess was surely innocent of any wrongdoing. The earl looked honestly distressed by her suspicions. Mr. Camden, arrogant though he was, had impressed her as an honest and responsible man. Faverill certainly seemed capable of such a prank, but would he attempt to play it in these circumstances, around these relatives? Juliette wanted to believe them.

"But . . . then where did the man go who was up in the gallery?"

Before Mark could reply, the countess said, "I have it! That scapegrace used the servant's stairs, of course. There is a panel hidden in the wall that admits entrance to the gallery. There are several such servant's stairs. But though they are hidden for aesthetic reasons, they are not secret, and do not give access to any bedrooms."

Mark nodded his agreement. "If you had not scurried away, you would have heard me explain to Mrs. Patchfield and her daughter. Uncle Ramsey could move unseen by us from the cellars to the attics through the servant's stairways and service halls. But Miss Berceau, none of those have access to individual bedrooms." Mark's forehead was furrowed in concern that she believe him.

"But . . . but . . . what made those noises that I heard?"

"*C'est le revenant*," Marie intoned. "Mademoiselle, we must depart this house of spirits, I beg you."

The earl said, "Like most old structures, particularly those made of a variety of materials, the castle is capable of producing quite a cacophony of sound as the temperatures change at night." Lord Hammerswold took Juliette's hand. "Miss Berceau, I hope you will accept this explanation and stay with us. To stand accused of plotting to spy on and terrify young girls would be quite lowering, you know."

"It's a damned impertinent insult, is what it is," Faverill growled.

Juliette ignored him, her attention focused on the earl and countess. She searched the earl's eyes. They were direct, honest, and almost desperate in their appeal. She understood perfectly well that his concern was for his wife, who looked anxious and unhappy. She turned and looked to her companion and her cousin for counsel.

Susan nodded her head. "I expect, dear, that Marie's

maunderings had your nerves upset, or you never would have suspected such a thing."

Adelaide nodded her head vehemently. "It is infamous of you to accuse the Camdens of such! I declare, I am mortified."

"Rightly so!" The viscount stepped closer. The look on his face was both angry and lascivious. "You are a bit of a cheeky baggage and want taming. Perhaps our ghost thinks me the man to do it—"

"If I were you, Jared, I'd say no more." Mark's voice was a deep rumble of warning.

All of Juliette's returning composure fled again. "That is another thing! Ever since I came here, I have been accused of being a scheming, lying person, a baggage, a bluestocking, a—a—theologian. Well, Addie may stay, but I will not. I have too much self-respect to continue to take any more such abuse. Marie and I will depart tomorrow. Susan, you may remain with Addie if you think it best!" She stormed from the room and down the hall.

"A . . . a theologian?" The countess repeated plaintively. "What on earth!"

Before Juliette could quite close the door to their suite, it was caught and flung open again. She whirled to see Mr. Camden and Viscount Faverill in the doorway. "Get out of here, both of you," she snapped.

Quite as if she hadn't spoken, Mr. Camden entered. He turned, then, blocking his cousin's way. "Not now, Jared. Your style of diplomacy mightily resembles the perambulations of the proverbial bull in the china shop."

"But she might be the one, Mark." Faverill made as if to push by, but Mr. Camden was stronger.

"Both of you leave, at once," Juliette demanded, but the cousins continued their discussion unheeding.

"And if she is, you've queered it entirely, you chucklehead. I'll be to your room directly for some frank conversation." The minatory stare Mark gave the viscount caused him to pull away reluctantly.

"Express my apologies to Miss Berceau, will you? Didn't mean to distress her." Faverill craned his neck, trying to catch Juliette's eye.

"Yes, yes, now go." Mark pushed him the rest of the way out of the room, but was unable to close the door, for Susan and Adelaide were waiting impatiently for entry.

"May I ask what you think you are doing, Mr. Camden?" Susan gave him her most fearsome chaperone's glare.

"You can't leave, Julie," Addie began. "I won't go, I won't. It will start a storm of gossip, and who knows what harm will occur to our hosts and to us!" Sweeping past Mark, Adelaide faced her cousin, tears in her eyes.

"We'll never be accepted in the *ton*. You've insulted the Earl of Hammerswold and his lovely wife, and the viscount, and . . . oh!" Blonde curls flying, Addie ran past her cousin into the bedroom beyond.

Susan was obviously torn between Adelaide's need of comfort and Juliette's need of chaperonage.

"Miss Campbell, give me just a few minutes alone with Miss Berceau, and I am sure—"

"Certainly not, Mr. Camden. But . . . I do wish you could convince her to stay." Susan frowned thoughtfully. "I shall go calm Addie, but the door to the bedroom will be wide open."

Mark smiled. "I shall hold the line, Miss Campbell."

"I have nothing to say to you, Mr. Camden." Juliette was surprised to find herself alone with him. *Why didn't I escape to my room while I had the chance?*

"Miss Berceau, you seem to me to be a reasonable person. My grandfather and I both have assured you—"

"You and your cousin accused me of being a scheming, lying—"

"You accused us of being pranksters and spies." Mark crossed to where she stood by the fireplace.

Julie felt the justice of this accusation, but was too angry to back down. "Then we are even, sir." She attempted to move away; he reached out and caught her hands, turning her to face him, and suddenly the whole world changed.

The room became too small, too warm, too electric, like the air just before a summer thunderstorm.

"Yes, we are even, Miss Berceau. That is just my point. We have each thought the worst of the other, for no very good reason that I can see. Can you not forgive me for my transgression, if I forgive you for yours? Can we not start over?"

Stunned by his proximity, Juliette couldn't answer. He was wearing silk pajamas and a robe that revealed a triangle of thick black hair at the neck. This close to him she could see the stubble of his dark beard. She was startled by her desire to explore this man's textures.

A knowing look crept into his black eyes. He tugged her closer and leaned forward.

"Harrrumph!"

They both turned toward Susan like sleepwalkers startled from a trance.

Choosing to ignore their improper proximity to one another, Susan joined her persuasions to Mark's. "That seems an imminently sensible approach, Juliette. Your suspicions do the earl's family no more credit than theirs do you. Instead of nurturing a family feud that will surely result in scandal, why not begin over?"

Self-consciously pulling her hands from Mark's strong grasp, Juliette smoothed them on her dress. "Yes, I suppose, but so help me, if Viscount Faverill or you hint even one more time that I am trying to entrap him—"

"We won't! I am quite cured of such a notion, and from the way he followed you here, I suspect that he belatedly realizes that you could be a prime candidate for his hand."

"That is only slightly less distasteful to me, Mr. Camden!"

"You truly would not welcome his suit?"

"No. And don't ask me why, sir, or I shall tell the truth with no bark on it!"

Mark threw back his head and laughed. "No, don't. I should be obliged to be offended, out of familial pride! Well, then, shall we cry *pax*?"

He held out his hand. Juliette took it, marveling again at the powerful effect his touch had on her. She looked down at his hand. Ordinarily she would not touch a man's hand with her own without gloves in between. Would all men's touch be as thrilling? *Does he feel anything? Is this powerful attraction only on my side?*

She lifted her eyes for a hint, and found his gaze, blacker than ever, warmly roaming her features. He slowly, deliberately raised her hands and pressed his firm lips to the back of each.

"I am looking forward to beginning again, Miss Berceau."

"I, too."

He started to turn her hands over to kiss the palms. Susan's loud throat-clearing made him jump guiltily, and he stepped away. Turning to the red-haired Scotswoman, he bowed. "Until tomorrow, ladies."

"The nerve of that man. He all but made love to you!" Susan bustled to the door and turned the key in the lock.

"Yes, wasn't it wonderful?" Juliette turned about in a dreamy whirl.

"Oh, Juliette, don't fall in love with Mr. Camden. He's got to marry well."

That brought Juliette out of her golden reverie. "You are right! I had best take care, for he is possessed of a great deal more charm than is good for me." Speaking what she knew she should believe, Juliette hoped her usual practical nature would enable her to conquer these longings that now assailed her.

"How is Adelaide? Will she speak to me?"

"Now that we are staying, I am sure that she will, but you are in for a scold."

"I expect that I am. I even deserve it, a little. Where is Marie? I want her to go down and make a tissane. I have the headache."

Both women became aware at the same time that their maid had not followed them from the countess's sitting room.

"I'll get her, and the tissane. She is likely to be useless as yet. You see to Addie."

Wondering at his own boldness with Juliette Berceau, Mark made his way to Jared's room, determined to impress Jared with the necessity of avoiding insulting her further.

His grandfather was lecturing Jared on another topic.

"Come in, Mark," he boomed. "I've been attempting to make Jared understand his duties as a host."

Jared was at his most conciliatory. "I do understand, Grandfather. I'm to be polite and attentive to each of the young ladies in turn."

"Get to know them," the earl urged him. "Think what their effect on the earldom would be. You need to understand, Jared, that I would never have comprehended the extent of my duties if NiNi—"

"Yes, yes! You've told me many times. She taught you to care about the land and the tenants, not just the rents. Though I've never understood why you bother so much with either, when you could move the tenants off, hire a few shepherds, and build up our sheep herds—"

"Sheep would not prosper in all of our holdings." Mark's voice revealed his exasperation at having to explain over and over the need for diversity in their crops.

"Then why not exchange them for more land in Scotland. Get it cheap there, run off the crofters—"

"We're getting away from the subject," the earl said hastily.

"Anyway," Jared drawled languidly, "the ghost's job, ain't it?"

"What?"

"Huh?" The earl and Mark both stared at the viscount.

"Figuring out who the right bride is. His job. I'll just let the old boy point her out to me. Mean to follow his advice, you know, so there'll be no more repeats of that episode this summer." Jared shuddered at the memory of the stroke that had left him temporarily speechless.

In utter exasperation Mark shouted, "And what if the

ghost's choice is Miss Berceau? You've thoroughly alien-
ated her with your insults, not that your stock stood high
with her anyway, because of your reputation."

Jared looked worried momentarily. "Tried to apologize,
didn't I? But you wouldn't let me! No, pushed me right out
of the room. Wanted to talk to her yourself. Which was
more important, that you apologize, or me?"

"As I said, your apology could well turn into another insult. You don't seem to understand how to deal with a
woman of strong character."

"Well, once we're married I'll know how to deal with
her." The light of battle flared in Jared's eyes. "Won't play
off her airs on me then."

"No wonder Miss Berceau thinks you'll make a poor sort
of husband," Mark said with a grimace.

"Does she? I will be more careful. Shouldn't show an
untried filly the whip before mounting up. Keep it out of
sight until well in the saddle!"

"Jared!" The earl thundered his disapproval. "You're
talking as if you were about to ride a half-broken horse, not
seeking a bride you will love enough to reform yourself
for."

Jared gave his grandfather an enigmatic look before continuing his response to Mark's comments. "But you're
wrong about getting one of them to marry me. Any of them
will. That's what they're here for. Women want a title,
Mark. A title, and wealth too, if they can have it. You of all
people should know that."

Mark winced. He did not like being reminded of his one-
time fiancée's decision to back out of their engagement
when he made it clear he would not leave his position as
manager of his grandfather's holding to enter government
service. She had urged him, "The earl can use his influence,
and you can use your talent, to advance. You'll have a title
too, someday, even if you don't inherit Hammerswold,
which you probably will, for Jared has no inclination to
wed."

It had been the first time he had realized she thought he

might one day inherit. "With my uncle and Jared ahead of me, that is extremely unlikely. I thought you understood that, Patricia."

"Jared is over thirty and showing no signs of settling down. Look at him. Have you ever known a heavy, hard-drinking man like him to live to old age?"

The discussion had continued off and on for several days. At the end of it, Patricia had not convinced him to leave Hammerswold for a career in the government. Instead, he had convinced her he was content to remain title-less, and determined to continue serving his grandfather. She had ended their engagement.

"Kind of you to remind me, Jer!"

"Just so. Mean it to be kind. In case you are thinking this prickly bluestocking theologian is the woman for you. You know perfectly well if I offer for her she'll have me, no matter how lofty the principles she holds up. If nothing else, she'll see it as her duty to reform me. No woman could resist that challenge, eh, Grandfather?"

The earl was studying Mark with a worried eye. "You're not becoming involved with Miss Berceau, are you? Because I expect Jared is right on the money for once. However she may protest, she certainly would accept a proposal from Jared. She wouldn't be here otherwise. I'd hate to see you hurt again, son. Moreover . . . think what the implications would be for Hammerswold, if she should be the ghost's choice for Jared and you've courted her for yourself."

Not having thought of this angle before, Jared was suddenly indignant. "Damned right. You keep off, Mark. No poaching. After Patricia you said you wouldn't marry till I had an heir, so as not to find your wife had been hoping for the title when she married you. Keep to your plan! Give me your word you won't seek to engage Miss Berceau's affections, or any other of these gels, for that matter."

Mark stood. "I'm not looking for a wife, Jared. You know that. But you must treat these young women respect-fully, or else—"

"Absolutely! I shall be a model of virtue from this moment forward. I want your word, though! No luring the ghost's choice to you. A man might conclude you are trying to inherit the title that way."

"Jared! What an unfair thing to say. No one can fault Mark's loyalty." The earl's voice shook with indignation.

"Then he won't mind giving me his word." Jared's jaw locked stubbornly as he stared at his cousin, whose face had darkened with anger.

"I am not scheming for your title, Jared Camden. That you think it makes me wonder if loyalty only goes one way in this family. Still, here is my hand on it."

# Chapter Eight

Juliette moved quickly through the formal gardens close to the terraced west front of Hammerswold. She wished to explore the landscaped paths designed by Lancelot Brown that swept down over what had once been part of the bailey and the curtain wall. The rubble left by Cromwell's cannon had been smoothed and planted to lead the eye pleasantly down the hill toward the abbey ruins.

As her feet flew, scrunching the gravel, she marveled at how well she felt, considering how long she had lain awake after returning to her bed last night. The longer she had lain there, the more embarrassed she had become about her accusations of the Camdens, because in her sleepless tossing and turning she had the opportunity to hear for herself that the castle was full of strange sounds, from pops and squeaks to creaks and metallic clanks. The latter she had finally identified as part of the roof drainage system stirring in the breeze. So much for chain-draped ghosts from long-ago dungeons!

"Yoo-hoo! Miss Berceau!"

The voice came from the wide covered veranda that fronted the west wing. Juliette was sorry that her morning isolation had been interrupted. Still, there was no help for it. She turned toward the voice and the hand waving above a tossing rosebush. A few steps revealed that it was none other than the countess who called her.

"Lady Hammerswold! What are you doing out here all alone?" Juliette quickened her steps, glad of the chance for a private apology.

"All of the others are upstairs for the tour of the gallery, as I thought you were, too."

Juliette felt a little twinge of guilt that none of them had thought of keeping the countess company. She dropped down in a cool wrought-iron chair beside the countess's wheeled chair. "No, I had to help get Marie packed and away this morning."

"Oh, dear, what a pity," the countess murmured.

"Yes, it is very sad to see someone so disturbed, though she never gave the least evidence of it in London. She is an excellent worker, and a genius with hair."

"I meant it is a pity you sent her away. I had hoped to quiz her about the others."

"Sent her away? Oh, no, ma'am, you misunderstand. She insisted on going. She was terrified of seeing other ghosts. But do not say you believe her astounding visions?" Juliette admired the countess, but she could not admire this propensity for the occult.

"I thought I had succeeded in reassuring her that the spirits that live at Hammerswold never bother us."

"You have seen more than one spirit?"

"Not I. I never see such things. But others—oh, mostly Irish or Scottish servants—see them, have done so through the ages. None has done so in ten years or more, though. They mostly see them when they first arrive. But we've not had any new servants here since my accident, until this gathering. Jared keeps the castle more as a hunting box than a residence, and I prefer the smooth, flat paths Winton and Mark have constructed for me at Faverill. I can propel by own chair about there."

Juliette forced back a laugh at the reference to the vast Hammerswold castle as a "hunting box." "I am quite bewildered," she said, not knowing which of several questions to ask first. The countess seemed such a clearheaded woman otherwise. She heartily wished to change the subject, but the countess was enthusiastically explaining.

"You see, the servants who see them soon grow used to them and stop noticing them. Or the ghosts lose interest and stop hanging about, I don't know which. It is very perplexing! The gray lady that Marie saw last night was last seen by a footman in the ballroom fifteen years ago. We thought she had left us. I would so like to know if the cook carrying the chicken still visits the central portion of the castle. He is one of our oldest, you know."

Juliette gasped. "That is what she was referring to! She kept fussing about the *'homme avec un poulet et un couperet.'*"

The countess clasped her hands in pleasure. "Then he's still here! Doubtless Marie feared his cleaver."

"She was sure he would murder her in her bed."

"Do you still doubt there is something to it, my dear?" The countess sobered, the shrewd hazel eyes studying Juliette carefully.

"Indeed I do!"

"Then how do you explain Marie's having seen ghosts that have been seen before?"

"Servants gossiping, teasing, finding a susceptible soul to frighten. Why, you said yourself you'd never seen any ghosts."

"No, my dear, I said I'd not seen these various spirits that linger in the air. The Ghost of Hammerswold is of quite a different sort, and I have definitely seen him." The countess's chin lifted and her mouth firmed.

"I . . . I see." Desperate for some other topic—had the whole world become demented?—she turned to the sweeping view of the valley before them, with the abbey's ruins in the right foreground. "It is magnificent!"

"Isn't it?" The countess turned, too. "It is my favorite sight in the whole world. I'm praying that we have good weather for Halloween. So far, we've been blessed with a late summer. I only hope this fair weather continues. There'll be a full moon that night, as there was the night I became engaged to Winton. Nothing is more romantic than St. Mildryth's in the moonlight."

Juliette sighed. "I can well imagine. It is romantic even in the morning light. I can't wait to explore it."

"Then you must let me be your guide this afternoon!"

The masculine voice startled both women. The countess shook her finger at the viscount, who had come to stand beside her. "Naughty boy, creeping up on us that way."

"I was seeking Miss Berceau. I expected her to be upstairs taking that boring tour." Faverill crossed to where Juliette sat and took the seat beside her. His face and voice were pleasant, not betraying in the least any sense of ill-usage because of the peal Juliette had rung over his head last night.

Juliette was relieved to see the viscount in such an agreeable mood. She smiled and arched an eyebrow at him. "No, I already had a tour, as you recall."

She darted a look at the countess, who shook her head and muttered, "That rascal, Ramsey! Where is he?"

"Grandfather says he has searched high and low. The servants are looking, too. He'll be found soon, NiNi. How is that maid of yours, Miss Berceau? Never saw anyone with the ability to see spirits who exercised it so reluctantly. Unusual, that, for a Frenchie to have the sight."

"It is a gift she would gladly give to someone else! She insisted on going back to my uncle at Solway this morning."

"Ah! Pity, that! I was hoping to use her to smoke the old boy out. Oh, well, expect he'll show himself at the right time, eh? Now, shall we plan an expedition to the abbey for this afternoon?"

"Oh, yes! I mean, that depends upon your grandmother's plans for us."

Both looked hopefully at the countess. "It is an excellent idea," she responded. "I think a picnic in the courtyard this afternoon might be pleasing to all of your guests, Jared. We should take advantage of this perfect weather."

"Miss Berceau and I had hoped for a private party," the viscount argued.

"Had you, indeed?" The three seated on the veranda turned to find Mark Camden, a stern expression on his face, just behind them. With him were most of the young ladies.

Sylvia Patchfield and Adelaide were on either side of him.
"What a very proper notion!" His voice dripped with scorn.

"For shame, Jared," the countess said. "Please forgive
him, Miss Berceau. He has grown too rackety by half."

Roses flagged Juliette's cheeks. Mr. Camden was looking at her as if *she* had wished a *tête-à-tête* with the viscount. *So much for putting away his insulting suspicious-
ness*, she thought, standing up.

"I understand, Lady Hammerswold." Juliette infused her
voice with a *soupçon* of regret. "But a properly chaperoned
outing to the abbey will be delightful, Lord Faverill." She
smiled at the viscount warmly. If Mr. Camden was determined to continue to see her as casting out lures to his
cousin, she'd give him some cause!

"If you will excuse me, my lady? As we are without a
maid, I expect Adelaide and I had best go up and look to
our wardrobes."

"My dears, you cannot do without a maid. I will assign
one of ours to help you." The countess twisted to catch
Mark's eye. "Betty, I think."

Both girls expressed their gratitude appropriately. As
soon as she was able to make her escape, Juliette slipped
through the window into the spacious salon behind them.
Addie hastened after her, and when they were out of hearing, observed in a peeved tone, "You said you were going
to help Marie pack, not that you were going to plan private
parties with the viscount!"

"Stealing a march on you and the other girls," Juliette asserted, lifting her chin and stepping past her obviously jealous cousin with a sniff.

Mark Camden stood in his stirrups, surveying the lively
scene before him. The three carriages bearing his grandparents and most of the other chaperones were just pulling
away from the front of the carriageway. More than a dozen
high-spirited horses were milling around their grooms or
testing their riders' control as the younger men and women
mounted up.

Mark carefully checked each young girl and her mount, hoping to spot any trouble before it started. Miss Whitten's showy roan gelding seemed to have been selected more for its looks than its tractability. But Lord Tremayne appeared to have taken her under his wing, so Mark, relieved, continued his survey. There was Sylvia Patchfield, conferring intensely with her groom somewhat apart from the crowd. He was picking up the horses's hooves one by one, frowning, as she spoke to him. Mark decided to see if she needed another mount.

As he walked his horse toward Sylvia, he continued his survey. Adelaide Beasley was mounted on a horse of pale cream color from mane to tail. Cunningly chosen to match its owner's hair, the gelding was also calm and well-mannered under her hands. Their groom had turned to toss Miss Campbell onto a sturdy Welsh-bred bay.

Mark had promised himself he would pay Miss Berceau no attention, but could not repress the desire to see how she was mounted. He casually turned in the saddle enough to study her. She was already up, gathering her reins and speaking encouragingly to a small brown mare that stood calmly in the chaos of horses and riders.

Mark chuckled. Was it in some spirit of satire of her blonde cousin that she had also chosen a horse the same color as her hair? The animal reminded him of her owner in more ways than one. Totally without surface show, she seemed sound, sturdy, and competent. The dished-in muzzle and huge liquid brown eyes bespoke some Arab blood, just as Juliette had that faintly exotic French background. Mark lifted amused eyes to find Miss Berceau looking at him. She quickly looked away, tilting her firm chin proudly.

He had blotted his copybook with her again this morning. And for what reason? He had known perfectly well that any suggestion of a private picnic with Jared had not come from Miss Berceau. *A fine one I am to lecture Jared on manners,* he thought.

Promising himself to look for an opportunity to apologize, Mark continued his survey of the women's mounts just as Jared, Sir Beauford Montrose, and James Betterton rode up to Miss Beasley and Miss Berceau. After a few moments of confusion, they led the exodus behind the carriages toward the abbey grounds.

Mark continued toward Miss Patchfield, though her groom had apparently given her horse his seal of approval. Thus he was in a position to observe that the lush blonde exchanged a look with the groom that was entirely out of keeping for a mistress and her servant. The intimacy this hinted at caused Mark to take a closer look at her groom.

He was a tall, strongly built man of a gypsy-like complexion, more handsome than was wise in the groom of a young, unmarried girl. He nodded to his mistress as if agreeing to some instruction of hers, before tossing her up. She put her heel to her white mare's side and quickly claimed the escort of Victor Makepeace, easily distracting him from the ample charms of Miss Harpwood.

Later, after an elaborate picnic in the one-time infirmary, the most complete building still standing on the abbey grounds, Mark slipped into a seat by his grandmother. "Does Jared really think you planned all of this on an hour's notice at his whim?"

"Hush, Mark. He's actually behaving himself. He and Miss Berceau seem to have come to some sort of accord."

Mark's mouth curved downward. "So I notice."

"I am so pleased. I do not know them well enough to be sure yet, but of the young ladies present, she seems to stand out as a very capable and conscientious person. Her cousin is also an admirable young woman, of course." The countess studied the two cousins as they strolled across the grass on the arms of their escorts, Jared and Mr. Betterton.

"Yes, Miss Beasley asked some intelligent questions during the tour of the gallery this morning. I fear most of the young ladies lost interest when they realized that Jared had left."

"I am sorry, Mark. It isn't fair—"

"Now, NiNi, you know I am quite accustomed to being ignored by eligible young ladies." In spite of his words of denial, Mark looked gloomily toward where Jared was helping Miss Berceau to a comfortable seat on a blanket under a towering shade tree.

He'd lost the attention of many a fair young charmer to his older, more highly placed cousin. Usually it did not bother him so much. But Jared had apparently been right. Miss Berceau, given the opportunity, was basking in the viscount's attentions, quite as if she had not voiced disdain for him yesterday. Mark did not regret giving his word to his cousin not to try to engage her affections—no, not in the least. So why this dull throb of misery as he watched her flirt with Jared?

"If you'll excuse me, NiNi, I think Miss Campbell has been abandoned."

"Yes, do see that she is entertained." The countess's smile approved of her grandson's offer. She could always depend upon him to help her with the wallflowers.

Mark felt that he had been well rewarded for his kindness toward Susan Campbell. She was, he discovered, an extremely well-informed woman who could hold her own in a conversation with a man without any show of the pomposity or archness that caused so many bluestockings to be disliked. A half-hour's walk took them from the abbey's history to the best breed of sheep for the climate of northern England. Mark only remembered her status as companion when their perambulations brought them back to the group seated under the trees.

"Oh, poor Julie. I wonder what they are discussing to make her look so down-pin."

Mark turned at Miss Campbell's spontaneous comment. Two other young men and Sylvia Patchfield had joined Jared and Miss Berceau. Adelaide and Victor Makepeace had left the group to stroll together. Juliette was seated with her back against the base of an ancient oak, with two huge, gnarled roots framing her figure. Jared was seated sideways in front of her, so that she was, in effect, penned in.

"She looks almost ill," Mark snapped. "What is wrong?"

Miss Campbell shook her head sadly. "She is, I think the military men call it, hoist by her own petard."

# Chapter Nine

"Blown up by her own bombs? Now what can you mean?" He looked thoughtfully from the woman on his arm to Juliette. That particular military expression indicated some tactic on Juliette's part that had gone wrong. The cloud that had settled over his emotions when Juliette began to flirt with Jared lifted abruptly.

But Miss Campbell, realizing what she had given away, retreated. "I meant only that if she *will* engage hunting gentlemen in conversation, sooner or later that conversation will turn to hunting."

"She does not approve of hunting? But I believe they are discussing boxing." Their steps had brought them within earshot of Viscount Faverill's loud voice.

"Juliette detests violence as a means of pleasure, sir, whether it be in hunting animals or beating men."

"Dare I guess how she came by such opinions?" Mark asked, chuckling at Miss Campbell's disapproving tone of voice.

Susan smiled. "I only encouraged her natural inclinations, sir."

"Well, then, I'd best rescue her, for Jared will prose on forever. 'Tis one of his favorite subjects."

"She is well able to look after herself." Susan attempted to guide their steps away from the group beneath the giant tree.

Instead of allowing her to direct him, Mark detached his arm from hers. "Nevertheless, gallant knight is riding." He swiftly reached the group. "Miss Berceau, your companion tells me you have some expertise in fall mushrooms. There are some I would have you examine before I take them to our cook."

Not waiting for her consent, and over Jared's objections, Mark reached past his cousin, holding out both hands.

"Now see here, Mark, just getting to the good part. Telling 'em about that mill outside of Cheltenham last year. You know, the one where Granite Gordon stuck his spoon in the wall."

"Not for ladies' ears, Jer." Mark scowled admonishingly at his cousin. Juliette had lost no time putting her hands in his, confirming her companion's suspicions that she wanted rescue. Mark tugged her up and half-lifted her past Jared's legs.

"Not true, Mr. Camden." Sylvia Patchfield's cheeks were flushed with excitement. "I find it quite stirring, Surely you wish to hear the outcome, Miss Berceau?"

"I thank you, Miss Patchfield, but edifying as this conversation is, I am always fascinated by the study of mushrooms." She slid a sideward glance at the blonde that had Mark suppressing a chuckle.

After a few paces separated them from Miss Patchfield, Mark spoke. "So you *are* an expert on mushrooms, my girl. Spot one on the most elevated ground, can't you?"

"I shouldn't have said that, and least of all in *your* hearing." Juliette turned her head away.

"Now, whyever not?"

"Because I do not want to cause Miss Patchfield to come under your censure as I have done yet again."

Mark was leading her away from the others at a rapid pace. "I have been wanting to speak to you. To apologize. Of course I knew you weren't contemplating a private picnic with Jared, I—"

"Then why did you hint at it?" Juliette stopped and lifted eyes trembling with tears to meet his. "I thought last night we had agreed . . . and then, I had such good intentions of apologizing even more—"

Mark yearned to soothe away the tears gathering on her

lower lashes. "I don't know why." He sighed. "I think I was jealous."

Juliette's mouth fell slightly open again. Why was this man forever stunning her into silence? Why did her heart beat so at the way he looked at her? And why was she so unwise as to welcome these manifestations of attraction to a man who must be on the lookout for a rich wife?

But Juliette was not feeling particularly wise. She encouraged him to continue. "J-jealous?"

Too late, Mark remembered his promise to Jared, to himself, not to become involved with this woman. *Drat. She gets past my guard so easily.* Shoving his hand nervously through his hair, he shifted abruptly to a jolly tone. "Yes, indeed. My cousin is forever luring the young ladies away. If there was to be a picnic, I wanted to participate!"

The look she gave him at this obvious attempt to avoid explaining himself was so reproachful he changed tactics. "Actually, I had read him a thundering scold the night before about behaving with propriety. What you saw coming to the surface was my vexation at his most improper suggestion. Jared seems to want to reform, but not to have much idea of how to go about it. That, I suppose, is where his wife will prove her worth."

"Oh." Juliette turned away, disappointed. Clearly Mr. Camden regretted having said he was jealous, and was determined to change the subject. She replied indifferently, "A wife may be able to help him if he truly wishes to reform."

"But where were you this morning?" Mark asked, changing the subject. "Did Uncle Ramsey—or the ghost, as the case may be—tell you all you wished to know of our gallery?"

"I had to help our maid pack and arrange for her transportation back home."

"You couldn't bear to have her around?"

"She was most insistent on going. I think she was about to take leave of her senses. At least now we know why she was willing to leave London to come to the country."

"What do you mean?"

"Marie is an expert dresser, especially gifted at dressing hair. She can command a high wage in London; Aunt Lydia had to pay very dearly for her. Yet when we abruptly left for the country, she came with us at quite a normal maid's salary. We wondered why. She explained last night that she always sees ghosts wherever she goes. When she heard that Solway was only recently built, she decided to see if she could find relief from those annoying *revenants*."

Mark couldn't help laughing at the expression of disgust on Juliette's face. "And did she?"

"Indeed, yes, or so she says. She begged me to explain to my uncle, so that he would not fire her for abandoning her charges. But how can I explain such a thing, when to me it is so much silliness?"

"That is a conundrum." Mark's grin faded. "I find it hard to doubt, though, that something causes these repeated sightings of the very same apparitions at various times in history, by people who could have no knowledge of previous sightings."

"I find it hard to believe that previous sightings are not discussed over and over again with such relish that new servants are quickly indoctrinated, and in the case of the susceptible, made hysterical, by them."

"A convincing argument." Mark smiled warmly down at her.

"While we are on the subject of last night." Juliette continued, blushing under the warmth of his regard, "I apologize again for that terrible slander against you and your cousin! How silly I was to accuse you of spying behind my wall just because of that noise, when I later realized the whole house is like a percussion section in an orchestra. Once everyone settled down, I could hear the castle creak and clank!"

Mark grinned. "It could have been dozens of ghosts."

"I'm sure Marie agreed. But I slept much better than she, secure in my knowledge that it was only timber shifting and metal contracting."

"Dear little rationalist." His black eyes caressed her face; his voice was tender.

"Oh!" Juliette's cheeks bloomed. She stepped away from him, but not as quickly as she should have.

"Excuse me! With you I seem inclined to forget myself." Mark's face flushed too. *What is the matter with me?* he wondered. *I don't seem to be able to keep a resolution for three minutes at a time.* "Would you care to tour the chapel?"

He offered her his arm. She hesitated. "I've been wanting to do that very thing from the minute I caught sight of it, but—"

"We won't be alone."

"We won't?" The faintest regret colored her tone.

"No, the others have started this way."

Juliette looked back and saw that indeed a general advance was occurring. In the vanguard, the two stalwart footmen carried the countess while the earl strode at her side. Sylvia Patchfield was on one arm of the viscount, while Adelaide was on the other.

"In that case . . ." Smiling sweetly, Juliette took Mark's arm.

Juliette held her bonnet in place as she tilted her head far back to take in the remains of the nave of the abbey cathedral. Saying nothing, she turned slowly in place.

Mark watched her reaction with pleasure. Her silence, the awed look on her face, expressed very much what he always felt upon entering this once-sacred place.

When she had completely turned around, Juliette wordlessly took his arm again and strolled down the central aisle, looking to right and left. When they reached the front of the sanctuary, he surprised her by lifting her onto what once must have been the altar, then joining her there. "There are some features you can see best from this vantage point," he explained.

"I think the original inhabitants would have been most

shocked to find a woman in this position, sir," she admonished him, but her eyes twinkled.

"I think they would appreciate the spirit of reverence with which you observe the ruins."

"Does it not make you a little sad?"

"Always. Particularly when I think of the many good works the church did for the poor of the area."

Chattering behind them warned them that the sanctuary had been invaded by the others. Mark leapt down and held out his arms to Juliette. She trustingly went to him. He reluctantly eschewed the chance to hold her close for an instant, honoring her trust. Taking her hand, he led her down the left transept.

"Come see the courtyard. That is where the Halloween ball will be held, weather permitting."

Moments later they were in a vast open area framed by high, unevenly weathered stone walls. The ground was completely covered by smoothly polished, expertly laid stones, obviously quarried from the abbey itself. No blade of grass nor twig of tree littered the polished granite.

"Now I understand how there can be a ball here. I've been wondering. You've restored it." Juliette glided across the stones in a trial dance step or two.

"Yes. In fact, if you look closely you'll see that all of St. Mildryth's, like this courtyard, is in some sense a fraud." Mark waved to his grandmother, who was just being carried in through another wide door.

"A fraud?" Juliette stopped dancing to stare at him.

"Yes. Look closely at the walls. Go back and look again at the portion of the roof arches that survive."

Pleased at being presented a puzzle, Juliette returned to the chapel ruins. She stood in the doorway for along time, studying the ancient structure.

"It's been repaired and reinforced?"

"Just so! Several years ago my father convinced my grandparents to halt the inexorable decay process as much as possible, lest the abbey become like Dunwich Friary in Suffolk, just a few rocks battered by the elements. Mr.

Franklin's invention has been a great help, and I am proud to say it was I who suggested we try it."

"Mr. Franklin?" Juliette's eyes sought out the tallest points on the sanctuary roof. "I see them! Lightning rods!"

"Before their installation we lost several good-sized chunks each year to lightning strikes. There had seemed little point in supporting the taller structures before, but now we've braced them as unobtrusively as possible, and even repointed some of the stonework."

"I think it is admirable of your family! You spend your money and effort to preserve one of the nation's treasures!" Juliette turned the full glory of her smile on Mark.

The effect of those golden-brown eyes looking so warmly into his own was almost overwhelming. Mark found himself clenching his fists for control. There was nothing he wanted more than to gather this sweet young woman into his arms and kiss her. This improper notion could not, of course, be acted on. They were surrounded by giggling females and sharp-eyed chaperones, for one thing. There was that damned promise to Jared for another.

"I cannot take any credit for it, for I am only following in my father's footsteps, and carrying out my grandfather's wishes."

"But you do so willingly, I am sure."

"Most willingly. I consider it a sacred trust."

"Then St. Mildryth's is safe!" Juliette lifted her hands as if to embrace the magnificent ruin.

"As long as my grandfather is alive, at least."

"What? Won't Faverill continue the preservation?"

Mark took her hand and led her back into the church, as most of the others had drifted into the courtyard by now.

"I am not sure. There is no telling with Jared. He is given to sudden starts like his father, to great sentimentality like his mother, and to great profligacy like several previous scions of the family tree. That is why my grandparents hope he will chose a wife who can steady him and reinforce what is good in his nature."

"Until today I scarcely would allow there to be good in

his nature." Juliette knew she should retrieve her hand, but ignored propriety's warnings. "He has been a charming host this morning, though I do not share his enthusiasm for blood sports."

"Oh, he can be charming when he wishes!" Mark sighed and released her hand. "Hammerswold will be the winner if Jared has succeeded in winning you over, for you will make a wonderful countess, likely the best choice he could make, come to that."

"Indeed, no. Adelaide would be much better, for she welcomes the opportunity!"

"But you said—"

"Only that he is not quite as hopeless as I thought him to be. He is still a gamester, a devotee of low sports, and, if what I have heard hinted at is true, something of a rake. After all, we women swear to love and honor our husband, as well as obey him. How could I commit my life so wholly to such as Faverill?"

"Most of the women I've met seem untroubled by that challenge," Mark insisted, trying to squelch the little spurt of hope that her words raised.

Juliette shook her head. "How sad for you, Mr. Camden, to have such a low opinion of females as to believe that Lord Faverill's title and wealth would outweigh all else."

"I see that principle in action constantly." The memories of his broken engagement brought a grim look to his countenance.

She frowned and reversed direction. "I would be the last to try to deprive a man of his principles."

He caught up to her. "I've done it again. Insulted you, and without the least intention. Please forgive me."

"I do believe it was accidental—this time." Juliette's smile was rueful. "Tell me—you and Faverill are so different. I wonder what made him the way he is?"

Mark chuckled. "In a way you might blame our family ghost. Jared was orphaned at an early age and raised by his mother."

Juliette blurted out, "So this supposedly wise ghost chose Lady Faverill!"

"You've met Aunt Helen?"

Embarrassed at her unguarded speech, Juliette nodded her head. "Forgive me, sir, I meant no disrespect."

He waved his hand dismissively. "Aunt Helen occasionally inspires awe by her utter silliness, but rarely respect! Since you know her, I needn't explain to you how Jared came to be spoiled and petted into complete irresponsibility. I, on the other hand, was reared with the responsibilities of the Hammerswold holdings always in view. My father loved the land, loved his older brother. They worked together like a perfect team, and I was raised to succeed him."

"Only you doubt that you and Faverill can work well together. Yet he seems to respect you."

"I believe he does respect me, in his way. But . . . Let me tell you a story. When Jared was eighteen, he got into some noisy scrapes that convinced my grandfather he needed to take the boy in hand. He brought him to Hammerswold over Aunt Helen's objections, and put him into my father's care, to educate in estate matters. Father decided he should start by learning about sheep.

"Jared spent three months being drilled in the management of sheep, yet today in a thirty-minute conversation your companion showed me more true knowledge of the subject than Jared could ever boast. All he retained of his learning was that sheep were economical to raise and thus usually profitable. From then on, whenever my father would mention problems with other crops or investments, Jared would immediately proclaim that we should rip out the hedges, throw out the farmers, and bring in more sheep. I have horrible visions of Hammerswold as one vast ocean of sheep." He chuckled at the image.

Juliette laughed with him, but clearly she understood the continuing anxiety under his laughter. "You would probably be long gone by then."

"True. My grandparents have tried to get me to promise

to stay with Hammerswold no matter what, but there are circumstances that might make that impossible."

"You couldn't stay and watch him ruin it . . ."

"Or bankrupt it . . ."

"Or turn it into some vast hunting preserve . . ."

"You understand me perfectly."

"What I don't understand is why everyone admires the ghost's choice so much, if he is believed to have chosen such a mother for Faverill."

"Oh, but that's just it! The ghost never chose. Hasn't made an appearance since convincing NiNi to marry grandfather! My Uncle Frederick was too impatient to wait, so they tell me. He married Helen Percival at the age of twenty-one, regretted it by twenty-two, and went to his eternal reward by twenty-three. That is one reason Jared is so determined that this house party will bear fruit. He is not terribly concerned with the prosperity of the earldom, but he wishes for longevity, you must understand!"

Juliette paused again. In another ten feet they would be in hearing of some of the others of the party. She knew she was losing her heart to Mark Camden. She knew, too—for hadn't he just confirmed it?—that he must marry well, having no independent means. Worse, he was firmly convinced that she was as determined to wed his cousin as any of the other young women, in spite of her protestations to the contrary. Still, that hope that springs eternal bubbled up in her, urging her to try make him understand her feelings.

"I hope this house party does bear fruit for him. I wish for him a wise, warmhearted woman whom he can marry to his very soul's advantage. But it won't be me, Mr. Mark Camden. I could not love a man I could not look up to. And I could never marry where I do not love."

# Chapter Ten

Julie was mortified by Mark's silent reception of this speech. *He doesn't believe me, or he doesn't care. He probably thinks that I am boldly setting my cap for him.* Her embarrassment was deepened by the knowledge that with the least encouragement she would do just that.

"I hear Susan calling," she choked out, and almost ran away, leaving Mark Camden standing as if turned to stone.

Mark was at war with himself. Deeply touched by her words, he felt an elation that his wooden expression did not reveal. Here was a worthy, attractive woman, for whom he felt an almost primitive longing, and her behavior indicated that his interest was returned. If she could be believed, she would not marry Jared for his title and money.

But his joy was diluted by concern. What if she should turn out to be the best countess for Jared? Wasn't it his duty to help his cousin win her? Wouldn't it be betrayal to court her himself? *NiNi and grandfather would be aghast,* he thought. *And I gave Jared my word.*

Thus, while he wanted nothing more than to pursue Juliette and begin a serious courtship, wisdom and family loyalty dictated that he remain in the background, awaiting events. Surely his affections could not be too much engaged now to draw back, but many more hours like this last one and he would not answer for his hungry heart.

As for Miss Berceau, she might find that her opinion of his cousin, already improved by their morning activities, might change in his favor. If he set himself to the task, Jared could be a most engaging man. Though Mark thought the possibility remote, it was conceivable that Jared might actually fall in love with her, and under that benign influence mend his ways, as his grandfather had done before him. Mightn't she grow to love him then, thus answering her principal objection to the match? *Do I have the right to lure her away from the chance to marry so well?*

No matter how he lectured himself, however, the idea of Juliette marrying Jared gave Mark pain. With an oath, he flung himself away and walked rapidly through the sanctuary and back up the hill toward Hammerswold.

Juliette, forcing herself to calm down, joined some of the other young people. Gradually she became aware that the conversation had let to purposeful movement, and she was being pulled along with the group.

Where are we going?"

"Gracious, Julie, have you been air dreaming? We have been discussing the Ghost's Walk these last five minutes. Now we are going up there ourselves."

Julie followed Addie's line of sight and saw a long flight of stairs, narrow, steep, and with only one landing, climbing up the south wall of the courtyard. At a right angle to it at the top, across the colonnaded entryway, there was a wide, walkway whose high walls were notched, like a castle battlement.

There were few things Juliette loved more than a view from a height. She picked up her pace, eager for the climb.

"I'm not sure you should do that, Addie." Susan's voice followed them. "You know you tire easily, and then you are not fond of heights."

"I shall keep to her side, Miss Campbell, to see that she is safe." Mr. Makepeace passed Susan and caught up to Adelaide.

"Why, thank you, Mr. Makepeace." Addie tilted her head to smile up pertly into Victor's face. "I began to wonder if you were going to favor me with your presence again this afternoon."

"The favor is mine, but one I hardly dared to wrest from the great Lord Faverill."

Juliette grinned as she walked ahead of her cousin. Addie gave every indication of a growing interest in Mr. Makepeace, in spite of her efforts to flirt with Faverill.

"I'll escort you up, shall I, Miss Berceau?" The viscount stepped away from the group that had gathered at the base of the stairs.

"Why, no, Lord Faverill, though I thank you for the thought. I have no fear of heights. Miss Patchfield looks to be expecting your escort."

"Take you both up, won't I?"

The stairs looked too narrow for this feat. Juliette waited until Faverill had turned to offer his arm to Sylvia, and then bounded up the steps first. "I'll wait for you on top," she called gaily.

Shrieks of fear, whether pretend or real, accompanied the progress of the more reluctant female climbers. The stairs were in good repair, as Juliette would have expected, given what Mark had told her earlier. Where the railing had collapsed long ago, new wooden inserts had been placed for safety. Still, they *were* steep stairs, and because they went up and up with only the one interruption, gave the appearance of great height.

Julie gained the top and eagerly crossed the walkway. Standing in front of one of the notches, she was rewarded by a magnificent view of a long river valley flanked by woods and charming stone-boundaried fields. The river Leven glinted in the afternoon sun as it snaked through the valley. Here and there the thatched roof of a cottage added a human element to the landscape.

She was still looking her fill when Faverill puffed up beside her. "Gad, what a climber you are, Miss Berceau. Not even breathing hard!"

Juliette turned reluctantly, sorry to drag her attention from the view. Her eyes moved on to Miss Patchfield, a little surprised that the buxom blonde had made it up the stairs. She too was winded, though she was trying her best to be ladylike and not pant. Beads of perspiration dotted her upper lip.

The look she returned for Juliette's smile was pure venom. "So masculine a strength. I never could have made it without a strong man to lean on!"

The others in the group began straggling up. Mr. Fotheringay's staggers had as much to do with too much wine at the picnic as the exhausting climb. Miss Whitten and Miss Stephens-Hill were encouraging one another to shiver in fright.

Juliette was relieved to see that Addie was one of the ones who had turned back. She was inclined to get the nosebleed if she overexerted herself, and climbing such a steep flight of stairs would certainly have exhausted her.

"What do you think of the Ghost's Walk, Miss Berceau, Miss Patchfield?" The earl appeared at the top of the stairs and crossed over to where the others stood.

"The G-ghost's Walk?" Mr. Fotheringay looked around in alarm. "Wh-why is it called the Ghost's Walk?"

"Because the ghost likes to pace back and forth here," Jared gleefully informed his friend. "He pitches those he dislikes over the edge!"

"Never told me that, Jer!" Fotheringay shoved his way through the little knot of people rudely, his walk less than straight, and staggered down the steps to the jeers of his friends. "Pay you out for this, Jer, see if I don't," the inebriated young man's aggrieved voice floated back up as he hastily disappeared from view.

Juliette reluctantly smiled as the others laughed. She thought it shabby of Jared to alarm his obviously terrified friend and then ridicule him.

"Why *do* they call it the Ghost's Walk, Lord Hammerswold?" Sylvia Patchfield asked.

"Because the old boy is often seen strolling here, especially on moonlit nights. Since he and his descendents did their best to pull the abbey down, it is surprising that it is his favorite place to haunt, but there it is. There's no accounting for a ghost's whims."

"Does he, ah, attend the Halloween ball from this vantage point?" Sylvia looked up and down the crosswalk with great interest.

The earl smiled. "He's been known to do so!"

"Well, Miss Berceau, Miss Patchfield, I daresay it is a good thing neither of you is afraid to climb the stairs. What a good way to encourage the old boy to appear, eh? Entice him out with a sacrificial virgin, like the dragons of old!" Faverill laughed heartily at his own joke.

"What a ghastly comparison," Juliette sniffed, laughing in spite of herself. Sylvia's amusement was more unrestrained. She leaned heavily against Faverill, giving him a clear view of her cleavage as she giggled.

Miss Whitten stiffened and looked most perturbed at this conversation. Next to her, Miss Davies turned beet red.

"Remember your manners, old son," the earl cautioned.

"Pah. No milk-and-water misses for me, eh Miss . . . I say, can't we do away with all this 'Mr. and Miss' stuff? Together for so long, we all ought to be on a first-name footing, eh? You hear me?" He raised his voice. "Everyone—first names."

"I thought you'd never ask, Jared," Sylvia cooed.

Juliette nodded her head graciously, though she privately thought it past the line for Faverill to give everyone there the freedom of her name without her permission.

Shouts from below ordered them to come down, as the party was breaking up. Juliette hung back, hoping for a few minutes of privacy. The earl seemed disinclined to leave her. "I shall be down directly, my lord," she assured him. I just want a moment or two."

He nodded. "I shall wait at the landing. That way you can at least fall no farther than that."

Juliette thanked him, then turned eagerly back for a last look at the valley. Just so had monks and nuns, lords and ladies, and ordinary townspeople stood for centuries, looking out over the valley, or down upon the entrance to the abbey. For this, she realized, was what she stood upon. The vast open arches had once held stout wooden doors that could be barred against enemies. The ancient road had led to these gates, and on this walkway the abbey's guardians had hailed friend or foe, received warning of approaching thunderstorms, or merely caught a breath of air on a hot summer's day.

Juliette felt such a breath just now, pleasantly cool on this unseasonably warm October day. She lifted her head and sniffed the fragrant breeze. Without knowing why, she glanced abruptly over her right shoulder. It had almost seemed as if someone had approached her. But no one was there. She stared for moment, a little shiver possessing her. This ghost-story madness was catching, like a cold, she decided, giving her head a little shake. With amusement curving her lips, she turned and started down the stairs to join the others.

The countess did not come down to dinner that evening. Exhausted by her afternoon excursion, she took her dinner on a tray. Lady Stephens-Hill took her place as hostess. Mark had followed Juliette's suggestions in the seating arrangements, except that Juliette found herself seated next to Lord Faverill. Jared had given her to understand that this was at his request.

Thus it was that she had the opportunity of being right next to Jared when he sat down, exuding a loud, long noise more suited to the privy than the dining room. She tried desperately to ignore it, but it seemed to go on forever. At last the viscount stood and ostentatiously removed what appeared to be a leather cushion, ending the noise. He began to howl with laughter.

Around the table most of the female guests, the earl, and Mark were just as shocked as Juliette was. But Jared's cronies, especially Fotheringay, laughed wickedly and knowledgeably. Sylvia, after a moment or two of surprise, began giggling behind her handkerchief.

When he had recovered a bit from his first wave of laughter, Faverill shook a fist at Fotheringay. "So it's to be practical jokes is it, you makebate?"

"Just paying you back for the Gh-ghost Walk business," Fotheringay choked out over his final gasps of hilarity.

"This is disgraceful. I never! Lord Hammerswold, if you cannot guarantee that my Gilda is not exposed to any more such insults, I shall . . . we shall . . ." Mrs. Whitten stood up, ready to march from the room.

The earl's face had turned puce. "You most assuredly need not fear, madam. There will be no more vulgar pranks during this gathering. I hope that is clear to each and every one of you!" He looked around the table like a hawk deciding which chicken to rend into pieces.

Faverill looked sullen. "Just a joke."

Fotheringay stammered, "Meant no harm, sir. I only—"

"Quite. If we are ready to dine, gentlemen." Once more the earl's look quelled dissent, and the meal commenced. But it was a stiff, awkward affair, and Juliette was glad when Lady Stephens-Hill stood to lead the ladies out.

The earl came with them, after pausing a moment to whisper an admonition in Faverill's ear. "I want to go up and check on Regina," he explained, bidding the women good evening.

The ladies were left to themselves then. Mrs. Whitten immediately began castigating the viscount. "I am of a mind to leave tomorrow. My Gilda is used to better than this. That man and his friends are not fit for society."

"I do not think he is truly wicked, ma'am," Sylvia asserted. "Do you, Juliette?"

Juliette thought he might be, but contented herself with saying, "He is the most immature man I have ever met. My cousins are ten and twelve and might well have been more embarrassed by that prank tonight than Faverill was."

The ladies murmured various levels of agreement with this assessment. "It would take a very strong woman to settle him down," Susan asserted.

"Or one who would appreciate and enjoy him for what he is," Sylvia snapped. "Not every woman in the world sees it as her duty to reform her husband. Some of them see it as their duty to make them happy."

None of the mothers and chaperones could acquiesce to such a permissive view of the dissipated viscount's future. Sylvia came in for a deal of censure, even from her own mother.

At ten o'clock, Lady Stephens-Hill sent for the tea tray, and when the gentlemen still did not join them, she suggested they retire for the evening. Apprehensive mothers and chaperones agreed. The men would not be fit company for young ladies after lingering this long over their port, telling raw jokes to one another.

Ordinarily Mark would have put a stop to the heavy drinking that took place after the ladies left. But he was in a deep slough of despond, which left him little energy for policing the exceedingly jolly party that developed. In fact, he had recourse to the port much more than was usual, as he tried to escape the endless round of painful thoughts that assailed him over Miss Juliette Berceau.

He had gone down to dinner determined to be polite but distant, and found himself receiving the exact same treatment from her. It was for the best, but it hurt him, to a depth that surprised him and made him reassess his afternoon's conclusions. But he was unable to resolve the conflict between duty to Jared and attraction to Juliette. The fact that he had no doubt it was she the ghost would prefer was, he realized, a measure of his own admiration for her.

When Jared and his friends finally rose and staggered to the billiards room for a game of high-stakes billiards, Mark ordered the butler to notify him if there should be a problem, and barricaded himself in the library with a bottle of brandy, determined to drink himself into utter oblivion. He was very close to achieving his purpose when Hopewell rushed in to announce the appearance of the Ghost of Hammerswold.

# Chapter Eleven

Julie leaned on the balcony railing outside her bedroom and gazed down the hill toward the ruins of St. Mildryth's. Now that she had seen them up close, she realized that her view was through the ribs of the sanctuary roof. The line of stone just beyond and below the broken ceiling arches must be the walkway upon which she and the others had looked out over the valley this afternoon. The light of the waxing moon, low on the horizon, threw its silhouette into dark relief.

*If only I were there now, on the Ghost's Walk, with* . . . She stopped her thoughts with an effort. Judging from his response to her this afternoon, she had no hope for sincere romantic interactions with Mark Camden. The man enjoyed flirting, but obviously it was but a social game with him. He became remote at any hint of seriousness.

A muffled shout reminded her of the bacchanalia in progress below. *They'll all be hung over tomorrow morning,* she thought. With a weary sigh she turned to go in. Last night had been eventful rather than restful. She was in need of a good night's sleep.

Something caught her eye as she turned. She stopped to glance over her shoulders. For a moment it had seemed to her that a dim gray figure was moving along the Ghost's Walk. She blinked her eyes and looked again. Wasn't someone slowly pacing the walkway? But how could she see anyone from here?

Juliette shook her head. *One thing this trip is proving,* she thought with amusement, *is that I am not as lacking in*

*imagination as my family has always insisted, for it would
not be difficult at all for me to imagine that I saw a ghost
walking there.*

Rather than remain to study the possible apparition, Juliette closed the balcony doors and tumbled into bed. She was asleep the instant her head hit the pillow.

"Wake up, Julie, oh, wake up, do!" Adelaide was shaking her. Juliette put up a floppy hand in protest and turned away grumbling.

"Grouch! You're missing the ghost. Everyone else is seeing it and you're missing it. Wake up!"

"Wh-what time is it?" Julie finally sat up.

"Twelve o'clock. Wake up. The ghost is on the walkway at St. Mildryth's. Everyone can see it!"

"What took them so long?" Julie muttered, pulling on her wrapper.

"You've already seen it? And didn't tell me? And went to sleep?" Adelaide's astonished indignation lifted her voice two registers.

Julie could see that Susan was standing on the balcony, clutching her robe around her against the night breeze. "Yes, I saw it just after we turned in. I expect one of those jackanapes hung a sheet from the lightning rods or some-such."

"Well, then, how did that sheet travel from Sylvia's room through the air to the walkway?"

Juliette had gained the balcony by then. She stopped and laughed at Adelaide's assertion. "Is that what she told you?" Then she turned to look past Susan's shoulder.

"Oh!" She hastened to the edge of the balcony. "That is quite something!"

"Not what you saw earlier?"

"No, indeed." Juliette stared in amazement. A very bright, glowing white object was moving at a ponderous pace across the walkway, periodically obscured by the sanctuary's roof columns as it progressed. Whatever it was must be very tall, ten feet or more, and much sharper-edged than Juliette would ever have imagined a ghost to be. Its shape was a triangle with the base beneath their line of sight, and the apex replaced with a round "head" that sported enormous dark eyes and no mouth.

A hubbub of noise announced that the other balconies were occupied with gawking women, and below a loud commotion preceded a general charge of inebriated young gentlemen down the steps and along the road to St. Mildryth's. As they whooped into the night, Julie tried to make out their identities. Just then a lone masculine figure walked slowly onto the top step and then stopped. Juliette recognized Mark Camden by his characteristic gesture of thrusting his hand into his hair. In a few minutes he was joined by the earl, who also merely stood, observing.

"Why don't they go, too?" Addie wondered.

"Because those rowdy young men will surely frighten the ghost away." Susan nodded sagely. All three women returned their gaze to the bright white figure. It had begun moving in the other direction, back along the walkway. As they watched, it suddenly disappeared.

"Oooh!" Disappointed exclamations sounded from the balconies.

"Just as you said, Susan." Adelaide rubbed her eyes. "What was it, I wonder?"

"Why, do you not think it the Hammerswold ghost, dear?" Susan's teasing smile could just be made out in the dim room.

"Perhaps." Doubt vibrated in Adelaide's voice. "Julie, what do you think?"

"I'm not sure exactly how it was done, but I'm sure it was not of supernatural origin! I am going back to bed." Juliette yawned mightily and suited action to words.

"But don't you want to hear about Sylvia's remarkable confrontation with the ghost in her room a little while ago?"

"She will tell it over and over. I'll hear it tomorrow. Doubtless it will gain in the retelling! Good night, sweet."

She kissed her cousin, glad that the younger girl's miff with her had passed.

Julie proved to be a prophetess. When she went into the morning room, the usually sparse breakfast crowd had grown to include most of the viscount's friends as well as the viscount himself.

Juliette entered the room just behind Lord Tremayne, who had heretofore not been seen belowstairs before noon at the earliest. Sylvia was holding forth, with the viscount hanging on her every word. When Julie entered, the buxom blonde crowed, "Only guess who visited my room last night, Juliette?"

Lord Tremayne chortled, "Jared, of course!"

Sylvia gave him a scathing look. "How dare you, sir!"

"Take care, Tommy. Show some respect!" The sight of Jared looking morally indignant was almost too much for Juliette. She turned aside to the breakfast buffet, choking back a laugh. She was surprised to find that Mr. Camden had joined her and was lifting the lid on the kedgeree for her.

"Good morning, Juliette," he greeted her quietly. "I understand we all are under orders to use first names now."

"Good morning, Mark." She smiled, but felt a renewed wave of irritation at the viscount. Mark was the one man of the group she might have derived great pleasure from granting that right. That tender moment was stolen from them both by Faverill's fiat. Though his behavior yesterday made tender moments between them extremely unlikely, she reminded herself.

"I hear you slept through our ghost last night."

"Not exactly." Her plate full, Juliette turned to the table to find Sylvia's eyes following her. "I was awakened from a sound sleep to view an impressive apparition on the Ghost's Walk."

"Then you did see it, Juliette? Did you speak to it? Hear it speak to you?" The blonde threw her a challenging look.

"No, indeed. I was too sleepy last night for late-night vis-

its. But I would love to hear all the details of your encounter. It sounds fascinating."

Juliette tried to imbue her words and expression with sincerity, but as Mark took his place opposite her, he winked
at her, very nearly destroying her composure.

She apparently convinced Sylvia, however, who launched
into a voluble explanation.

"He came into my room just as that other ghost came
into yours last night, through the paneling. I was just doz-
ing off when a bright light awoke me."

"You must have been terrified." Lady Stephens-Hill
looked sympathetically at Sylvia.

"At first I was. I declare my heart was racing. But he told
me to be calm and of good spirits. His voice was so kindly,
I could not be afraid of him."

"And so she sat like a good girl and conversed with him.
Isn't she amazing!" Mrs. Patchfield beamed at her daughter.

"Whatever did you converse about?" Juliette was genuinely curious.

"Oh, he asked me my ideas on the role of a countess in
society, how I would behave toward tenants, my ideas on
housekeeping, and so forth."

"Housekeeping!" Elizabeth Harpwood laughed. "Doesn't
he know that ladies of the *ton* don't concern themselves
with housekeeping?"

"He is, after all, a very old ghost," Mark said seriously.
"It is natural he would have old-fashioned ideas."

"Oh, yes. I collect when he was alive the countess was
the chatelaine and carried dozens of keys and all that!"
Elizabeth wrinkled her nose in disdain.

"Well, and so she should be now," Sylvia asserted. "I
was raised to know all the details of housekeeping and to
supervise servants, and so I told him. He appeared to be
most satisfied with my answers."

The other girls around the table had long faces. Their
mothers looked even more disappointed.

"And so you were named the next countess. Well, that is

taken care of then. I wish you happy, both of you." Juliette was utterly sincere. No more unwanted attentions from the viscount, nor accusations of trying to entrap him from anyone else. She slanted Mark Camden a look that said "So there!"

"Well . . . not exactly." The viscount looked reluctant to contradict her. "Mean to say, *I* haven't heard from the old boy yet."

"Oh." Juliette looked from the viscount's sorrowful countenance to Sylvia's triumphant one. "Well, I am sure that you will be hearing from him soon!" *Particularly if Sylvia and her unknown assistant can think of how to manage it.* "But tell me how the ghost got from your room to the ghost's walk, or was the thing on the walkway a prank?"

"Oh, t'was no prank. Just as your maid did last night, Juliette, mine awoke while I was conversing with the ghost. She took fright and began to scream. He rose up, floated to the window, and then sailed out. I ran onto the balcony and watched him sail through the air until he reached the walkway. My maid saw it too; you can ask her."

"I don't doubt she'll confirm every word!" Julie ducked her head to avoid seeing Mark's smirk.

"Of course she did." Mark's smile grew wider. "Poor creature was in spasms. Thought we'd lose her today as we did Fotheringay and your maid, but she has been pacified. My grandmother explained to her that all of our ghosts are benevolent, and she expressed a wish, in fact, of apologizing to the old gentleman."

"Lost Mr. Fotheringay?"

Victor explained. "The sight of that . . . whatever it was . . . on the walkway last night completely overset poor Algernon. He scrambled upstairs, roused his servant, packed, and left before first light."

"How dreadful." Juliette felt sorry for the young man, so badly frightened by so silly a scheme.

Adelaide came skipping into the room. "The countess has proposed a sketching expedition on Rosethorn Hill as our entertainment today. She has asked that all who want to go be prepared by eleven. Of course we will have an al fresco luncheon taken to us there."

Juliette rose eagerly. "I'm so glad. I was hoping to have this opportunity. I have heard that there are picturesque views to be taken in three directions from that point."

"Not to mention Hammer's Pepperpot," Mark said. "Our rock formation is considered a close rival of the Bridestones or Roseberry Topping."

Sylvia threw down her napkin, pouting. "I don't like to sketch trees and hills! I prefer to draw people and animals."

"I will pose for you," Jared offered eagerly.

"Will you count his sketch as an animal or a person?" Beauford jeered above the hoots of Jared's other cronies.

Watching this byplay, Juliette thought gleefully, *The viscount has clearly turned his attentions to Sylvia. I may be able to enjoy this visit after all!*

Mark's feelings were more complex. He was pleased to see Jared wasn't singling Juliette out, yet chagrined at the apparent success of the scheming, totally unsuitable Sylvia Patchfield. The thought of such as her one day becoming the Countess of Hammerswold was enough to turn his stomach.

"I wonder what they are going on about?" Susan's musing voice caused Julie to glance briefly toward Elizabeth, Carolyn, Millicent, and Gilda, who were in intense, low-voiced consultation on a large boulder a few feet away.

"I really can't imagine." Julie was indifferent to the young girls' behavior. She was intent on completing the detailed drawing she was making, from which she would paint a watercolor, and perhaps one day a large oil painting.

"They're plotting something."

"Hmmmmm." Julie carefully drew in Hammer's Pepperpot, standing like a giant's toy straight above Rosethorn Hill. Silhouetted against the valley below, it was a fascinating rock formation.

"They keep looking at the viscount and Miss Patchfield—"

"They certainly can't like the way he is now devoting himself exclusively to her." Julie took out her watercolors and began washing in color to assist her memory of the scene.

"They've also given you and Addie some peculiar looks."

"I wonder why? We're being ignored by Faverill!" Julie smiled vaguely.

"I am pleased that Addie is not more upset. She seems to be quite content to have Mr. Makepeace's company."

"Could be a match forming there," Juliette's attention came completely away from her drawing at last. "I've thought from the first that she was interested in him, and now he seems very attentive. I only hope her father will not be too disappointed if she fails to snare the viscount."

"Lord Paxton *should* be pleased. Victor will be a baron one day, and well-heeled." Susan's brow knit with worry.

"Yes, but just how much like the viscount is he? You can tell a great deal about a man by the company he keeps."

"Precisely."

Both women frowned anxiously at Addie, who was seated on a rock a few feet below them, sketch pad in hand, with the attractive Victor Makepeace looking up at her adoringly.

# Chapter Twelve

Dinner that evening once again found Julie sitting beside Mark. Sylvia was in the place of honor next to the viscount, smugly absorbing all of his attention.

Julie's dinner companion on her right was Mrs. Harpwood, who had hardly deigned to address a word to her since she arrived at Hammerswold, clearly seeing her as beneath notice. The formidable matron continued this cold formality at the dining table, once again throwing Juliette on her own resources, as Mark's attention was absorbed by his other dinner partner, Mrs. Whitten.

*It is fortunate that the earl's cook is excellent,* Juliette mused, *for I seem condemned to eat my dinner in silence.*

Mark at last escaped his other dinner partner. He turned to Julie with a smile. "What did you think of Rosethorn Hill?"

Relieved to be freed from her solitary state, she turned to him. "The view is all that was claimed in Patterson's guidebook, and the Pepperpot is fascinating."

"Shall I expect to see your sketches after dinner?"

"Modesty and maidenly reserve prevented me from bringing them downstairs," Juliette protested, stifling a giggle. "However, like all the young ladies, I have them ready to hand just inside the door of my room, in case they are called for. I warn you sir, you must be very clever tonight, if you are not to spend the entire evening poring over dozens of amateur pictures of the same view that Mr. J. M. W. Turner took to such perfection, and which hangs over the mantel in the Prince of Wales's drawing room."

"Thank you for the warning. But I should indeed like to see *your* efforts."

Juliette inclined her head in agreement, cautioning him, "I make no claim to talent. My artistic endeavors afford me great enjoyment, and I am content with that."

Sylvia's distinctive laugh carried across the table, engaging their attention. She and Jared were completely absorbed in a private joke.

"So, you have lost your place, have you?" Mark arched a dark eyebrow at her.

Juliette was irritated to see that, in spite of all she had said to him on this score, he was studying her features as if looking for signs of disappointment.

"La, sir. I am not finished yet! Her ghost was more convincing than mine, but I think I know how it was done. Now all I have to do is find a scene painter, and a confederate who doesn't mind walking about in the middle of the night on a high stone wall carrying lanterns and stretched canvas!"

The dark head drew back in astonishment. "A pretty good guess, very close to my own."

"Who is her confederate, do you know?"

"Sylvia has a very devoted groom. He claims to have been sleeping during the incident, of course."

"Of course." Juliette's eyes danced with laughter.

"So! Why did you not say something this morning to cast doubt on this apparition, before Jared had got the matter firmly fixed in his head?"

"A misstep, sir. I shall recover." She turned her entire attention to the potted lamprey on her plate.

Mark chuckled. "You know, I do believe you mean to stay silent."

"You cannot tell me you or your grandparents accepted that ridiculous performance as genuine. Far better for *them* to disillusion Jared than for me to do it."

"They tried, as did I. But as we could not account for the

presence of the ghost in Sylvia's room, or explain to Jared's satisfaction how it managed to fly through the air and land on the walkway—"

"I collect I am the only one he accords the honor of thinking capable of lying."

"Jared would rather believe it of you than her, I am sorry to say."

Juliette's spirits plummeted. *Then he is sorry that I am no longer looked upon by Jared as a potential wife.* This idea depressed her so thoroughly she couldn't continue her conversation with him. She turned, determined to make Mrs. Harpwood speak to her, even if all she got for her efforts was a set-down.

Juliette's unhappy expression sent Mark into the doldrums. A few moment's gloomy rumination on her reaction convinced him that she must be very disappointed, in spite of her bravado. *All of this pretense that she isn't interested must hide a really deep-seated desire to be Jared's wife,* he thought.

The next morning Juliette was quietly eating breakfast. Mark, Susan, and Lady Stephens-Hill were also at table.

Suddenly Addie burst into the room, blonde curls bouncing. "It is famous! You'll never guess!"

"Your manners, dear." Susan couldn't quite put aside her role as governess.

"Elizabeth saw the ghost last night!"

Mark looked up, startled. *Miss Harpwood, the plump young girl with the ravenous appetite?* A sudden mental picture of her and Jared spending a lifetime vying for the choice delicacies at the table forced him to cough into his napkin to avoid a rude laugh.

Lady Stephens-Hill's eyes bulged. "Surely not! What makes you think so?"

"She told me. She wanted to know what to do."

"Do? Do? What *can* one do?" There was a slightly hysterical note to Lady Stephens-Hill's voice.

"What did you advise her, Adelaide?" Juliette studied her cousin with interest.

"I told her she should tell the earl and the countess what happened. She protested she had no proof, as both her mother and her maid slept soundly through the whole thing."

Juliette nodded wisely. "That is true. Without a hysterically screaming maid, she is at a bit of a disadvantage."

Adelaide stifled a giggle behind her hand.

"Juliette," Susan protested, though she looked none too far away from laughing herself.

Mark's amusement broke through in a crooked smile.

Lady Stephens-Hill saw nothing humorous in the matter. "You did the right thing," she said, standing. "I am going to see that the earl and the countess are informed."

Mark dropped his serviette on his plate and pushed back his chair, sparkling eyes on Juliette, who ducked her head to keep her composure.

"Shall we go see what happens?" Addie was prancing with eagerness to entice her cousin and governess away.

"I wouldn't miss it for the world." Taking one last hasty sip of her morning tea, Julie joined the general exodus out of the room.


"And then he asked me about my housekeeping skills, just as he did you, Sylvia." Miss Harpwood sniffed disdainfully. "Silly of him, but I was too polite to tell him so. I said that I hoped the countess would teach me all I needed to know."

Lady Hammerswold smiled benignly at her. "Of course I will. That is . . . did he tell you he had settled on you?"

"Oh, no, my lady. He only wished to make my acquaintance, he said." Elizabeth spoke most respectfully to the countess, but she cast Sylvia a pert sideward glance and then turned to the viscount. "He said you should consider all your alternatives carefully before making a decision, Jared."

Jared's return look was not encouraging, being more like

a glare than anything else, but he raised from his chair enough to sketch her a bow.

At that moment, Carolyn stepped forward, hands on her hips. "Well, the ghost visited me last night, too!"

A great hubbub greeted this news. Lady Stephens-Hill put her hand on her daughter's arm. "You didn't tell me this, child."

"I didn't wish to make a great piece of work of it, Mother. After all, he didn't name me the next countess either, only asked me a bunch of tiresome questions. But if Elizabeth is going to brag of it as if it were some great distinction—"

"Then I will, too!" Gilda Whitten spoke up. "I saw him and had the same conversation with him."

Mark's eyes turned back to Juliette just as she looked at him. The flash of shared amusement between them warmed him to his toes.

"Well, Millie," the countess asked, addressing the shy, quiet girl standing on the fringe of the group. "Did you too have a visit from the ghost. I think you must have, from the look on your face."

Suddenly Millicent Davies began to cry. Great tears rolled down her cheek silently. "What is wrong, Millie?" her mother demanded.

"I . . . I don't like to say. That is . . . oh! I don't know what to do."

"If you have seen the ghost, you must speak up," her mother urged her. A note of exultation lifted her voice.

Millie hung her head and nodded.

"When, child?"

"Last night, Mama. It was very much as with the others, though I . . . I was afraid at first. But he was ever so nice."

"They are lying!" Mrs. Patchfield shouted angrily. "They've gotten together and made this up because they are jealous of my Sylvia."

"Mother!" Sylvia put a restraining hand on her mother's arm and whispered in her ear. After a moment the matron relaxed.

"Forgive me for saying that. All of this talk of ghosts is so unsettling."

"Well, what about you, Adelaide?" The earl's face was carefully neutral.

"No, indeed, sir! I neither saw nor heard a ghost."

"You are the only one who lacks that distinction, it would seem."

"Well, I expect I am not under serious consideration, then," Addie replied, sliding a quick glance at Victor, who was watching her response alertly. "Besides, properly speaking, Juliette didn't see him either, did you, dear?"

"Indeed not. Perhaps he was afraid I'd throw water on him, too." Juliette winked at her cousin.

"What am I to do? What do you think, NiNi?" Viscount Faverill turned to his grandmother anxiously.

"It is all quite remarkable." The countess looked to the earl for guidance.

"Indeed it is. Well, at least we shan't have to worry about whether the ghost is going to appear this year, shall we?" Lord Hammerswold rubbed his hands gleefully.

"But he hasn't appeared to *me!*" Jared's voice rose to a frustrated wail.

"But he will, Jared. You must be patient." His grandmother patted his flabby cheek reassuringly. "Just do as he suggests, for he clearly is wise to insist that you get to know each of these fine young women. In time it will be clear whom you should marry."

Jared looked ruefully at Sylvia. "Thought it was all settled," he pouted.

Sylvia surprised everyone by reinforcing the countess's advice. "The choice of the future Countess of Hammerswold cannot be made lightly. Soon enough you will hear from the ghost's own lips whom you should marry."

Once the incident had been chewed over as much as it could, the group in the countess's room scattered to begin the long process of selecting just the right outfit for the day's planned visit to Stokesley.

Juliette announced her intention to pass up this outing in favor of beginning her painting. "My study was not so detailed that I can use it once I have forgotten the view. I must begin work while I still have it up here." She tapped her head.

"In that case, you must set up your easel in the Queen Anne salon," suggested the countess. "It is my favorite room for needlework, for it has a marvelous east light. Mr. Turner pronounced it a perfect painter's studio. He painted our view from Rosethorn Hill there, you know, as well as several others taken in the neighborhood which have been exhibited at the Royal Society. You can set your easel up there and leave it until you are finished."

"I accept eagerly, ma'am. While I am painting, perhaps you will join me? You could bring your needlework?"

The countess seemed well pleased with this invitation, though she hesitated to accept. "But will you quite like it, my dear? Won't conversation distract you?

"Not at all. I haven't the least hint of artistic temperament, I assure you, and I love to have company while I am reworking a sketch."

Almost all of the other people had left the room by this time. Juliette leaned down to whisper near the countess's ear, "Perhaps you will explain the secret of the maze to me. I expect we will be challenged to go into it soon, and I confess I do not like that sort of thing. It makes me apprehensive, not knowing how to extract myself."

The countess looked at her consideringly. "I too was used to dislike situations I could not control. Yes, I will tell you. It will be amusing to see you reach the center ahead of everyone else."

"See, ma'am?"

"From my bedroom window I can look down into the maze, thus enjoying some of the fun."

As Juliette entered the hall, she found that Mark had waited for her. "So you are not going into Stokesley?"

"No, your grandmother and I have a *tête-à-tête* planned." She smiled at him. "I must commend you upon your family ghost, sir. What an extremely methodical *revenant* he is, to be sure, interviewing the candidates one by one for the position." The way his full lips curved at this sally did strange things to Julie's heart.

"He would make a fine estate agent." Mark put his finger to his lips. "If he would but be more regular in his attendance upon us, I could entrust him with the hiring of the servants, a chore I despise."

Juliette yearned to continue trading quips with Mark, but she began walking swiftly down the hall. *I enjoy his company too much. This way lies sorrow, for the man has no interest in me, except as a possible wife for his cousin.*

Mark kept up with her easily. "Tell me, did the other girls invite you and Adelaide to participate in their little plot?"

She shook her head, chuckling. "Not me, at any rate. I think not Addie either. They had their heads together on Rosethorn Hill yesterday while I was sketching the view and Addie was sketching Mr. Makepeace. Perhaps the stars in her eyes as she looked at him convinced them she would not wish to join in."

"Well, you bear your disappointment admirably. Did you have no temptation to invent your own ghost story?"

She looked up angrily, to find that there was something almost tender in his smiling eyes.

"No, do not rip up at me. I know the answer. You are an honest little rationalist!" He started to chuck her under her chin but instead drew a line with his knuckle up to the center of her bottom lip.

Thrilled to the bones, she pretended indignation, tossing her head and hastening down the hall. She stopped at her door to find him still staring after her. His hair was so rumpled it was clear he had just thrust his hand through it. Instead of slamming the door as she had meant to, Juliette lingered a moment, looking at him, and then quietly entered, a foolish smile on her lips.

# Chapter Thirteen

The weather continued fair for several days, though the nights grew slightly chillier. The young people took full advantage of this halcyon period by occupying themselves during the day with outdoor activities, including long, rambling rides about the countryside, bowling on the lawn, croquet, and cricket. Twice the gentlemen went shooting while the ladies sketched.

The awkward imbalance in numbers since Mr. Fotheringay's departure caused few problems because Jared was dutifully trying to court all seven young women. Save for Victor, his cronies were lacking in matrimonial ambitions. Thus there was little pairing off; activities were undertaken as a group.

Mark usually made up one of the group, when estate matters permitted. Normally he would have regretted the time spent in such aimless pursuits, but he welcomed the opportunity to get to know Juliette better without betraying any partiality for her. He found his admiration for her grew, and with it his impatience about keeping his word to his cousin. Unfortunately, the more he observed of both her and the other young women, the more convinced he was that she would make the best wife for the heir to Hammerswold, which meant sooner or later the ghost was going to draw Jared's attention to her.

As for Juliette, she learned that her sense of humor was so compatible with Mark's that when anything amused her she had only to glance at him to set them both laughing. She cautioned herself over and over to keep a tight rein upon her emotions, though she permitted herself to view Mark as a friend. He seemed to welcome this role, so they dealt comfortably with one another.

As Juliette had expected, exploration of the maze was on the list of things to do. On that particular morning, Mark was out checking on some sheep that had cleverly thrown themselves over a hill and become lodged in a ravine.

As a result of the countess's coaching, Juliette felt confident that she could find her way quite handily, so she experienced no anxiety when the female contingent was sent one by one into the maze unescorted. Jared and his friends made it into a regular horse race, with bets placed on who would be the first one out, the last one out, the order in which they would emerge, and every other permutation they could think of. To encourage their "fillies," elegant ivory fans were offered for first and second place.

In spite of the countess's naughty encouragement, Juliette disdained to take advantage of her knowledge to win. Instead, she wandered slowly through the high green tunnels, admiring the statuary scattered in alcoves along the route. She located the secret shortcuts and exits the countess had told her about, the ones the gardeners used.

"For it would be too time consuming," Lady Hammerswold had explained, "For them to have to run the entire maze every time they wished to trim the topiary animals or place bedding plants in the flower beds."

Jared was at the center of the maze when she made her leisurely way there. He was alone.

"There you are," he huffed at her. "Last one, you know. Never took you for a flat!"

"Forgive me. I was enjoying the statues and plantings. Have you been waiting long? It really wasn't necessary."

"Yes, it was. Someone must see who arrived in the center first and last, after all. Got a monkey on it, don't you know? Come sit down by me and rest a moment." He patted the carved marble bench welcomingly.

Juliette received this suggestion without trepidation, having no concern that he might molest her. Though he had decided that it was his ghostly ancestor's wish that he court all of the young women, he clearly preferred Sylvia, and just as clearly found Juliette a drab little thing.

"Thank you. I will be happy to rest a bit. Pity there isn't a fountain, for I am perishing of thirst."

"There is," He pointed. "On the other side of that topiary deer. But come sit beside me first."

She eyed him a little askance. His insistence rang warning bells in her mind. "I am quite thirsty, sir. I believe I must avail myself of the water first."

The fountain depicted nymphs cavorting in a lily pond. A brass frog sitting on the side of the pond spouted a perpetual stream of water for the convenience of the thirsty.

She bent for a long, refreshing drink, and then turned to find herself staring Jared in his waistcoat. There was quite a lot of it, for he was very stout. He put his arms around her.

"Lord Faverill!"

"Thought this was a good opportunity—know you must be as curious as I—all the others were." He bent his head.

*He's trying to kiss me,* Juliette thought. A giggle broke from her. "Part of the interview process, I take it? What a methodical family you are, first and last. Well, Jared, as flattered as I am to be considered part of your court, you must surely realize that—" She attempted to elude his grasp as she spoke.

"Come now, 'tis only a kiss. I am considered an excellent lover, you know. Any number of my mistresses have told me so."

*He's been drinking!* Vaguely alarmed, Juliette leaned as far away from his pursed lips as she could, pinioned in his arms as she was. "I am sure you are quite an expert on that topic, but it is not a fitting subject for young ladies. I hope you didn't upset Adelaide with this start."

"By no means. She was curious as a cat. And quite a charming armful, let me tell you! And Sylvia—mmmm!" The viscount smacked his lips. "Now that Gilda —nothing. Cold as a mackerel. Just what I'd have expected from Miss

Prunes and Prisms. Come, Juliette. Let's see how you com-
pare to your cousin."

"I respectfully decline this disrespectful invitation, my
lord." With that, Juliette gave him a mighty shove. Unpre-
pared for such forcefulness, Jared stumbled backwards, hit-
ting the edge of the lily pond with one foot. For a few
seconds he balanced on the other foot, arms turning like
windmills. Then gravity won out, and he plunged sideward
into the water.

Alarmed at the unintended result of her effort to be free,
Juliette waited until she was sure the viscount was unhurt
before she turned on her heels. She was a good runner,
even in skirts, as she had already proved in cricket. She
also had the element of surprise. She could hear the viscount thrashing his way out of the water as she rounded the
first turn out of the maze.

His loud, pounding steps behind her told her he was in
hot pursuit. He knew the maze better then she. *Must find
one of those exits,* she thought, eyes searching. *There it is!*
She ran straight for a decorative obelisk, and slid into the
curved niche of trimmed hedge behind it. Sure enough,
there was a little door, painted green. She stooped down to
pass through, for it came only to her waist.

Quickly she shut the door behind her. Seconds later she
heard the viscount's steps thundering past. He sounded
angry as well as out of breath as he called for his victim to
return.

Dusting herself off carefully, Juliette looked around. She
was near the succession houses. A pleasant garden path led
back toward the castle. Laughter bubbled up out of her. She
couldn't wait to tell Mark.

Mark was not amused.

After dinner he approached her with an invitation to
walk in the garden while the company at large was engaged
in charades. They moved down the broad steps that led
away from the Prince of Wales drawing room, and Juliette's heart raced at the thought of being alone with him.

Well, not entirely alone. Susan had taken up an observation post on one of the ornate wrought-iron chairs that graced the porch.

Mark, glancing back to see where she was looking, smiled. "The ever-vigilant Miss Campbell. She is a very devoted chaperone. Nothing escapes that cool blue gaze."

"Jared succeeded in escaping it this afternoon." She leaned a bit on his arm, savoring the strength of him, and the spicy masculine scent. She felt his muscles tighten beneath her hand.

"What do you mean? Did he insult your cousin? Did he insult you?" Alarm and anger increased the volume of Mark's voice. "I am most curious to learn what happened this afternoon. I heard that Jared came out of the maze dripping wet, with a lily pad filling in where his hair has disappeared on top. I was told you went into the maze and never came out. I would have been alarmed had I not seen you talking with Mrs. Hopewell before dinner."

"Shhh. This is for your ears only. I am sure Jared did not think of it as an insult. More in the line of careful shopping, I should say. He sat in the middle of the maze and kissed the girls one by one as they arrived. Rather like Georgie Porgie, I think, though I don't know if all of the girls cried. I rather think Sylvia did not." She grinned mischievously.

Instead of answering with a grin of his own, Mark grimaced. "This . . . this is beyond anything. I'll have his guts for garters."

"Now, please do not cause a fuss," Juliette said in a soothing tone. "I took no harm."

"Was Adelaide upset?"

Julie shook her head. "Not really. She regards him as harmless. I think she was interested in making some comparisons of her own. I might add, the results were very much in Victor's favor."

"That sounds like Mr. Makepeace has succeeded in evading Miss Campbell."

"It does, doesn't it?" Julie frowned. "I cautioned her, and she promised me she was behaving as she ought."

"Apparently you did not find Jared's kiss—or was it kisses—agreeable?" Mark stopped and turned to face Julie. Darkness did not hide his intent expression.

Indignant, Julie turned her back on him and started toward the castle. "As if I would let him—"

"Didn't you?"

"No, indeed! How did you think he got into the lily pond?"

"Now we are getting to it!" Mark's anger began to ebb. "You pushed him into the pond and ran away. A fleet-footed rationalist." His hand on her elbow stopped her forward momentum. She turned back to him, mollified by his approving tone.

"Yes, and oh! It was so funny, Mark. He couldn't find me and I could hear him huffing and puffing, full of astonished indignation that I would refuse the opportunity!"

Mark allowed a tiny quirk of his lips at this image. "That *would* be a surprise to him, the way young ladies are fawning over him! I'm amazed that you should manage to outwit him in a chase through a maze he's played in since childhood, when you've never been there before today."

"Not so amazing when you realize that the countess's bedroom has an excellent view of the maze, and Lady Hammerswold was kind enough to give me some hints . . ."

The quirk deepened, bringing an attractive dimple into play. He offered her his arm and they resumed their stroll. Mark was very thoughtful. "It would be a mistake," he said at last, "to view Jared as a harmless buffoon. He is my cousin, and family loyalty bids me be discreet, but I must tell you I do not trust him to hold the line with any unchaperoned girl."

Julie lifted troubled eyes to his. "He is truly that bad?"

"No more than many another of our class, naive theologian. Were you not in town long enough to know how very unreliable some of the most tonnish young bucks are?"

"No. It is a lowering thought."

"No stolen kisses in the gardens?"

She giggled and wrapped her arms around herself in a mock shiver. "No, indeed, for it was still quite cold then."

"Nor in any dark hallways, or convenient antechambers?"

"Ours was a very brief season, sir." She looked up at him from under fluttering lashes.

"Minx. I'm sure you regret your lost opportunities."

Abruptly Julie became completely serious. "No, never. I think a girl's first kiss is a very special event. It should be given her by the man who will be her husband, in token of mutual affection."

He turned to her again. In the torchlit shadows of the formal gardens she saw those black, black eyes go even darker as they looked into her own. His hands came up and gently rubbed her arms below the puffed sleeves of her muslin gown. Juliette's heart began to pound. She thought he was about to give her that first kiss and the declaration it would imply.

"I knew you would feel that way about it, Julie. I wish—"

At that crucial moment a loud clap of thunder startled them. They both turned toward the west, to see that a storm was hastening over the valley.

He released her arms and stepped away. "We'd best go in, before lighting strikes!"

The combination of amusement and tenderness in his voice made her doubt it was the electrical storm he was warning her about. She nodded and fluttered her eyelashes at him coquettishly. "It could be dangerous."

His lips curved appreciatively. "Oh, yes, dear rationalist. *Very* dangerous." He took her elbow and turned her hastily toward the lighted porch where Susan waited.


"It was too much to hope that the weather would remain fair. It so rarely does this time of year." Regina sat at her window, her husband at her side, gloomily watching the rain beat down on the maze.

"There is a week to go until All Hallow's Eve. It may yet be clear. And there is always the ballroom."

"Of course." The countess patted her husband's hands. "But no full moon on the Ghost's Walk."

"He's also fond of the library. That's where I saw him, and where you saw him the first time."

"Yes, Winton." A secret little smile briefly lifted Regina's lips. "Isn't it wonderful how well Jared has behaved since the night of the ghosts?"

The earl chuckled appreciatively. "Indeed, yes. Those clever girls."

"Unfortunately, none of them will do," the countess sighed. "Miss Harpwood will be obese and encourage Jared's gluttony. He'll be dead by forty with her as a wife. Miss Davies is not merely shy, but timid. She'll be dominated and imposed upon by her husband and everyone else."

"Not the sort likely to lead Jared to an improved way of life," the earl agreed.

"As for Gilda Whitten, she is entirely too straight laced and prudish for Jared. She hasn't even the slightest sense of humor. Miss Stephens-Hill is too much like her cheeseparing mother. She won't encourage Jared to keep up the properties, especially the abbey. As for the tenants' welfare if she were to be countess . . ." Regina shook her head gloomily. "I think Adelaide and Juliette are the most worthy of the young ladies."

"Do you? Unfortunate, for Juliette seems utterly indifferent to Jared. And as for Adelaide, while she is always polite when Jared favors her with his attention, she is much more enthusiastic about Victor's company."

The countess frowned in concern. "I've noticed. If only Jared understood those young ladies' true worth, he might spend more time with them and win one of them over."

"He still favors Sylvia above any, perhaps because he saw *her* ghost himself."

Both of them began laughing. "The silly gudgeon." The countess sobered. "I do believe Sylvia is the one I'd least like to see him marry. Her deception was planned well ahead of time, with a confederate, yet."

The earl frowned. "Yes. Mark suspects her groom. She is just such a one as the ghost warns against. How did you come to invite such an unsuitable creature?"

"'Twas that silly Helen's doing. Mrs. Patchfield was a bosom beau of hers from her youth. She invited them and then informed me. I am only glad Helen did not decide to join us. She would have spent her time encouraging the match!" Lady Hammerswold frowned and turned to stare morosely at the rain-soaked view.

The earl studied her with concern. She never complained, yet he knew that her physical condition was deteriorating. Worrying over Jared was using up some of her precious strength. Where was that damned ghost? *It appears that it's going to be up to me. Time to act,* he thought.

"Your grandmother is concerned that this weather will deprive you of the opportunity to meet the ghost."

Jared eyed the earl over his glass of port. He'd been summoned to the library for a private talk with his grandfather. "I've wondered about that too, sir. Perhaps I should go wander around in the keep at midnight."

"That's a possibility, though he rarely shows himself there. Why not try here in the library? Much warmer and more comfortable."

Jared sat up straight. "That's right, you saw him here, once, sitting in front of the fire taking his ease."

The earl nodded. "Puffing on a pipe, smoke everywhere, though I'd only just had the chimney worked on. Called me a right fool for pursuing Susan Mortimer, which I was! Only I couldn't get Regina to take me seriously, you see."

This was an old family story to Jared. He stopped his grandfather's flow of reminiscence with a question. "Didn't NiNi see him in here, too?"

"Yes. When I couldn't convince her that I'd quit my rake-hellish ways, he appeared to her in that old mirror on the wall, and told her she shouldn't hesitate to marry me!"

Jared walked over to the old mirror in its ornate gilded frame. The beveled glass was so badly chequered with age that it was of little use as a looking glass. "I guess that's why you refused to have the glass replaced when that decorator wanted to."

"Everything is just as it was. A blazing fire, the old mirror on the wall. After your guests go upstairs tonight, why not sit here and give him a chance to appear."

Jared's lower lip protruded. "I suppose."

"Why this reluctance?"

"Know there's no chance he'll chose the one I prefer. He'll think Sylvia too fast by far. Probably want me to wed Miss Prunes and Prisms, or the little theologian. Or Adelaide. Now, *that* wouldn't be so unpleasant for me, but Victor would doubtless object."

"You must listen to what he has to say. Remember, there is more at stake here than a light woman's favor—"

"Sylvia ain't no light woman! Wish she were. No more kisses for me, she said, until I'd made my choice!"

"I only meant, in the past you've looked at females strictly from the point of view of the pleasures of the flesh. Undoubtedly that is important, but in the wife of my heir, it is only one of many considerations."

Jared looked even more resentful at this, but nodded his head. "Don't need to say any more. Made up my mind to do as the old boy tells me, and I will. Don't have to like it, though."


Jared entered the library silently, nervously. He had no real fear of the family specter, just a healthy awareness that he was about to come in contact with something outside normal experience. A careful survey of the room revealed no gray presence.

He sat down on a leather sofa and made himself comfortable. His grandfather had indicated he might have a while to wait. A brandy bottle and glass sat nearby to comfort him during his vigil. He poured himself a generous measure, not by any means the first of the evening, and began to talk to the room at large.

"Are you here, eh? Doubtless you've been wondering

when I would show up. That is, you haven't exactly tried to get in touch with me, but I know before I had that apoplexy this summer I wouldn't have been interested, so I guess you thought you'd just be wasting your breath."

There was no answer. The room was quiet except for the faint crackling of the fire and the tick of a clock.

"Hope you won't pick out someone too proper, you know. I mean to say, you know how a man is. He needs a woman who heats his blood. For heaven's sake, don't pick that fat Harpwood female. And I hope—"

"It is for me to talk, and you to listen."

The voice was thin, reedy, but full of authority.

"Eh! What? Where? Can't see you. Show yourself." Jared's eyes were darting around the room.

"You can hear me. Listen well! The Earl of Hammerswold must devote himself to the land and its people. It will not be enough for you to marry my choice of wife, if you do not mend your ways as well."

It was a sermon he had heard from his grandparents many times. "Oh, of course. Always meant to, soon as I'm the earl. No need for it till then, though, eh?" Jared stood and began moving toward the mirror. "You in there?"

"If you seek me here, you will find me. Come no closer. There is danger if you see too much."

Apprehensive for the first time, Jared stopped in his tracks. He was about three feet from the mirror. He could see, not his own reflection in the cracked glass, but whirling smoke through which a shape could dimly be seen.

What he could make out revealed clearly that the fringe of hair, the white moustache, the heavy white eyebrows were just exactly as Juliette Berceau had described them. The ghost did indeed resemble his Uncle Ramsey, but no flesh-and-blood creature could get inside a mirror!

"So Juliette Berceau *did* see you in the gallery! I suppose the theologian is your choice, then."

"You know in your heart which of these young women is worthy and which is not! Miss Sylvia Patchfield you must put from your mind." The voice in the mirror grew more sepulchral, and began to waver.

"Knew you'd say that! Well, there's nothing for it! But which one shall I marry?"

"Miss Berceau will make you an outstanding countess. Her cousin, Miss Beasley, is equally worthy. You must exert yourself to win the affections of one of these women." The smoke began to swirl thicker and thicker, and the shape within it to disappear. As it faded, the reedy voice whispered over and over: "Miss Adelaide Beasley. Miss Juliette Berceau. Miss Adelaide . . ."

# Chapter Fourteen

Juliette furtively crept from the servant's entrance on the east wing, her cape wrapped around her and her head covered by the hood. It was early morning on the fourth day since the weather had turned rainy, and the clouds this morning were thinner, as if the sun was trying to come through. Tired of being cooped up indoors, she hastened to the maze, looking behind her again to see that she wasn't followed. She wanted a private moment as well as exercise.

Three days ago Viscount Faverill's behavior had suddenly changed, and the change had been a sore trial for both Juliette and her cousin. He had ceased paying the least attention to the other female guests, in favor of Addie and Juliette. Addie, in particular, was pestered by his ponderous gallantries.

Poor Addie. She could no longer spend most of her time giggling over Victor's jokes and fluttering her eyes at his flirtations. Victor had become increasingly resentful of Jared. Addie was torn. She still retained a healthy respect for the concept of being a viscountess who would one day be a countess. Yet clearly she had developed a *tendre* for Victor Makepeace.

Susan counseled her to encourage the viscount as her parents had ordered. "For, dearest, you haven't committed yourself to Mr. Makepeace—indeed he hasn't even offered for you yet—so you are free to make the best match."

Applied to for guidance, Juliette gave her the opposite advice. "Jared is a shallow, self-centered man. Even when he is being agreeable, as he is now, he is not so very agreeable, is he?"

Adelaide shook her head vehemently. "And the thought of his kiss makes me shudder." She looked over her shoulder to be sure their chaperone was out of earshot.

"Only consider what he will be once you are wed and the honeymoon is over. It is not to be thought of."

"Still, Juliette—to be a countess one day! To be mistress of this magnificent house, and Faverill Springs, and half a dozen other properties. And think of all the good I could do. I could start schools for the tenants' children . . ."

She seemed like a shuttlecock in a game of badminton. At last, Adelaide wrote her parents about her dilemma, and now nervously awaited their answer.

Julie, too, had written them, a long letter detailing all she had seen and learned about the viscount, in the hopes that the title would have less luster in their eyes once they knew the kind of man he was.

As for Jared's clumsy attentions to her, she had continued to be polite but distant. It was not Jared's new enthusiasm that upset her so much that she felt she must get away by herself on this misty, foggy morning when she could barely see in front of her face.

It was Mark.

Since that magic evening in the garden, when she had been sure he was about to kiss her, he had become distant again.

She knew he kept an eye on her when Jared attempted to get her alone, but he was equally watchful of all the other young ladies, so she took no comfort from that.

"Foolish, foolish girl," Susan had scolded her this morning, on seeing the circles smudging her eyes from lack of sleep. "I told you he must marry well, and what have you done? Gone and lost your heart to him, that's what. And I thought you the practical one. I could just shake you."

"I haven't lost my heart to him at all," she had insisted. "I could, easily enough. But I see now that you were right, and I have been unwise. I shall do better."

But as Juliette moved quietly through the dew-drenched maze, she knew that Susan had the right of it. She had lost her heart to him, completely and irrevocably. In fact, she loved him so much she felt ashamed of her desire to marry him. It wasn't fair that such a fine man as Mark Camden should one day be dependent on such as Jared. He deserved a wife with a dowry large enough to purchase land of his own. And that wouldn't be penniless Miss Juliette Berceau.

Though she had seen no sign that such was his intention, she wondered if perhaps he would make a match of it with one of the other girls. *It is only reasonable for him to use this gathering to find a wealthy bride,* Juliette thought. *Sylvia is vastly wealthy. Elizabeth and Carolyn are both plump in the pocket, and Gilda said she would inherit a fine estate, as she is an only child.*

Frowning at the thought, Juliette entered the center of the maze. She gasped, awed by what she saw. Every single leaf of every tree and every blade of grass was spangled with hundreds of tiny drops of dew. The statues and fountains were dew bedecked. Even the stone walkways were paved in dewdrops. Still swirling about were strands of the foggy mist that had been so heavy earlier, but a beam of sunshine had broken through to illuminate the scene so that it looked to be spangled in diamonds instead of dewdrops.

"Oh!" she turned slowly around, tilting her head to enjoy the sight of the green walls of the maze and the trees above, all shimmering with dew-diamonds in the light. Each step broke hundreds of the tiny droplets, leaving her footprint's dark watery outline.

"It's beautiful, isn't it?"

"Who spoke?" Julie whirled around. She saw no one.

"I can't be alone anywhere," she muttered. Aloud, she insisted that her companion show himself.

"Your wish is my command." The slight shift in position of the voice made her turn her head toward the nymph fountain. A moment ago she would have sworn there was no one there, but now she saw a shape. Like herself it was shrouded in a cape and hood. It was a man, not much above herself in height, leaning on a cane. *The gray of the fabric must blend in with the fog enough that I didn't see him before*, she thought.

"You gave me quite a start. I thought I was alone."

"And wished to be so." The man started toward her. He spoke in a raspy but kindly voice.

"Yes, I did. But now I am glad to have someone here to share this exquisite sight with me." She swept her arm around. "It won't last long enough, I expect, to go and rouse anyone else."

As the man drew closer, she confirmed her first thought, which was that she did not know him. He looked familiar, though. He was not an elderly man, but his face was gray, almost as gray as his cloak, as if he were ill. His clothes, too, were gray. Even his eyes seemed colorless. He wore a gentle smile, and limped terribly, even with his cane. Surely he offered her no danger.

He took the seat in the center of the garden, the one that Jared had sat on as he attempted to lure her into kissing him. "Won't you join me?" he asked. "We can sit here and enjoy this beautiful sight for a while, before the sun drys it."

Juliette nodded and crossed to him. "I hate to walk on it, though. Every step destroys some of it." She dropped down on the bench beside him. They sat companionably side by side for a long while, listening to distant birdcalls and to the soft dripping of excess moisture from the shrubbery.

At last the elderly man spoke. "You came here with a troubled spirit. Would it help to talk about it?"

Juliette shook her head. "I don't think so, though I thank you . . ." Suddenly she recalled she didn't know who he was.

"Are you Uncle Ramsey? And if so, who was that I met in the long gallery, for surely you are not one and the same, though you do nearly resemble one another."

"We have not met before. I am another uncle, if you will."

She looked at him sharply. "Next I suppose you will tell

me you are the ghost, come to convince me to wed Faverill!" She stood. "I resent this kind of trickery, sir!"

"You would make an admirable countess."

"But I won't. And Addie shan't either. She loves Mr. Makepeace, and at any rate, Faverill would make her miserable."

"Regrettable! But Faverill has made his own bed, and doesn't deserve a good woman to lie in it with him."

"You surprise me, sir. I made sure you were plotting to convince me—"

"You must convince Mark Camden that his cousin is responsible for his own fate."

"I certainly cannot presume—"

"I thought you loved him. Am I mistaken?"

"Really, sir. I cannot . . . who *are* you?"

The gray eyes looked at her directly, compellingly. "Mark Camden may do Hammerswold and himself great harm if he cannot accept that Jared's fate is of his own making."

*Why?* Juliette wondered, moved in spite of herself by her companion's urgency. *Why was Mark's attitude of so much importance to the future of the earldom? What did she have to do with the matter? Perhaps . . .* A chill ran up her spine as she considered the implications.

"Sir, I cannot, will not do such a thing, even if you were a messenger from beyond, which I don't believe. Mark must decide for himself—"

"You wouldn't want him unless he chose you over Hammerswold. There is a touch of selfishness in that, child."

"I do not agree. I will not enter into any but a true marriage, where there is equal affection on both sides. You imply that Mr. Camden has stood back from me in the belief that his cousin should wed me. If that is true, obviously any feelings he has for me fall far short of love."

"I expect I must be the one to tell him." Her companion's shoulders drooped as if this required more effort than he could expend.

"I do not want a husband who cannot make up his own mind, I tell you!"

"Yesss." The latter part of the word became a long, sibilant sigh. "I feared you would respond so. At least I can put you on your guard. There is danger here."

"Are you threatening me?" Juliette stepped farther away from him.

"Dear child, by no means." His voice grew softer, slower. Each word seemed to be a great effort. "You . . . must . . . avoid . . ."

"I think you are ill, sir. Let me help you inside."

"You cannot . . ." He lifted his hand as if to ward her off.

"No, I collect I could not lift you. I will find someone to help you. Wait here, sir. Do not despair."

"Stay," he whispered. "I . . . must . . . warn . . ."

The gray-cloaked, gray-faced man seemed to have shrunk as he sat, hunched over, in the dew-drenched garden. In fact, he looked even grayer than ever. *He is in pain,* she thought, *possibly even dying.* Not heeding his request, she hastened to the exit by which she had escaped Jared. As soon as she stepped out of the maze, she began to call, "Someone help me! Please, is there anyone around?"

"Juliette? What is the matter? The deep voice she loved sounded to her right and she whirled to see Mark dismounting from his stallion. He brushed dew drops from his shoulders as he turned.

Her heart began to race at the sight of him in the boxy riding jacket designed rather for comfort and function than for elegance. His riding breeches fit him like a second skin, and the fact that the boots that encased his long legs were scuffed did not detract from the masculine impact he made upon her.

*He is so dear to me.*

Arrested by the expression of tenderness and admiration on her face, Mark stopped. He had been avoiding Juliette since the morning after he had nearly kissed her in the garden. He had gone to his grandfather to tell him he was planning on offering for her, and found Jared closeted with the earl, laying out a campaign to win either Juliette or Adelaide as his bride. He had eagerly told Mark of the ghost's appearance in the mirror. Mark had heard the ghost's advice with a sinking heart.

Since then Mark had held back. Conscience would not allow him to ruin Juliette's chance of being a countess, nor Jared's chance of winning a bride who would benefit not only him but the earldom. Though he hoped against hope that Jared would woo and win Adelaide instead, he knew even without the ghost's endorsement that Juliette, of all the young ladies present, was the best suited to such a position of responsibility. Surely the misery he felt at the thought of her as Jared's bride would fade in time?

But it hadn't begun to fade, and now he found himself facing her, quite alone, by a dew-drenched shrubbery, and the temptation to kiss her was almost overwhelming. He reached for her and she grabbed his hand, but her purpose was not the same as his.

"Come quickly. I think he is sick. Surely such pallor couldn't be just makeup. Even his eyes . . . please hurry." She tugged on his hands to hurry him through the little door into the maze.

"Who are you speaking of, Julie?" Ducking through the door, Mark followed her swift short steps easily, keeping one small hand in his.

"A man . . . perhaps Uncle Ramsey, but . . . oh! He never told me his name, either. A relative of yours. I think he intended to convince me he was the ghost. I should be furious with him! But he looks so ill!"

They hastened into the center of the maze, and there Julie stopped short, causing Mark to run into her. He put steadying hands on her shoulders, and to his complete surprise, she leaned fully against him, pressing her hand to her heart. He could feel her trembling.

"Oh! He's gone. But where . . ."

"Where did you leave him?

"Sitting on the bench there. He must have gone back another way. But he could collapse. We must find him! Oh, which way did he go?"

"We should see his footprints," Mark observed looking around the area.

Julie stared at the ground. There was less dew than before, but it was as Mark said. When they looked behind them, their steps could be seen. On the part of the path that Juliette had trod when coming into the maze, her footprints could be seen.

Walking carefully, studying the ground as they went, they approached each of the eight exits from the center of the maze. No other person's footprints could be found.

Beginning to have a sharp sense of *déjà vu*, Juliette wailed, "But I know he was here. I first saw him by the nymph fountain. Let's look there." They approached it cautiously, studying the ground carefully.

"There they are!" Triumph and relief filled Julie's voice as she spied his footprints. "I'm so glad to have found them, else you'd have thought me demented!"

Mark frowned over the faint prints. The dew was beginning to evaporate, leaving a film of moisture instead of the millions of tiny beads of water. "Small footprints, very close together, as if their maker were unsteady on the feet. What is this?" He pointed to the small round print beside the footprints.

"That is his cane. He was limping horridly. See, they go to the bench. We sat there together and talked. You can see my prints too."

Mark didn't move toward them. "Yes, I see." He looked intently into the puzzled golden-brown eyes lifted to his. "A cane! Describe this man to me."

"No! Don't look at me that way. It was a real man, I say! He looked ill, he left footprints. We must find him."

"Julie, where are his prints leading away?"

Julie circled around. There were no prints on the other side of the bench. The prints she had made as she left him to find Mark crossed the stranger's, but there were no prints to indicate which direction he had taken when he left the bench.

"He . . . he must have stepped in mine."

Mark lifted his eyebrow at this. "His are broader. Besides, wasn't he too fragile to follow in your wider-spaced footprints? Where are the prints of the cane?"

"Oh!" She stared long and long at the evidence, watching her feet as she moved carefully this way and that, in hopes of seeing something she had missed.

Mark, too, was investigating. At last he turned to her. "He seems to have vanished into thin air."

"I wonder how he did it?"

Mark grinned. "Ghosts are very clever creatures."

"Codswallop! I won't listen to this nonsense!"

"Tell me what he looked like. Better yet, tell me what he said to you." Mark was completely serious; indeed, his tone was quite as compelling as the stranger's had been a few minutes earlier.

"No, no, no, and no! I did not see a ghost! You may tell your relative I am quite vexed with him. He has played off this trick once too often. Well, it did not succeed with me. I am going to go home, and take Addie with me if I can. And—Mark Camden?

"Yes?" The expression on Mark's face was difficult to read, but Julie thought she saw suppressed amusement there.

"Mark Camden, if you know anything about this, if you had anything to do with this contemptible trick, I am very disappointed in you!" She turned on her heel and ran straight across the wet lawn toward the nearest exit to the maze.

Unmoving, Mark watched her go, a myriad of emotions roiling in him. Amusement was certainly one of these. He threw his head back and laughed. *Stubborn little rationalist! "How did he do that" indeed!* How he loved her!

This thought sobered him immediately. He loved Juliette Berceau, to whom the Ghost of Hammerswold had just paid a visit. Despair filled him. If the ghost had appeared to her it could have been for only one reason—to urge her to accept Jared.

Clarity did not bring with it easy acceptance. *The woman I love, married to Jared. It is too much to ask!* Mark strode out of the maze, needing more than ever the long lonely gallop he had promised himself this morning.

# Chapter Fifteen

When Juliette returned to her room, she was surprised to find that Addie and Susan had already gone down to breakfast. This gave her a chance to write a second letter to her uncle, this one a scathing denunciation of the Camdens for unprincipled behavior. The very idea of men pretending to be ghosts to manipulate young women!

She didn't understand the point of this prank, though. If the man in the maze had been the real ghost, his purpose was clear. But there wasn't any such thing as a ghost, so why would anyone pretend to be a ghost, only to confirm her in her belief that neither she nor Adelaide should marry the viscount? Why would anyone encourage her to try to convince Mark that he should court her himself?

What point could there be, other than the pleasure of alarming and upsetting a hapless female? Unless there was some insanity behind this prank? Juliette drew in a sudden breath of alarm. The gray man's warning, "There is danger here," took on a new and sinister meaning.

Alarm gave impetus to her pen. She must convince her uncle to let them come home! When she finished her letter, she took it down to be posted.

After breakfast there was a treasure hunt scheduled. The countess was pleased that the sun had broken through. "I had made up clues for both an indoor and outdoor hunt, but the outdoor one will be ever so much more interesting."

Juliette drew Lord Tremayne for her partner. He was such a slow-top that they were well behind the others, so she was surprised to come up on James Betterton, Adelaide's partner, standing alone by an equine statue.

"Where is Adelaide?" she asked.

"I wish I knew. When the clue at the stable separated us, I found my way here quite easily. Apparently her instructions were not so simple."

"No clue at the stable separated us," Tommy asserted. "Is it fair when people have different clues?"

Trying to keep her alarm from her voice, Juliette asked, "Do you have any idea where her clue sent her?"

"I think she went in the direction of the maze."

*The maze! They are going to try to play that ghost trick on Adelaide.* Julie was furious at the idea. Addie would be terrified. "Why don't you and James team up, Tommy, and I will find Addie and partner her."

Lord Tremayne readily agreed. It was humiliating to have to rely on a woman to figure out the clues for him.

Juliette moved through the maze as swiftly as she could, calling, "Addie? Addie?"

As she neared the center, she began to hear sounds of a woman weeping. She doubled her pace, arriving in the open out of breath to see her cousin seated on the bench in the center, sobbing despairingly.

"Addie! What is it, dearest?" Eschewing the rock pathways, she hurried straight across to her cousin.

"Oh, Julie, I am so unhappy!"

"What has made you cry? Tell me."

"I have met the ghost! The Ghost of Hammerswold. And he told me I should wed Jared! But now I know I don't want to. I love Victor! Oh, my heart is breaking!"

"When did this happen?"

"He only just left. I think he heard you calling and disappeared."

"No! I will have this madness stop! Don't cry, Addie. That was no ghost. Come with me!"

Grabbing her astonished cousin by the hand, she pulled her along. "The closest exit, the one the gardeners use to enter the maze near the succession houses, was likely the one he used. If we hurry, we can catch him, with his limp."

"Limp?" Addie's question was breathless.

Julie stopped. "He did limp and use a cane, did he not? And look quite gray and ill?"

"No, not at all. For an elderly man he seemed in prime form. A very elegant Elizabethan gentleman, he was."

Julie stamped her feet. "The beast. It was a disguise, not illness! Well, we will still find him."

She resumed her mad race to the little door behind the obelisk. Ignoring Addie's questions about it, she urged the girl through, then followed her. A quick scan of the area revealed no one, not even a gardener.

Juliette's eyes moved from the garden path to the succession houses. "I should have thought of them before. The perfect hiding place."

Addie panted, trying to regain her breath. "Wh-what are you talking about?"

"Don't you see? He must be staying in the succession houses. That is why no one has seen him. Let's go!"

"The ghost? Julie, I r-really don't want to ch-chase a ghost."

"Not a ghost. Uncle Ramsey. Come on, Addie, we are going to track this villain to his lair." Once again she caught up Addie's hand and began to half-run toward the long row of greenhouses.

Their path took them through a row of huge, stately elms. A blur of motion seen near one of them halted Julie. Addie bumped into her.

"There he is. I see him too," Addie whispered, staring at the tree. Just the edge of a man's coat could be seen protruding behind the massive trunk.

"Quietly. I want to surprise him."

"But Julie, do you think there is any danger?" Addie tugged on her cousin's wrist, trying to dissuade her.

"Indeed I do, and he is the one who is facing it." Fury impelled her to break free of her cousin and begin to run.

A face peeked around the tree and the drew back. Then a

little man with white hair ran away so fast his hat fell off. His coat flew behind him, and Juliette managed to catch a handful of it.

They both went down in a tangle of limbs and petticoats. Confusion reigned for several minutes as the man tried to free himself. Finally, gasping for breath, they both struggled to their feet and stood facing each other, he poised for flight, she equally poised for pursuit.

She recognized the man as her guide to the art gallery. "It is of no use to flee, sir. We know you are human—see, there is a little blood in the scratch on your head."

Her antagonist clamped his hand to his head. "Vixen! Where's your respect for your elders?"

"How can I feel any respect for one who spends his time sneaking about, terrorizing young women into marrying where they don't wish to—"

"I protest! I only sought to advise—"

"Frightening maids—"

"I never frightened one maid. Nor did I frighten Miss Adelaide, only upset her. I had not realized the extent of her attachment to Mr. Makepeace, or I would not have tried to persuade her—"

"What is going on?"

They all turned to find Mark reining in his winded stallion beside them.

"Do you have to ask? I have found your family ghost, sir! He has had a very busy morning, but not, I think, a profitable one. And now, Addie, let us go and pack. We will order a post chaise. This is no place for decent people!" Lifting her firm chin, Juliette turned away. Behind her she heard Mark exclaim, "Uncle Ramsey! So you *are* here!"

Tears ran down her cheeks. She wanted to believe Mark had no part in this. She wanted it so very much, but she doubted her wanting it could make it so.

*         *         *

"Your desire to return home is understandable, but you must wait for Lord Paxton to send his carriage," Susan told Juliette and Adelaide firmly.

"We can't stay here now. I couldn't face them! It is all so very peculiar and frightening." Addie's pretty face reflected her confusion.

"It will be very awkward, Susan," Juliette said in her most reasonable tone.

"I don't care, we can't hire a chaise and leave without Lord Paxton's permission!" Susan's folded arms and firm voice indicated her determination to carry her point. She was distracted by a scratching at the door. She opened it to a footman with a note on a silver tray.

She read it, forehead knit. "It is from the countess." Juliette took it from her outstretched hand and read it aloud.

"Dear Miss Beasley and Miss Berceau:
    You are understandably upset by the events of the morning. Would you please do me the honor of coming to me at one o'clock, at which time explanations will be demanded and apologies tendered.
    Regina Camden, Countess of Hammerswold

"I should very much like to hear these explanations!" Addie bounced from her bed. "Susan?"

"So should I," Susan said. "Julie?"

"This seems like *déjà vu* to me. Yes, I suppose we must go and hear what they say."

Once again Mark, Jared, the earl, and the countess faced Julie, Addie, and Susan in the countess's sitting room. Ramsey Camden was also there, his face sadly scratched. His rumpled Tudor costume proclaimed that he, unlike the girls, had not had an opportunity to change.

The countess's face was composed but she looked as if she had been crying. The earl's expression was grim. Jared was looking cross. Mark was stone faced.

After they were seated, the earl began. "We owe both of

you an explanation and an apology. It is my fault, entirely. You see, the ghost had not put in an appearance in so many years that I began to believe he had abandoned us. Ghosts do fade away, I'm told. It was time for Jared to marry, and he was wanting to marry a worthy wife."

"I was wanting to marry the ghost's choice," Jared snapped.

"Yes, of course, you wanted the ghost to select one for you, but I decided that we couldn't wait anymore for that to happen. You *are* three and thirty, after all. I've tried to explain to you, Jared, that the point of the ghost's appearance is to help the heir select a suitable bride, something he *could* do for himself if he were wise enough. The ghost doesn't create of her a talisman, a lucky charm to ward off all harm. At any rate, what with our family ghost having taken French leave, and you insisting on his participation before chosing a bride, I decided to take matters into my own hands."

Ramsey Camden joined in, speaking softly. "I had recently arrived home from Italy, and he asked me to keep my homecoming a secret so I could help him." He held out his hands in supplication. "We meant no harm. We thought all of the young ladies at this house party would be eager to wed Jared."

The earl nodded. "All we had to do, we thought, is select one who would be a steadying influence on Jared, one who would have the common interests of the people of the earldom at heart, not her own selfish pleasures."

Lord Hammerswold shook his head in puzzlement. "It never occurred to us that not one, but two, and clearly the two most suitable, would reject him."

"They haven't rejected me," Jared interposed, his *amour-propre* wounded. "They may now, after this fiddle-faddle, but thus far I've been busy courting them. I haven't offered for either, so stands to reason I haven't been turned down."

The earl cleared his throat. "Yes, well, your suit didn't seem like it was prospering to us. Miss Berceau seemed particularly resistant to your charms, so Ramsey and I lured

Miss Beasley into the maze so he could have a talk with her. Meant to fill her mind with all the good things that being the countess included. But she became upset and began to cry, so he gave it up."

"I know it was wrong, but we meant well, truly." Ramsey looked pleadingly at Adelaide and Juliette.

"Is that all you have to say to us, sir?" Juliette was scowling fiercely. They had not explained *her* "ghost." She glanced at Mark, who still looked as if carved in stone.

"Perhaps if you told them why you did it, Win?" The countess's voice was tender.

He reached for her hand. "Thing is, Regina ain't been well lately. Not stout at all. Worrying her head about the succession. Two grandsons, both unmarried, neither of any inclination to marry. There's Ramsey, too, but he's never seemed likely to wed, and getting on in years now. She was afraid she would die without seeing the heir."

"And I was hoping to atone for a terrible mistake fifteen years ago, by helping to make her happy now." To everyone's acute discomfort, Ramsey put his head in his hands and began to cry.

The countess leaned over and patted his shoulder. "Now, Ram, I never blamed you for that accident—"

"Blame myself. Riding like a fool, never looking to see who might be coming along the road. Knew that particular spot was too narrow." Ramsey lifted his tear-streaked face to the three women. "Jumped a fence right in front of their curricle, causing it to overturn. Crippled, and by me!" Again he began to sob.

Tears hovered in the countess's eyes as she turned to the girls. "I am not pleased that they both chose such dishonest means to try to please me, but I hope perhaps you may find their reason sufficient to forgive."

"Of course, ma'am." Adelaide crossed to her side and knelt down, taking the countess's wrinkled hands in her own. "I do understand their feelings."

Juliette stared at them. Of course she was moved by this tale, but curiosity tormented her to know how Mr. Camden had made himself look younger but deathly ill when he appeared to her in the maze, how he had managed his trackless disappearance, and most importantly, why they had hinted that it was Mark, not Jared, she should be concerned with.

Before she could open her mouth to demand a full confession, Jared spoke, apparently very much of the same mind as she. "I suppose you did all of this other ghost stuff, too? The screaming maids, the lights, the ghost pacing on the walkway?"

"None of that was of our doing," the earl said. "Most particularly not that ridiculous thing on the walkway. The young girls made up their ghost sightings, I am sure."

"And the mirror," Jared demanded, his voice rising almost hysterically. "The mirror, too? I made sure *that* was the real thing, but now I see it was Uncle Ramsey, somehow."

The countess gasped, "The mirror?"

The earl's face went deathly pale.

"In the library. I went in there at grandfather's suggestion. He saw the ghost in it once, as did you. He said I should sit in there and wait for it. And sure enough, it appeared, and told me whom I should marry. Told me to court Adelaide and Juliette." Jared gave a half-bow from his chair to each of the young girls, then scowled. "Particularly spoke against Sylvia, but now I see she's the only one has actually seen the ghost. It's a fine thing when one's own relatives play such a trick on one!" He stood to begin agitated pacing of the room.

The countess put a kerchief to her mouth. "Not the mirror, Winton! Where I first saw the ghost that told me to marry you?"

This time it was the earl who had tears in his eyes. "I had hoped you would never find out. This is, I know, a blow to you. Perhaps you would allow me to explain in private."

"By involving these young women in your deceptions you have forfeited that right. Now let us have a full confession and no roundaboutation!" Her firm, angry voice startled Juliette.

"The mirror is mounted on the wall in front of the hidden treasure room. I replaced the mirror with a glass. A smudge pot to emit copious smoke, some gauze to disguise his features—"

"Don't be too hard on him, Regina," Ramsey pleaded. "He did it because he loved you."

"Yes, and because of that I forgave him long ago. But previously, he had actually seen the ghost. He knew I was the ghost's choice, and he knew I cared for him, though I hesitated to marry him. To supplant the real ghost! To presume to tell Jared he must court a young woman of your choosing! Such arrogance! Even if you were going to do such a wicked thing, I cannot imagine why you would do so before Halloween, when tis most likely that the ghost will appear."

"Forgave me long ago? You knew?" The earl looked oddly relieved for one whose behavior had just been so roundly condemned.

"Of course!"

"But how? When? You seemed so frightened it quite smote my conscience. Surely you couldn't have pretended to such fear."

"At first I was frightened, but something about the voice, even the way he had disguised it . . . and the faint smell of smoke seeping in. But it wasn't until I had met the *real* ghost that I knew for sure. It was he who helped me over my last qualms, including soothing my concerns over your dishonesty for playing such a trick on me. And now, all these years later, I find you once again involved in wicked, dishonest . . . Mark, were you in on this?" She turned abruptly on her youngest grandson.

"No, ma'am."

"He knew nothing of it. I didn't think he'd go along with it." The earl's voice trembled. "Can you ever forgive me?"

Mark's deep voice rumbled into the countess's long,

pregnant pause. "Have you told us all, Grandfather? Every single prank?"

The earl sank back into his chair, his hands biting into the arms. "Yes, all. Every last thing!"

"And you, Uncle Ramsey? No further deceptions without Grandfather? No hiring of others to assist you?"

Ramsey shook his head. "Wasn't the sort of thing you'd dare trust servants with."

"How about you, Jared? No little charades to help persuade a reluctant young woman to look upon you with favor? No pranks to amuse yourself and your cronies?"

Jared was clearly bewildered. "What are you getting at, Mark? I am the main victim in all of this, not one of the perpetrators."

"You swear to that on your honor?"

Jared's expression firmed, and he looked his cousin directly in the eye. "On my honor as a gentleman, Mark."

"What is all of this about, Mark?" Lady Hammerswold leaned forward in her chair.

Mark's black eyes blazed at Juliette as if willing her to speak, but she was silent. "I think there was one other ghostly sighting, and I wanted to try to account for it."

Jared nodded wisely. "You're speaking of the night Sylvia saw him in her room, and we all saw him on the walkway. Like I said, only authentic sighting. But odd that he'd pick her. Mean to say, like her myself. Has a bit of fun to her, not so much propriety and—" Mark's hand on Jared's shoulder stopped him from uttering any unflattering reflections on Juliette and Adelaide.

The earl stood and struck his right fist into his left palm. "Surely you are not such an idiot as to believe that ridiculous bit of theater."

"Stop it!" The countess was almost weeping. "You are a fine one to speak of ridiculous theater."

"Hear, hear!" Jared stood, hands on his hips, glaring at his grandsire and uncle. "Seems I can trust *her* better than my nearest relatives!"

There was an unhappy silence in the room. Juliette's determination to bring up the gray man in the maze faded. Seeing how very upset the countess was, she decided not to add any further to the woman's distress. Her own curiosity was at an end—it was clear to her that the earl and his brother had conspired in that "ghost" too. Their agonized embarrassment was such that she wasn't surprised they didn't wish to confess to any more.

Now Mark was pressing the point. Why? She firmed her lips. She was heartily sick of the whole business.

When Mark saw that she would not speak, he moved to his grandmother's side. "NiNi, you look tired. Would you like to lie down?"

She patted his hand as it caressed her cheek. "Yes, I expect I had better. Perhaps I'll just stay in bed forever. I shan't be able to face anyone after this."

"I thought as you retired, you might like to invite Adelaide and Juliette in for a look at the portrait of the first Earl of Hammerswold."

Her crinkled, pain-drawn hazel eyes searched his. "If you think best."

"I think by now we may safely conclude that they won't pretend to see his ghost where they do not." Mark turned his inscrutable dark gaze on Juliette.

"That is an excellent idea!" Juliette's chin came up. "We can lay all thought of ghosts to rest, then, can't we, Mr. Camden!"

# Chapter Sixteen

Mark bowed gravely to Juliette. No twinkle of amusement lit his dark eyes. He turned the countess's chair and wheeled it into her bedroom, positioning it before a curtained picture frame.

"We do not keep it on public display because it was painted when he was quite ill, shortly before he died. It distresses some to see it," the countess explained. She nodded to Mark, who pulled the cord.

The portrait was of a well-dressed Tudor gentleman, painted by Hans Holbein. Juliette felt a buzzing in her brain at what she was seeing. She sank down upon a dainty dressing chair while she let the portrait's details sink in. The picture was dark and cracked with age, yet it was possible to see that its subject strongly resembled Mr. Camden. But even more strongly did he remind her of the man in the maze, even to the point of looking extremely ill.

Could any makeup in the world have transformed the elderly but healthy and spry Ramsey Camden into the bent, gray-faced, wasted-looking man who stood portrayed at full length above them, leaning heavily upon the same dragon-headed cane that her morning visitor in the maze had used?

"Well, Juliette?" Mark's voice was insistent. He believed she had seen the real ghost. He probably believed the ghost had pleaded with her to accept Jared's suit. *He wants me to tell them. He wants Jared to court me. He is willing for me to marry Jared, to benefit Hammerswold,* she thought. Misery flooded through her.

Her spine stiffened. "It is true what you said that first day in the long gallery. Your uncle Ramsey does indeed have the look of your ancestor about him. I expect it was indeed you, sir, who gave me that informative tour of the family art collection?" She turned to Ramsey for confirmation.

"I never meant for you to see me. Tried to sneak out but got caught. Just scouting out possible locations if we needed to do a bit of haunting later." He chuckled, but when his amusement was not echoed by the others, subsided.

"Then it was this incident you and Juliette needed to clear up, Mark?" The countess looked anxiously between her guest and her grandson.

"So it would appear, NiNi." Mark's mouth was set in a grim line.

The earl's relief was palpable. "Well, then, that is that! And I swear to you there will be no more such charades." He took his wife's hand. She smiled at him, rather sadly, but it was clear he would be forgiven.

Juliette stood. "Lady Hammerswold, I think I speak for Adelaide and Susan when I say we shall not speak of these events. It appears to me that these malefactors have learned their lesson."

"Thank you, dear." The countess pulled her hands free and held them out to Juliette, who stepped forward to take them. "If there is anything you wish to speak with me about in private, I would be delighted to—"

"You are very kind." Juliette meant it. The countess had become very dear to her. Her throat tightened as she looked into the deep hazel eyes and knew, as did her husband and grandsons, that she was too fragile to remain in this world for long. She seemed to sense that Julie was holding something back, and the temptation to confide in her was great. *How frail and pulled she is looking.* It was time to end this distressing meeting.

Suddenly she remembered the alarm-filled letter she had penned to her uncle. The last thing the countess needed was Uncle Ronald descending on them in a fury. "If you will excuse me, ma'am, I must stop something from leaving in the post."

"By all means."

Juliette hastened downstairs and found her letter still awaiting Lord Hammerswold's frank. She retrieved it and tore it up. She would not grieve the countess by leaving early. Indeed, there seemed no need now. With the earl and Ramsey exposed and thoroughly ashamed of themselves, and Jared having no ghostly authority to continue pestering Addie or herself, there was no reason why they should not remain until after the Halloween ball.

The hardest part would be dealing with Mr. Camden, who knew perfectly well there was unfinished business other than the encounter with Ramsey in the long gallery. As to what she was to believe about that man in the maze, Juliette found her mind would not work on the problem, but shied from it like a high-strung horse from blowing leaves. *And no doubt as substantial a problem, too,* she comforted herself. *I know a rational explanation can be found.*

That evening the viscount, deprived of ghostly advice, was polite and attentive to each of the young ladies in turn. He even suggested a musical evening instead of leading his troops into billiards or deep play at cards.

It was an enjoyable evening except that Juliette kept feeling her eyes drawn to Mark's. Each time Juliette looked his way, she found his dark gaze on her, his expression serious. Finally, when the tea trays were carried in, he stepped to her side and asked her, *sotto voce,* to walk with him in the conservatory on the morrow.

"I have some unanswered questions. Perhaps you do, too?" His dark eyebrows lifted in interrogation.

Juliette did, though she found it took courage to admit it to him. A wild surmise formed in her mind. Had *he* somehow arranged that impersonation of the ghost in the maze? If so, why? "Susan won't permit me to—"

"Your chaperone, of course, may attend us."

"Then I shall join you there after breakfast."

"Could we make it before? I would like very much to be as private as possible. The fewer who are up and about, the less likely it is to become a general entertainment."

She inclined her head in agreement, trying to look serene though her heart was beating frantically. *Was he at last going to offer for her? Had the day's events been some sort of test?*

Susan was not complacent about abetting Juliette in meeting Mark. "You'd just begun to resign yourself, child. Now you're getting your hopes up. I can see it by the hectic color in your cheeks," she complained.

But she allowed herself to be persuaded. She took a seat on a bench and began to read the copy of Shakespeare's sonnets she carried with her while Mark and Juliette strolled off down the graveled paths of the conservatory.

"First of all, I would like to apologize again for the behavior of my grandfather and great uncle."

"It has been forgiven in any case, but you do not owe me an apology, Mr. Camden." She peered at him meaningfully. "Do you?"

He shook his head ruefully. "I can't say I blame you for being suspicious of our whole tribe by now, but now, I swear to you, I have had nothing to do with any of these ghostly hoaxes."

"Including the one I saw in the maze at first light?"

"Particularly that one! That is what I wanted to ask you about."

Just then a delicate, delicious scent caught Juliette's attention. She realized then that they were in the orangery. "This smells heavenly," she said, bringing a blossom-bearing branch down for a close sniff. She sneezed.

"Oh!" She laughed self-consciously, searching in vain about her person. She had forgotten a handkerchief. "Perhaps Susan has—"

"Here. Pity you must wipe off the pollen. It adds a certain *je-ne-sais-quoi* to your appearance."

"I don't doubt it, and it isn't sophistication or elegance."

Juliette slid her eyes away from his admiring look and wiped her nose vigorously with his large kerchief.

"You don't need elegance, Julie. You have charm and a special presence all your own."

"You confuse me," Her eyes dared him to be serious for once.

"I confuse myself." He straightened away from her and continued in a brisk tone, "I wanted to know why you didn't ask Grandfather or Uncle Ramsey about that incident in the maze."

"I knew it must be them. It seemed to me that any more revelations would have been devastating to your grandmother. She looked as if she had taken all her constitution could stand."

"I thank you for it," he said gravely. "She was sorely disappointed in my grandfather. I had heard he was a sad rip when he was young; now I see he is not entirely reformed."

Julie nodded. "Reprehensible as it was, he had a good motive. He loves your grandmother very much. Also, he is devoted to Hammerswold, and is understandably worried about Viscount Faverill's propensities."

"Yes." They were walking again, slowly, and Mark seemed to be concentrating deeply on his steps.

"You, too, are devoted to Hammerswold."

"Very much so. Is that why you thought I might have created a ghost to encourage your interest in Faverill?"

She winced. His question implied that his goal was to see her married to Jared. "It is one possible explanation." *He has no idea that whoever or whatever was in the maze was more concerned with his future than Jared's.* Almost she was tempted to tell him exactly what that strange man had said. But she still found the idea of influencing him by a ghostly pronouncement, whether real or playacted, repugnant.

He was silent, pacing steadily, not looking at her. They reached the end of the orangery. He motioned her through the next door, but she hesitated, glancing back at Susan.

Mark's mouth firmed. "The door is open and she is an

alert chaperone. At any rate, you do not suspect me of planning to ravish you, do you?"

"No, indeed, sir. I just did not wish any appearance of impropriety that might create pressures you don't want . . . that is, we don't want—"

"I understand." He smiled. "Come! We are getting away from the subject. I know my grandfather and Uncle Ramsey had nothing to do with your ghost, Juliette, and—"

"How do you know?"

"I went to them after grandmother went to bed and made them swear it to me. Then I queried Jared again. None of my relatives did this, Juliette."

She scowled. "Then who? Why? and how?"

He laughed. "You simply can't accept that it might actually have been the ghost."

"Absolutely not."

"Yet you admitted once that such a thing as a ghost was possible."

"More because it seemed arrogant to state as a certainty that it was impossible, in front of your grandfather." She laughed. "Ironic, isn't it? I didn't want to hurt his feelings by saying that I believe ghosts are hoaxes, and there he was, planning on perpetrating a hoax himself."

"He saw the real ghost once. Grandmother did, too."

"How do you know?"

"Because they told me . . . oh! This is maddening. You carry rationalism too far. See here, you saw and heard something in the maze. Is it not irrational to deny the only explanation that fits the facts?"

"I still say someone did it to try to fool me."

He grabbed her by the arms. "How? How did he get there and leave without leaving prints in the morning dew? For that matter, how did he know you'd be there?"

Julie's heart stopped at the feel of his hands on her. The first hard grip quickly relaxed, and his thumbs began to play across her shoulders in a way that made her heart start beating again, slowly and heavily, pounding in her ears.

"I . . ."

His expression grew tender. "Why, Julie? There is some reason, some deep-seated personal reason why you refuse to even entertain the notion of a visitation by the Ghost of Hammerswold."

Mark hoped she would say that it was because she wanted nothing at all to do with his cousin, now or ever. Once he knew that she was entirely free of that ambition, even though the ghost had urged her to be Jared's bride, he would himself feel free to court her.

But Julie turned away, pulling out of his grasp and wiping at tears that started in her eyes. "You are right. It is something I just cannot accept, that the spirit of a family member can love his family so much that he returns from the afterlife to advise them."

Mark was silent, waiting, for clearly this was not all of the explanation, nor was it the explanation he had hoped to receive.

"You see, when my mother died, I was twelve. I was just becoming . . . ah . . . more mature, and full of fears and doubts. I needed her then. I felt abandoned by her, even angry at first, that she had died. Of course, I soon grew out of that. She didn't die deliberately. She didn't want to leave me. And she didn't stay away when she might have come back to communicate with me."

"Ah! That is the crux of the matter."

"Yes." Julie turned to face him, her face taut with grief. "Even today, I need my mother. If your ancestor can do it, why can't she? I know my mother loves me as much as any one person ever loved another. But she hasn't ever visited me, because she can't, because such things are just not possible."

"To believe they are possible is to believe your mother is doing less than she might for her daughter."

"Yes . . . I daresay it sounds a little selfish." She hung her head.

"It sounds very understandable, Julie. And much more convincing than your rational arguments." *She looks so sad.* Mark's heart turned over with pity for the feelings of abandonment she had carried inside herself for so long. He stepped up and took her in his arms. He had to do this. He knew he shouldn't, but he had to. She needed kissing as much as he needed to kiss her.

She lifted tear-spangled lashes and looked deeply, trustingly into his eyes.

*Jared be damned. The ghost be damned. Let them find their next countess elsewhere!* Mark lowered his head and touched his lips to Julie's. She stood unresponsive at first, clearly not knowing what to do.

*So innocent,* he thought, fitting his lips more firmly to hers. *So sweet.*

Then she began to return the kiss and the wonder of it swept over him. He put his arms around her and would have kissed her senseless, except that an insistent sound in his ear distracted him.

"Ahem. Ahem. Mr. Camden. *Ahem!*" The last urgent sound was accompanied by a solid blow to his shoulder. He sprang away from Julie, who staggered and looked dazed.

It was Susan Campbell pounding on him. "Sir, unless you have something pertinent to say to me regarding your intentions—"

"Susan, don't!" Juliette's dreamy expression gave way to sheer horror. "Don't. It was just . . . Mr. Camden was comforting me, that is all. I was telling him about my mother and began crying." The last thing Juliette wanted was for Mark Camden to feel obligated to offer for her.

But with her blood still singing from that kiss, part of her hoped mightily that he would rush into a declaration, that he would not feel trapped but, rather, delighted by the opportunity.

She was disappointed.

Mark flexed his shoulders and looked around, thinking frantically. *She looks so upset.* She had been concerned to avoid just such a situation, where propriety forced them into marriage. She obviously did not want to commit herself to him, at least not yet. Was it because of what the ghost had said to her? But if she gave credence to that, why hadn't she told Jared? He would have proposed to her on the instant. Confused, Mark drew away. *I will just have to await events, as I originally intended*, he decided. But the decision to do so came much harder this time.

Through gritted teeth he declared, "She speaks truly, Miss Campbell. It was a reflexive action. I have three sisters, and have often acted as father figure to them. I was intending comfort, but . . . somehow things got out of hand. But no one else is here but we three, so I am sure there is no harm done."

Susan's look could have frozen molten lava. "I am sure not, Mr. Camden. But I trust there will be no more repetitions of such behavior. Julie is deserving of your respect, and if I cannot make you take that seriously, I am sure her uncle, Lord Paxton, can!"

Mark lifted his hands in mock surrender. "Say no more. I am sufficiently intimidated."

Susan reached forward and caught Juliette's hand. "Come, dear, we've tarried long enough. You are going to need a good breakfast if you are going to go nutting with the others."

Juliette, firm chin held high, swept past Mark and up the conservatory path. He watched her until she disappeared through the door at the entrance without a backward look.

# Chapter Seventeen

There was time enough for Juliette to exhaust herself with weeping before the projected nutting expedition. She wanted to stay behind, but Susan refused to leave her alone just then, and couldn't allow Addie to go unchaperoned, particularly on such a ramble through tempting woodlands.

So Juliette laved her face in cold water, dressed in sturdy, warm clothes, and came downstairs with the others. To her relief Mr. Mark Camden was not among them.

Open carriages carried them through a spacious park, past the stone walls of Hammerswold's closest fields, past the thick hedgerows of older enclosures, and into an area where a charming small stream wound its way down a hill interspersed with coppiced woods, ancient oaks and walnuts, and numerous patches of hazel.

Leaving the carriages, they took the baskets that had been provided and spread out, shouting and romping like schoolchildren, to gather the nuts.

Juliette felt a bit sorry for the mothers who must keep track of their daughters in this situation, and even sorrier that the one with whom she might have been tempted into a minor indiscretion behind a thick stand of hazel was nowhere about. She wandered disconsolately toward the stream. Long patches of hazel overhung the banks.

"Here. Let me assist you, Juliette."

She jumped as the viscount spoke. He stretched out his curved walking stick, which she had taken earlier for an affectation, and hooked the flexible stalks, bringing them into reach of her hands.

"Thank you, kind sir." She tried to look enthusiastic as she stripped the tawny clusters from the stalks. Some of the nuts were so ripe they popped from the sockets as soon as she touched them.

"Gracious! Such bounty!" She hefted her basket, now almost half full.

"The season must have been unusually wet; everything is lush like this, all over the estate. My coverts are in peak form. I can hardly wait to see the fine foxes we'll hunt from these woods."

Jared looked around him with deep satisfaction. Juliette studied his face as he surveyed his kingdom. At least he had some feeling for the land, even if it was mainly as a source of recreation.

He even looked the part of a countryman now, in his buckskins and sturdy boots. His windswept blond hair for once did not owe its arrangement to the efforts of his valet. His eyes were the same yellow-brown as the nuts she had just picked, and for a change they were not red, nor underhung with dark bags bespeaking an evening of excessive drinking the night before. His pink skin glowed in the cool autumn air, and his cheeks were as rosy as a girl's. *If he were not so stout, he would be a handsome man*, she thought.

He glanced down and caught her eye. She looked quickly away, suddenly shy of him, wondering why he was here with her.

Jared chuckled. "Yes, we are alone. But I shan't take advantage. You'll see, I do know how to behave, and I mean to do so. Odd, isn't it. All these years I've seen my grandfather as a stodgy, straitlaced, morally unassailable man, and knew I could never be like him. Told myself I didn't want to. Yesterday I saw a glimpse of what he must have been like in his salad days—a disgraceful rakeshame not much different from me—and it has given me hope. If he can reform under the influence of a good woman, so can I."

Jared looked down at her, exuding sincerity. When she couldn't suppress a doubtful little frown, he asked, "Don't you think I can, Juliette?"

"I am a firm believer in the ability to improve oneself, given the desire and the will."

"Well, there you are!" He took her basket in his right hand and offered her his left arm. "Shall we see if there are walnuts to be gathered?"

His enthusiasm for this form of nutting was quickly worn out, however. He stopped, puffing, at the base of the tree, to visit with Sir Beauford and James Montrose.

Juliette moved in a wide arc around the tree, searching for her cousin and chaperone. Before long, they appeared from the direction where Juliette and Jared had picked hazelnuts. Victor was with Adelaide, holding her hand, in fact!

Susan didn't look disapproving nor Addie embarrassed. In fact, both women were smiling broadly. Victor, too, was smiling and looking tenderly into Addie's eyes. *What is Susan thinking of!* Juliette hastened over, to awaken them to their scandalous display.

"Oh, Julie! You must wish us happy," Addie whispered in her cousin's ear. "Pretend nothing is different, though. Victor must speak to my father before matters can be settled."

Juliette gave Addie a quick hug and welcomed Victor with a warm smile. "Then you had best quit holding hands, else the others are going to think the worst!"

Addie jumped away from Victor. "Oh, we must be more careful."

Victor grinned at Juliette. "I can't think there is much doubt of the outcome. I have written to request an interview with Lord Paxton as soon as the house party is over. In fact, I am to escort you home."

"I am so very happy for both of you." Julie's conscience smote her, for her feelings were not entirely joyous. Pain that she had this morning been denied just this happiness pierced her heart.

Susan walked with her toward the picnic, now being laid out under the stately walnut trees, her arm around Juliette's waist. "I saw you with the viscount earlier."

"Yes, and oddly enough he was being most agreeable. I had not expected that now his ghosts have been explained away."

Susan nodded. "Like many stupid, self-centered men, he has a shrewd notion of what is in his own best interest."

That cryptic comment went unexplained as they reached the picnic site. The chairs were already in place around several small tables, and wine was already poured. Juliette had not eaten breakfast, so she was able to do justice to the buffet of delicacies set before them, in spite of her aching heart.

Jared took it upon himself to fill a plate for her, and then sat by her side, glaring at Sylvia, who was flirting with Lord Tremayne.

"Do you love her, Jared?" Julie inquired softly, sympathetically.

"Hmmm? No! No!" His tone was vehement. "A fine-looking woman, but not what the future countess of Hammerswold should be, according to my relatives. Though I do wonder—after all, there is that ghost on the walkway ... ummm ... let us speak of you."

Jared asked her to tell him about her brave father's exploits against the French while fighting to liberate his country from Napoleon's tyranny. He grunted noncommittally when she said that neither her father nor his father before him had blamed the French citizenry for hating the brutal tyranny of the Old Regime.

Juliette was surprised. Most noble Englishmen were horrified by this view, seeing it as somehow a threat to their very existence. She ventured an explanation. "He said that Napoleon was just as bad, though, and a hypocrite too."

Jared grunted again, still covertly observing Sylvia.

Mischief made her continue, "Actually, he thought all of the English aristocracy ought to be guillotined too, and then both countries could start fresh."

"An excellent man and a brave soldier." Jared's tone of voice was that of someone humoring a tiresomely talkative child while he tried to read his paper.

"Thank you," she responded, shoulders shaking with suppressed laughter. *I hope I am not quite so obvious in my wish for a different partner*, she thought, before turning her attention to a particularly delicious custard.

She was not at all surprised when, after they arose from their luncheon, Jared claimed Sylvia and led her away into the woods in defiance of his grandfather's disapproving glare.

That evening Jared singled out Adelaide for his attentions. *Clearly he has decided to honor his grandfather's suggestions, in the absence of a ghost,* Juliette thought, studying the way he was attempting to cut out Victor. Now she understood his attentions to her during the nutting expedition, when he had obviously wished to be with Sylvia. Juliette frowned anxiously as she observed the viscount's behavior.

They had returned to find a letter waiting from her uncle, a letter that made her uneasy. Lord Paxton had written:

Winton Camden was a wild young man. Everyone shook their head when Regina Malmsey married him. But he has become as solid an example of the English ideal as you can find. Jared may well do the same. As for this ghost business, always thought it was folly. Juliette, you are the practical, sensible one. Keep your wits about you, Miss, and be sure your cousin does the same. I am going to join you in a day or two, to see that the two of you are taking advantage of this opportunity to attach the viscount.

Aunt Lydia had enclosed a short note scolding them both for their attitudes. She had ended,

> As for you, Addie, Mr. Makepeace is eligible, but your father will be vexed if you pass up an opportunity to marry the viscount. Do not disappoint him if possible. Juliette, if it should be you that he chooses, it would be all that is foolish for you to refuse Jared Camden with no other eligible match in sight. I will not have it, and neither will your uncle.

Juliette shuddered as she thought of these notes. Would her uncle absolutely force either of them to marry the viscount? He was her legal guardian, with as much authority over her as over Adelaide. Even if he didn't insist, the pressure he and Aunt Lydia would exert if either girl refused the viscount would be horrendous. Still, she thought she could stand out against them if she must.

But Addie? She was a bit more given to fits of temper than Juliette, but down deep she was an obedient, biddable daughter. Would she let herself be pressured into marrying the viscount? Would Victor, who seemed such a lackadaisical young man, persist in the face of parental disapproval?

She gnawed on her lower lip as she watched Victor walk off in disgust after Jared persisted in engaging Addie in conversation.

Addie was seriously agitated when they retired for the night. "What shall I do if Faverill offers? Oh! That Victor had already spoken to Papa!" She threw herself on her bed, moaning.

"It would not have changed things. Your father would not permit an engagement to him until after this house party is over, to see if Viscount Faverill offers for you." Susan spoke briskly. It was her duty so see that her charges behaved as dutiful young ladies of the *ton* should. Yet her frown revealed where her true sympathies lay.

"Perhaps I will be able to draw him off." Juliette stroked

her distraught cousin's forehead. "I believe his feelings entirely unengaged. I can only suppose he decided after the great ghost unmasking to depend upon his relatives to help him select a suitable bride. Whether it is you or I is entirely the same to him. If left to his own devices, he doubtless would marry Sylvia Patchfield."

"She is welcome to him. Oh, Julie, I don't think he will reform as the earl has done. He's only playing at being the complete gentleman. I wouldn't want you to marry him either." She hit her pillow angrily with her fist. "My parents are wrong about this!"

"I agree. Viscount Faverill is transparently interested in nothing but his own health and well-being. But I wouldn't marry him. My only thought is to hold his attention until your father accepts Victor's offer. In fact, I am glad he is coming here. It gives Victor the opportunity to speak to him sooner."

"I'm not sure it will work," Susan cautioned her. "You and he are like oil and water, Julie, and it is clear that he favors blondes."

"But you will *try?*" Addie looked anxiously at her cousin.

"Yes, love, at least long enough for Victor to be accepted."

Addie launched herself at Juliette, enveloping her in a hug. "Oh, best of cousins, I will never forget this!"

Mark barely listened to Elizabeth Harpwood's chatter. His attention was fixed across the table, on Juliette, seated as she had been for the last three evenings next to Jared, giving every appearance of taking pleasure in his company. On her other side was her uncle, who had arrived that day, beaming his approval of Juliette's dinner partner.

They had been a painful three days for Mark. After that fateful morning when Jared learned that the ghost in the mirror had been a hoax, his cousin had gone through a short period of indecision, vacillating between Adelaide and Juliette, but with one eye always on Sylvia. But abruptly, three days ago, Jared had suddenly and unmistakably fixed his attentions upon Juliette.

Mark had kept his word to Jared and stepped back to let him court Juliette out of dual conviction that she was meant to be the next countess, and that it would be selfish to stand in the way of her achieving that high position. But, illogical as he knew it to be, he found himself feeling hurt and betrayed that she was now apparently seizing the opportunity with both hands. He realized that he had held out to himself the hope that Juliette, who gave the ghost no credence, would ultimately refuse his cousin.

*Can't she see that this change in Jared is superficial?* He waved off an excellent roast pheasant. *As soon as he's won her, he'll be the same old Jared again. But perhaps not. Perhaps he's truly begun to care about her. The ghost must think she can turn him around, else why appear to her?* Miserably, Mark's thoughts chased themselves around in his head like the spit dog on his eternal rounds.

Their numbers at table were considerably swelled by new guests who had begun to arrive for the Halloween ball. Only two days away, the Hammerswold traditional entertainment was a popular one that brought friends from the farthest corners of England as well as the local gentry. The invitations had been accepted all the more eagerly because the countess's health had prevented them from holding the ball for several years.

After dinner he sat at his grandmother's side, eschewing the dancing she urged him to attend.

"We've so many eligible young men here now, I would only be someone to avoid," Mark told her with a faintly bitter note to his voice.

The countess looked sharply at him. She understood something of what had happened, though nothing had been said. *He's breaking his heart over Juliette,* she thought. For the thousandth time she found herself wishing it were Mark and not Jared who was the heir.

"Mark, I think we need to be private for a heart-to-heart. Will you come to me later?"

"With pleasure, NiNi!" Perhaps his grandmother could steady him, make him surer of his duty.

Regina surprised her grandson by her opening remark when he joined her at her bedside, where she was comfortably tucked up for the night.

"I want to talk to you about Juliette. Do you think you are doing quite the right thing, leaving the field entirely to Jared?"

Mark looked around to be sure the earl hadn't joined them yet. He decided he must make a clean breast of it, if his grandmother was to help him to do the right thing.

"What else can I in good conscience do? NiNi, there is more to it than just that Juliette is the best candidate to be Jared's bride."

"I know, dear."

"Juliette saw the ghost, I am sure of it."

"I know, dear."

"That morning in the maze, she saw someone. I helped her look for him. We found footprints that went nowhere, with the print of a cane beside them. He was there! I don't know what he said to her, exactly, but the fact that he sought her out—"

The countess put her soft, wrinkled hand to her grandson's cheek to stop the rush of his tormented thoughts.

He finally realized what she'd said. "You know? How? Did Juliette confide in you?"

She shook her head, a mischievous smile lighting her features. "I saw some most peculiar behavior in the maze that morning. First Juliette acting as if she were conversing with someone, though she appeared to be quite alone. Then you and she looking all about. He was there, all right, though she is too stubborn to admit it. How I wish I knew what he said to her."

"What who said to whom?" The earl leaned over Mark's shoulder to kiss his wife on her cheek.

Mark straightened up, surprised. He really didn't want his grandfather knowing about Juliette's ghost sighting. It was, after all, her secret to keep or reveal.

Regina responded, "What Victor said to Adelaide to make her glow so with happiness this evening!"

The earl eyed his wife suspiciously. "I seriously doubt that's what you were talking about." He moved a chair by Mark, who scooted over to make room.

"I've been wanting to say what an admirable thing you have done, my boy, to cease paying attention to Miss Berceau, whom I am persuaded you admire greatly. Another, lesser man, might have concluded that since she is the ghost's choice, that might mean you could inherit eventually if you wed her yourself."

"The ghost's choice? What makes you think that, sir?"

"Tch. Don't you think I knew the meaning of the unveiling of the portrait? You wouldn't have asked that it be displayed except for a very good reason, and I could read the reason in Miss Berceau's face. That fool of a grandson of mine! Mooning over Sylvia Patchfield, wasting his time with Adelaide Beasley, while ignoring Juliette! I put a flea in his ear, don't you know, that he'd best mend his fences with the ghost's choice before the Halloween ball."

Mark felt a dangerous tension building in himself. "I had dared hope his courtship of her now was based on awareness of her good qualities and a sincere desire to attach her."

"Oh, he wants to attach her, all right." A frown furrowed the earl's brow. "Though not for the most unselfish of reasons, I expect."

Suddenly it was too much for Mark. He had at last met a women he could love, one who had seemed able to return his affection without regard for his lack of fortune, and he was expected—expected himself—to let her go to a man who didn't love her, probably didn't even like her.

"I think I will return to Faverill Springs," he announced abruptly. "I am needed there, and I don't believe I can remain to see the prospering of Jared's courtship." He stood up, his face grim.

Mark looked his grandfather in the eye as the older man also stood, opening his mouth to protest.

"Indeed, sir, I doubt I can remain as your estate manager if Jared marries her. On that day I must leave Hammerswold."

# Chapter Eighteen

"No!" The countess cried out as Mark strode off. "He mustn't leave us. This is going wrong. Oh, Winton, what have you done?"

The earl was alarmed by his grandson's threatened departure, too, but the criticism stung him. "Done? I've done nothing!"

"Told Jared she's the ghost's choice when you don't know that!"

"I know she's seen him. What other purpose can he have had for appearing to her? And it certainly changed her attitude toward Jared. She's been quite enchanted by him since."

The countess bit her lip. She too had noticed Juliette's change of behavior, and wondered at it. "She had not seemed the sort to blatantly seek an advantageous match."

"Which is all the more reason to believe she is acting upon knowledge imparted to her by the ghost."

"Yes, but Mark—"

"Mark will come around. Hammerswold is his life. He would be like Antaeus, cut off from the earth."

"Worse and worse!" The earl's wife dropped her head into her hands and began to cry.

"My dear! It is time for your hot posset. You are overtired."

Regina allowed herself to be cosseted, but when her husband started to leave her, she called him back. "You must talk to him! Please, at least insist he stay through Halloween. Surely the ghost will appear at our ball and sort everything out!"

"These roses are magnificent!" Juliette savored the fragrance of the blossoms as Lady Hammerswold looked on. She and several of the other young ladies were in the still-room helping the countess prepare for the Halloween ball. Some of them were arranging the massive amounts of flowers that had been sent up from the Faverill Springs greenhouses to decorate Hammerswold for the coming festivities, and some were packing the baskets of fruit that the Hammerswolds traditionally gave out to the people on the estate and the nearby town.

At long tables nearby, the young gentlemen were engaged in a more onerous task. Under the direction of several estate workers, they were carving lanterns from turnips, beets, and potatoes. These were traditionally carried by the local villagers on All Hallow's Eve to frighten away any evil spirits that might be walking about. The countess planned to hang hundreds of them around the courtyard to give it a Halloween flavor for the ball.

Sniffing another fragrant blossom, the countess agreed with Julie. "Our head gardener is a genius. There was a time when he grew nothing but out-of-season fruits and vegetables in our greenhouses, but when I insisted on having fresh flowers for my tables year 'round, he learned all about blooming plants. There should even be some orchids somewhere."

"Here they are," Sylvia called. "So exotic. So voluptuous. I much prefer them to roses. Oh, Lady Hammerswold, I am looking forward so much to the tour of the keep this afternoon!"

The countess looked startled. "Tour of the keep! I am afraid not. Mark said it was in too great a state of disrepair to safely allow a tour by a large group."

Sylvia's eyes widened. "But Jared assured me that he would—"

"He doubtless is unaware of the problem. I will have

Mark explain things to him. I am sorry you have to be disappointed, Sylvia."

Disappointment did not seem an adequate word to describe the emotion written on Sylvia's face. "But we must . . . surely . . . couldn't Jared take just a few of us? I have quite set my heart on it."

Julie looked at Sylvia skeptically. *Since when did you become so fascinated by ancient buildings?*

The countess replied firmly, "No, my dear, that would not be fair, as most of our guests would wish to participate in such a tour. Perhaps another time."

Sylvia looked stunned. She turned away from Lady Hammerswold without a word.

*How rude of Sylvia. Can't she see how sorry the countess is to disappoint her?* Juliette studied the elderly woman surreptitiously as she worked. *She looks quite done in. All of the these guests and activities are exhausting her.*

Julie, too, felt exhausted from the strain of the last few days. At first it had seemed that Adelaide was doomed to be the only object of Jared's attentions. Julie's efforts to distract him had been in vain. But abruptly, four days ago, he had abandoned Addie in favor of Juliette, who kept her promise to her cousin by responding in an open, friendly manner to his overtures.

Her uncle, seeing that Jared ignored Adelaide, gave his daughter permission to accept Victor. But the relief Julie felt was diminished by his stern warning to her. "Faverill is about to offer for you, be assured he is," Lord Paxton had declared. "And he is behaving just as a gentleman should. There is no reason for you not to accept him."

Julie attempted to convince her uncle that Jared's true nature was hidden behind a false front. "He will be the most dreadful of husbands," she declared. But she failed to convince her uncle that she could not rehabilitate the viscount once they were wed. She, too, thought Jared would offer soon. He had hinted as much last night.

*I will refuse, and Uncle will be furious, and the Hammerswolds will be disappointed.* She would have to take a position as a governess somewhere, for even if her uncle did not disown her, she knew it would be impossible to continue living under his roof after defying him in this matter.

"The ball is tomorrow," the countess said, casting an anxious eye on the sunny sky outside the window. "Do you think this lovely weather will hold?"

She had asked the same unanswerable question several times in the last two days. Juliette smiled reassuringly. "I expect that it will, ma'am. There's not even the hint of a cloud as far as the eye can see."

"Begging your pardon, madam." Mr. Hopewell, the butler, bowed to the countess. "Miss Berceau's uncle asked her to come to the library."

Juliette's heart clenched in her breast. Was this the summons she had been fearing?

Juliette hoped her uncle would be alone in the library so that she could try to reason with him one more time. Surely if he knew she would never accept Jared, he wouldn't expose the viscount to the humiliation of a rejection.

But instead, she found Jared waiting with Lord Paxton. "Lord Faverill has my permission to speak to you," her uncle said, looking at her meaningfully before excusing himself. Juliette turned reluctantly to face Jared.

"Your uncle said you were hesitant about my suit, so I begged that he let me speak to you privately. Come here, Juliette." He motioned for her to sit beside him on a small sofa. When she had done so, there was little room left on it. The length of Faverill's thick thigh was pressed against her own.

"I want to reassure you that I have quite reformed my ways, and intend to lead an exemplary life in the future. I know I have not done as I should have in the past. I always had the security of knowing Mark would look after things, but now I have reason to learn all I can from my grandfather about estate management."

Juliette couldn't contain her gasp of dismay. "You speak as if Mark has left."

Jared looked narrowly at her. "He fell out with my grandfather about something and announced his intentions to resign his post shortly. But I—"

"What will become of him? Hammerswold is his life!"

"He'll make his way. A man of his abilities will be snapped up by some other wealthy man to run his estates. He will come about. It will work for the best in the long run. You find my cousin very attractive, don't you, Julie? Well, I don't begrudge you that, but until I have an heir I won't be a complacent husband, and even later, well, with my own cousin—deuced awkward, you know. Best he and I go our separate ways."

Jared said all of this in the tones of a man of the world speaking to a woman of the world. *He doubtless thinks this liberal view of marriage pleasing to me,* Juliette thought in disgust.

Something of her emotions showed in the disdainful look she gave him. He stopped and stared at her for a moment. "Now what's got you in queer stirrups? Don't tell me you wish I'd declare my intention to guard you like a dragon guarding a hoard of gold all of our lives? Dashed boring life that'd be, for both of us. Nor are you so fond of me as to demand fidelity, I think. No, I have read you well enough, and am not displeased with your practical approach.

"You'll make a conscientious countess, doing all those things NiNi used to do to keep the tenants content. Mark loves to blather on and on about the importance of keeping good tenants. Apparently they don't just grow on trees, you know." Having delivered this wisdom from on high with a condescending look, he added as an aside, "Though I don't understand why we need 'em! Wouldn't if we'd raise more sheep.

"And I know you'll be a good hostess, for you've assisted my grandmother here quite competently. You are not the most beautiful girl I've seen, begging your pardon, but I'm not telling you something you don't know. But you are quite the glowing specimen of health. You never seem to tire. Doubtless you'll present me with an heir and a spare with no difficulty. You have a good disposition, though I know you'll nag me when I backslide, as I will, of course, but I expect you to cut up stiff. What I'm marrying you for, hey? Wouldn't be right to be in a miff at you for doing as you should."

Juliette's disgust began to transmute into amusement. *What a charming proposal,* she thought. *I wonder how many hours he lay awake preparing this lovely monologue!*

"Ah! You begin to smile. You understand me. We understand each other. So, without further ado . . . " He began to fish in his waistcoat pocket for the ring he had hidden there.

Juliette held up a cautioning hand. "Lord Faverill. Please. Do not embarrass yourself—"

"Now, don't go acting coy. You mean to have me, else why have you encouraged me so? And your uncle is delighted."

"Just because I have been friendly to you, that doesn't mean I want to marry you."

Juliette decided that playing for time might prevent their stay at Hammerswold from coming to an acrimonious end. "It is true that you have begun to improve, Lord Faverill—"

"Call me Jared, my dearest." He took the uplifted hand and pressed it to his thick lips.

"But how do I know you won't fall into your old ways? No, I wish you to withhold your offer for six weeks. In that time—"

"Six . . . no, no, no! Far too long! I've put it off long enough as it is. The ghost will almost certainly appear on Halloween, to ratify my choice. I would like to make the announcement at the ball."

"There is no such thing as a ghost, Jared. But if there were I am very sure he wouldn't chose me."

"Naughty puss!" Jared winked at her. "You aren't fooling me, you know."

Juliette struggled to withdraw her hand, suppressing the urge to wipe it on her dress. "I am trying to be honest with you, Jared. I must decline—"

"Wait!" Jared's face was mottled with emotion. "I see you mean to refuse me. Perhaps you were told to see that I reform before our marriage? Very well, then, my angel, only give me hope——"

Suddenly Juliette regretted her cowardly attempt to delay the inevitable. She was piling deception upon deception. She could not be so dishonest, however expedient it might be. "I am sorry, Jared. I can't do that. It wasn't very brave of me to suggest waiting, for I truly do not think a delay will change matters. We simply will not suit."

Seeing she was about to close the door entirely, Jared hurried to change her mind. "I understand your reluctance. I will give you time. I cannot bear that you should refuse me. I have begun to be quite fond of you. A man in love sometimes has difficulty waiting for an answer."

Juliette resisted the urge to snort in disbelief, for she was sure the viscount had little love or even liking for her. "I really don't think——"

"Of course, I could petition your uncle to insist on the match," Jared mused. After a moment's hesitation he shook his head. "But NiNi wouldn't like that, I daresay. Give me six weeks. Well within that time you will know me better, and then you will gladly marry me."

Juliette knew she had to agree, for her uncle would be most upset that she had not accepted Jared outright. To refuse even to allow the viscount six more weeks to court her would infuriate Lord Paxton.

The smile Jared bestowed on her as he took leave of her was both patently false and somehow deliberately unpleasant, so it was with a great sense of disquiet that Juliette watched him leave the room. She remembered the warning of danger that the man in the maze had given her, and shivered apprehensively.

# Chapter Nineteen

When Juliette informed her uncle that she and the viscount had agreed that he was to have six weeks in which to convince her to marry him, he was predictably angry. "It was ill advised in you, my girl. He might shab off. Plenty of lovely young ladies here to tempt him."

"They are welcome to him, sir." Juliette was as disappointed in her uncle as he was in her.

"Ungrateful child. I should have known blood would tell. Should have married you to Squire Farnwell when he asked for you two years ago."

Juliette stared at Lord Paxton. "Squire Farnwell? This is the first I heard of it."

"He offered for you after your birthday ball when you were sixteen. In the worldly sense it was a good match. Should have accepted."

"He is over fifty. I am deeply grateful that you didn't."

"Well, now, show it by marrying sensibly. It makes me want to tear my hair to think of you refusing Faverill. How I wish he had continued to court Adelaide. She'd not have been so foolish."

Juliette bent her head and sighed. *It is a good thing I distracted Faverill from Adelaide,* she thought.

She would have liked to go off by herself and brood, but with guests arriving constantly and last-minute preparations under way for the Halloween ball, she knew the countess needed her help. She excused herself from her uncle and returned to the stillroom.

That evening Jared was as attentive as ever. He joined

her as soon as the men left their port to return to the ladies. Julie played chess with him at his insistence, defeating him easily.

"Showing your teeth, eh," Jared chuckled. "It won't discourage me, Julie. I am pleased that my children shall have a clever mother."

Blushing crimson, Julie stood. "That is beyond what is proper, Lord Faverill."

While he was profusely apologizing, she became dimly aware of a disturbance occurring elsewhere in the large drawing room. A glance told her that Sylvia, her mother, and Mark were having a heated discussion. Soon after the argument with the Patchfields, which resulted in their leaving the drawing room in a huff, Mark also withdrew from the group.

The next day was a frantic one. All morning Julie and Addie helped the countess with last-minute preparations for the ball. The other young women, either dispirited by Jared's continued courtship of Julie, or requiring all day to dress for the ball, did not appear.

The young men had become a veritable factory, turning out numerous vegetable faces, some fierce, some humorous. Mark installed the tiny lanterns inside them that would permit them to stay lighted in a breeze. To her surprise, Jared was nowhere around.

Addie examined one of the small lanterns with interest. "This must have cost the earth," she whispered to Julie.

"The countess sets great store by this ball. I think they are going to look charming." Julie held one large, grotesquely carved turnip up, trying to imagine what it would look like glowing in the dark.

As if reading her mind, Addie whispered, "It will look the way Sylvia looked last night when Mark firmly refused to give her a tour of the keep."

"Is that what the argument was about? I had been wondering."

"It is most curious, is it not? She ordinarily only shows

interest in those activities which will put her in direct contact with Jared. She is up to something."

"Perhaps she hoped to push me over the balcony!"

Addie shuddered. "Do not joke about such things, Julie. If you only saw how she looks at you sometimes."

*There is danger here.* Was that a voice speaking to her, or only a memory of what the old man in the maze had said? Julie shivered apprehensively.

"Does it frighten you by light of day? Then tonight is going to be quite a trial for you."

She looked up to find Mark standing by her, smiling. It was the first time he had directly spoken to her in days. Spirits lifting, she smiled back at him. "It reminds me of the toothdrawer my old nanny used to threaten me with whenever I misbehaved."

He turned away laughing, and tossed over his shoulder, "No wonder you are so well behaved."

Brief though the exchange had been, it buoyed Juliette through the remainder of the day. When the countess retired after nuncheon, she insisted that Addie and Julie do so too, so they would be rested for the ball. Lying quietly on her bed, Juliette found that her heart still raced at the thought of Mark standing beside her, smiling down on her. Surely he would ask her to dance tonight. Surely when no ghost appeared, Jared would leave her alone!

"Julie! Julie! Wake up, sleepyhead," Addie called, pulling on her shoulder. "Who would have believed you would actually fall asleep in the middle of the day! Betty has finished doing my hair and needs to start on yours. Susan is going to help me finish dressing."

Betty was not as good with hair as Marie had been, but Juliette was more than satisfied with the result. From high on the crown her thick, abundant curls trailed down her back and over her shoulder. Her mother's pearl-encrusted combs had been tucked in strategically. After Betty dropped the gauzy white net tunic over her pale pink satin slip, Julie fastened the matching pearls around her neck. The maid drew up the matching pink satin ribbons under her bosom and around her sleeves and tied them in dainty bows, then stepped back to admire her work approvingly.

"You look a treat, Miss, if I may say so!"

"You certainly may," Juliette smiled at her. "Whether it is true nor not."

"She isn't giving you Spanish coin, Julie. You are in your best looks tonight." Addie tripped in, looking ravishing herself in a white satin and lace confection.

"I only hope neither of you catches cold. Be sure to wear your wraps. The night air cannot help but be chilly." Susan handed the warm Norwich shawls to her charges. Julie's was a deep rose, Addie's a celestial blue.

"You are in looks, too, Susan," Juliette commented, surveying Susan's kelly-green gown. "That looks so well with your coloring."

Feeling well pleased with themselves, the three women descended the stairs to join the other dinner guests. It was the largest group that had sat down to dinner at Hammerswold since they had arrived. In the state dining room the vast table was let out to its full extension. An army of footmen served the succession of fine French dishes. Juliette was disappointed to find that she was once again at Jared's side, and could not even see Mark, who was seated at the far end on the same side of the table.

*It doesn't matter,* she promised herself. *He will surely ask me to dance. Perhaps, if he is at all encouraging, I shall tell him why I have tolerated Jared's courtship these last few days.*

She did not get the chance, however. Jared insisted on leading her out for the first dance, which was a waltz. He maneuvered their steps so that when it ended they were standing by the wide arches beneath the ghost's walk. "Come, Julie, let me show you the local's interesting custom on All Hallow's Eve. I think you will find it fascinating."

"I don't think I had better," Juliette demurred. "Didn't the jack-o'-lanterns turn out well?" She gestured at the dancing strings of lanterns that were spread everywhere, providing most of the light for the dance. They crisscrossed the courtyard, hanging from invisible wire strung from the walls. It was a fairy scene. With the right man she would have found it most romantic.

"You needn't be afraid. Look, others are going, too. It is considered *noblesse oblige* to look in on their dancing."

Juliette could see that other couples were filtering out of the courtyard. Catching sight of Addie and Victor drifting along with them, she decided that it was safe. "Very well. Lead on."

Jared's delight seemed disproportionate. "You'll never regret it, Julie. Never!" He led her along a lantern-lit path to the huge bonfire in front of the abbey.

"The locals build a bonfire on All Hallows Eve to keep the spirits away, and dance around it all night."

Juliette saw that the baskets they had filled the previous morning had been set on a large trestle table, along with other refreshments. Tubs were set out for apple bobbing, and a rowdy game of blind man's bluff was under way among the lantern-lit trees.

"The locals seem to be enjoying themselves even more than the people inside the courtyard," she chuckled.

"They have another custom on All Hallow's Eve that is even more enjoyable. I'll show you after we've had some punch."

He procured a large mug of what tasted like a well-aged cider. It was warm and spicy, and Juliette drank it down appreciatively. Beside her, Jared drank two, one right after the other, a large grin on his face. When she had finished hers, he set their mugs down on the trestle table.

"Come. Let me show you the most interesting custom of all." He took her hand firmly in his and led her around the bonfire. Abruptly he angled away from the fire and into the trees. Before she could dig in her heels he had pulled her out of the light of the lanterns.

"Jared! This is most improper."

"The natives care little for propriety. On All Hallow's

Eve one of their most honored traditions is an excursion into the dark to kiss their lovers." He grinned lasciviously at her and wound his arms around her as she tried to escape.

"I'll scream!"

"Half the females around the fire are squealing and screaming. No one will pay the least attention." He bent to kiss her, but she turned her head, presenting her cheek, which he bussed enthusiastically. "You look most fetching this evening, did I tell you?"

Juliette responded cooly, "I thank you, sir. Now release me. I wish to return to the others."

To her surprise he quickly agreed. "Let's go back to the dance, shall we?" But he led her farther into the darkness. Beginning to be alarmed, Juliette tried to break his grasp on her wrist.

"Not exactly the direction to the courtyard, old man."

With relief, Juliette turned at Victor's voice. He and Adelaide were hastening after them.

Jared didn't seem upset to find out that they had company. "It's a shortcut. You'll see. Follow me."

Julie thought he was lost, but her fear subsided with Addie and Victor right behind them.

Suddenly, amid a whooshing sound, a billowing white shape crossed their paths and rose rapidly into the trees. At the same moment a sepulchral voice called out, "Stop. I am the Ghost of Hammerswold. Go no farther."

Jared stopped immediately, and put a protective arm around Juliette. "He's here! Showing himself at last!"

Addie and Victor stepped to their sides. "What was that?" Addie peered anxiously into the dark.

"You heard it. It was the ghost. Speak, sir! You see that I await your advice."

"You do well, Faverill. I am very pleased with your choice. Miss Juliette Berceau will make an admirable wife for you. See you marry her forthwith."

Drawing in a sharp breath, Juliette peered up into the tree where the white object had disappeared.

"Sir, she is not quite sure she wishes to marry me."

"Miss Berceau," the voice boomed. "Do not fear to marry Faverill. He will reform, with your help and mine. Farewell!"

The barely discernable white object quivered and then disappeared from view.

"Whew!" Victor exclaimed. That was quite something." He glanced at Juliette questioningly.

"Oh, Julie. You really *are* the ghost's choice. What will you do now?" Adelaide turned troubled eyes to her cousin.

Julie stomped her foot angrily. "Do! Do! I shall climb that tree this instant and snatch down your confederate and his sheet if you do not admit that this is a hoax, Jared!"

"A hoax! It was not! Jared turned to his old friend. "Was it, Victor? You saw. 'Twas the real thing."

Victor shook his head. "Not a bad effort, Jared. Give you that. But since Julie don't buy it, and don't want you by half, I'll not go along with it."

Jared spluttered. "You're wrong. Adelaide knows it was real, don't you, my dear?"

Addie was peering into the dark above them. "We-ell, it *could* have been real."

Julie stormed toward the tree. "Boost me up, Victor."

"By no means. You girls fetch a lantern or two, and I'll climb up there. Unless I'm mistaken, I recognize the voice of Jared's man, Walters." Victor reached over his head, grasping for a low limb. "Unless you'd care to save me the trouble and confess, Jer."

"Damn you, Victor, I'll pay you out for this!"

Relief brought a smile to Julie's face. "Jared, give it up. You know, until this moment, I did not realize that you don't believe in your own family ghost."

"Wh-what do you mean?" Jared demanded indignantly.

"If you did, you wouldn't have needed to try to fool me. You would await his orders. What if he were real, and showed up later to point out someone else entirely? Wouldn't you feel a little foolish?"

This idea apparently had not occurred to Jared, who stood nonplussed.

Laughing among themselves, Julie, Victor, and Addie started back toward the bonfire that could be glimpsed through the trees. Jared followed slowly. Just before they stepped back onto the lighted path, he called out.

"A moment, Julie?"

She hesitated. "Why?"

"You're safe. Victor will come back if we don't return in two minutes, won't you, Vic?"

"Don't go far, Jer. None of your tricks," Victor warned him.

"On my honor."

Victor led Adelaide, who looked reluctantly over her shoulders at her cousin, back toward the path.

"I apologize for my actions, Julie. I know the ghost has already appeared to you, but I was afraid you were determined to ignore his advice."

"What folly! I've never seen a ghost, Jared. There really isn't such a thing."

"My grandfather said you had seen him in the maze. He saw it in your face when you cast eyes on the old boy's portrait that morning."

Julie shook her head. "It was another of their pranks, the earl and his brother. He must not believe in the ghost, either. I'm beginning to wonder if any of you do, except perhaps your grandmother."

"They both claim they were not involved in that sighting. It was the real ghost. If only you would accept his advice! Will you still give me six weeks, Julie?"

She sighed. It was pointless, but to keep the peace with him and with her uncle, she must agree. "I will, but no more tricks, Jared."

"I will not attempt to fool you again, I swear! Shake on it?"

She put out her hand, which he drew to his lips before turning and offering her his arm.

Thus it was that Mark found them, emerging from the

dark. Julie was leaning heavily on Jared's arm because of the uneven ground, and Jared was smiling down at her, telling her how he was going to pay back Victor for his defection.

As he watched Julie laugh up into his cousin's face, Mark felt a knife twist in his chest. He had come seeking her out of concern that Jared might try something dishonorable. He had hoped to rescue her in that case, and in any event to request a waltz. Angry at himself for caring, for letting himself believe that Jared's title and wealth wouldn't eventually win her over, he stalked off into the darkness.

Julie returned to the ball eager to find Mark, but he was nowhere in sight. She danced several times without enthusiasm. When it was nearly time for the supper dance, and Mark still had not appeared, Julie looked around, wishing for a way to be private. She especially did not wish to have supper with Jared.

As she looked about her, she noticed that the moon had cleared the ribs of the abbey and flooded the courtyard with light. This was her chance to see the river valley from the walkway in the moonlight. The stairs were roped off, but she easily ducked under the thick cords.

A dozen steps up and she was above the lights.

*Probably no one can even see me,* she thought, and found the notion of invisibility very attractive this night. Up, up she climbed, studying the swirling crowds below. When she reached the top, she crossed eagerly to the other side of the walkway, and sighed in delight. The moon lit up the whole valley below, turning the river into a ribbon of molten silver. In the distance storm clouds had formed, and in their purple-black depths could be seen frequent flashes of lightning.

Above the clouds, the stars shone in their myriads of thousands. Juliette had never seen a more magnificent sight, a composition of serenity contrasting with coming violence.

She shivered in the breeze, and drew her warm woolen

shawl around her. The splendor of the scene held her in place in spite of the chill, and she stood on the rampart, hair escaping in the quickening breeze, watching the storm slowly but inevitably roll up the valley toward them.

# Chapter Twenty

Having walked off some of his anger, Mark returned to the ball. It wasn't until he was in the crowded whirls of dancers that he realized the wind was whipping up. The flambeaux sputtered, the lanterns danced on their strings. He looked up to see wisps of clouds streaking across the moon's face. He reached his grandmother's side, where she sat on a dais that had been constructed for her benefit just as a mighty roar of thunder rolled in from the west.

"Mark! You're back!" She clasped his hands, her voice full of relief.

"Yes, NiNi. I just . . . ah . . . went out to the bonfire to greet the villagers."

Another tremendous clap of thunder startled them both. "We may have to adjourn to the castle," Mark said.

"Oh, no! And our ghost has not yet put in an appearance. Mark, I am so sorry about how things are turning out! I know Julie is being pressured by her uncle and Jared, yet there is no real proof that she is the ghost's choice."

He patted her hand consolingly. "Still, we know the ghost has appeared to her. Perhaps the ghost hasn't visited Jared because he is more than willing to marry her already." This thought, which consoled his grandmother, made Mark miserable.

A massive flash and almost instantaneous clap of thunder announced the rapid approach of the storm. A buzz of concerned voices followed. Then there was a change in the sounds of the crowd, and Mark saw faces turning toward the east. Instinctively he turned, too, and was dazzled by the sight that met his eyes. A bright, sparkling ball of pure light was passing through the abbey's ruined arches, moving from the east to the west in a slightly downward trajectory, glittering with unearthly splendor.

Mark had heard of ball lightning but never seen it. He had thought it a product of vivid imaginations. Unlike the lightning responsible for the thunder behind him, this phenomenon was silent. Unlike the sizzling speed of regular lightning, this was slow, almost leisurely. Instinctively his eyes traced its probable path. *It won't clear the walkway,* he thought.

Another brilliant lighting flash illuminated the walkway seconds before the ball slammed into it. They were the longest seconds of Mark's life, for clearly revealed silhouetted against the night sky was a woman, her back to the courtyard, gazing out over the valley. She was completely unaware of the danger sailing toward her.

*Julie!* Mark groaned. It was too late to warn her, even if she could hear him, which she couldn't, above the approaching storm and this crowd. She was doomed!

Frozen with fear, Mark saw the brilliant ball hasten to destroy the woman he loved.

At what seemed the very instant of impact Julie suddenly dropped from sight. In a shower of brilliant sparks the fiery ball slammed into the walkway.

There was an instant's hushed silence, closely followed by a hubbub of voices. Mark thrust his way through the crowd and tore off the cords that blocked the stairway. He dashed up the stairs, dreading what he must see.

At the top of the steps his eyes searched the walkway frantically. There was a gaping hole blasted in the farther wall. Thick smoke and powdered rock filled the air. Two feet away lay Juliette, face down, her clothing and hair on fire. Falling down beside her, Mark stripped off his evening jacket and began beating out the sputtering flames.

As soon as the fires were out, Mark pulled Juliette's inert body into his arms, cradling her against his chest. He could see that she was breathing. Her eyes were closed but fluttering wildly.

"Julie! Dear little rationalist. Speak to me. Explain to me that there is no such thing as a ghost. Tell me that ball lightning is an imaginary phenomenon." He accompanied his words with light slaps to her cheeks.

After what seemed an eternity, she moaned and then lifted her head to look around her in a daze. "Mark?"

"Yes, sweetheart. I am here."

She stiffened as her eyes fell upon the gaping hole in the wall. "What happened?"

"You were almost struck by a ball of fire. I do not yet know how you managed to avoid it."

Her face lit up with joy. "Oh, Mark! I heard a voice! I heard a voice and knew I was in danger. I knew I must fall down and roll away. I don't know how, for I didn't really have time to think about it, I just did it. Did the lighting rods fail?"

"Something a little more exotic than that, dearest. Ball lightning, going for you like a cannon shot. If you hadn't moved when you did . . ."

They both looked toward the hole in the walkway wall. "That's where I was standing. Oh, Mark, that voice saved my life!"

"Well, that's it, then!" Behind them, the earl eagerly proclaimed his opinion of events. "The ghost saved her life! There can be no doubt that she is the chosen bride."

Juliette turned to see that crowding toward them on the walkway were the earl, Ramsey, Jared, Sylvia, Susan, Adelaide, and Lord Paxton. She felt Mark's grip loosen and turned to see that his face was wracked by pain.

Jared knelt by Julie and Mark. "Now do you believe that you are the ghost's choice?"

"No, indeed! It wasn't the Ghost of Hammerswold that spoke to me, of that I am absolutely sure!"

"Nonsense. What else could it have been!" The earl scowled at her. "Mark, let her go. It is for Jared to attend her now."

Jared leaned forward to take her from Mark's arms.

"Not what, my lord, but who!" Mark relinquished her to Jared. "Wait, Mark! It was my mother's voice." But it was too late. Mark shoved through the crowd and disappeared down the stairs.

Jared struggled to stand up with her, then staggered.

"Put me down. I tell you, it was my mother, not the Ghost of Hammerswold, that saved my life."

"Rot! Our ghost has never given a more spectacular example of his approval of a female in over two hundred years," the earl growled.

Susan bustled forward. "We can sort out our ghosts later. Juliette must be checked over and treated for her injuries." Ignoring his protests, Susan helped Juliette escape from Jared's arms, and supported her as they walked toward the stairs. A crack of thunder and a splatter of raindrops helped in breaking up the crowd around her as people turned and hastened down the stairs and toward the carriages that the countess had already commanded to be brought to the courtyard entrance.

Mark was the first to reach his grandmother's carriage, where her two reliable footmen had already taken her. He leaned in to relieve her worry. "Julie is safe and not, I think, much injured. Jared has her in hand. I am going to Faverill, NiNi. I can't stay around for the announcement of their engagement."

"Mark! Not in this storm!"

"I will take shelter if it continues, but I think it will pass quickly." He strode swiftly away. A walk in the rain might help to cool his temper, for he found himself not so much anguished as furious at the ghost's having selected the woman he loved for Jared's bride.

Juliette was found to be remarkably unscathed by her adventure. Scorched hair seemed to be the worst of it.

"Even Marie would not be able to work around that," Susan observed ruefully as she cut away the burned hair.

"It is of no moment." Juliette fretted, "I am much more

concerned about this business of the ghost. Do you think it was some kind of divine sign, Susan? Adelaide?"

Adelaide avoided her eyes. "The fire seems to have destroyed your gown without doing you any great harm." She shook the sad-looking garment out in amazement.

Susan sat back on the bed and studied Julie's distressed face. "Can't you reconcile yourself to marrying him, my dear? It is not as if Mark were courting you. They say he has left for Faverill Springs. And it is an excellent match! Perhaps it *is* heaven sent."

"Would a higher authority intervene to insist I marry a man I don't love? To lie as I speak my wedding vows?"

Julie looked from one to another of her two dear friends. After a second Addie shook her head and turned away. Susan patted her hands. "You will make the right choice, of that I am sure. Now you must rest."

After Susan and Adelaide had left her alone, Julie fell asleep almost instantly. She slept for two or three hours, and then awoke abruptly, rested and feeling very clear headed. She pulled back the covers and walked to the balcony. The storm had ended almost as soon as it began, and the moon, now beginning its descent, bathed the scene in a golden light.

*It was my mother's voice.* Somehow this fact, which had awed and delighted her at first, kept recurring to her. It had a greater significance than she had first imagined. *If my mother can save my life by speaking to me from beyond the grave, then perhaps there can be such a thing as a ghost. And if there is . . .*

Her mind went back to the maze. She saw the events there in an entirely different light. *It was the ghost of Hammerswold I saw! And he wanted me to help Mark feel right about courting me. He didn't expect me to marry Jared! I will tell them tomorrow.*

Her decision did not make Julie entirely happy, for it still seemed wrong, somehow, that Mark was willing to stand back, passively awaiting the ghost's choice. He had called her sweetheart last night. But after the earl had proclaimed that the incident meant she was the ghost's choice, he had surrendered her to Jared far too readily.

*Though I love him, he surely doesn't love me. Whatever feelings he has for me, he puts Hammerswold first!*

Juliette slowly, morosely returned to her bed. She would have to refuse Jared, of course. But she still couldn't bring herself to attach Mark on the basis that she was the ghost's choice. Tomorrow was going to be a very difficult day!

*I am a prophetess,* Julie thought as she looked at the circle of angry faces around her. *A very difficult day indeed!* She faced the earl, Jared, her uncle, and Lady Hammerswold. Only the countess was not berating her. But her expression was so distressed that it was clear she, too, thought Julie should accept Jared.

Again the earl repeated his assertion that the ghost had chosen her in a most spectacular fashion.

"If you allude to the ball lightning, my lord, one might as well reason that he tried to destroy me!"

"He didn't cause it, he warned you of it!"

"No, my lord." Again Juliette explained, "It was my mother's voice that warned me."

"Ghost, schmost!" Her uncle Paxton slammed his hand against the arm of his chair. "You have been honored by a proposal of marriage by the viscount and you will accept him, my girl."

Jared complained, "Was there ever such a creature! It is just as it was when she saw him in the maze. She knows she is his choice, yet she refuses me! Surely you can talk some sense into her, Paxton."

"I shall, if I have to do it with the rod." Paxton advanced on his niece. He had never struck her, but just now he looked completely capable of doing so.

Julie drew in a composing breath. She would have to tell them about the ghost or they would never leave her alone. "You are correct, Lord Faverill. I now believe I did in fact see the ghost in the maze.

"Ha! Didn't I tell you!" The earl was exultant. The countess put her hands to her mouth to stifle a cry.

"Then why didn't you say so? Why are you still being coy," Jared demanded.

"I am not being coy. I didn't say so before because until I heard my mother's voice I didn't think there could be such a thing as a ghost. I now know better. But he did not tell me to marry you, Lord Faverill. Indeed, he said that neither Addie nor I were to do so, that you had not earned the right to marry a good woman, and that you were the master of your own fate."

"You are lying, and I know why. Could see it very well in the way you snuggled against Mark last night. Well, let me tell you, if you are hanging back because you hope Mark will offer for you, you may forget it. He has left Hammerswold for Faverill. He won't offer for you, knowing you are meant for me!"

"Jared!" At last the countess spoke. "I do not believe Juliette is lying. Perhaps you should take her words to heart."

"Regina!" The earl looked at her as if she were a traitor.

"NiNi!" Jared, too, at first seemed inclined to argue with his grandmother, but checked himself. He looked at Juliette's determined face and clenched fists.

"Very well, Julie. If that is the case, I still have six weeks to prove myself worthy of you."

Relieved but amazed, Julie allowed him to salute her by kissing both hands. He then bowed and left the room.

The earl continued to grumble under his breath, but the countess caught his hand to keep him from bursting out of the room after his grandson.

Lord Paxton shouted, "If you continue to be so stubborn, Missy, you had best begin planning to take charge of your own life, for if you reject my authority, I cannot have you under my roof."

Julie nodded. "I realize that. I am sorry for the rift, Uncle, but I cannot pledge before God to marry a man I do not love, or even respect."

Lord Paxton snorted. Without glancing at Julie he walked past her, almost knocking her down. Sadly she watched him leave the room. *I hope I will enjoy being a governess,* she thought. She curtsied to the earl and the countess. "I beg your pardon my lord, my lady, for the discomfiture I have caused."

The earl harrumphed and turned his back on her, going to stand moodily at the window. The countess beckoned her closer. "Julie, I will write Mark. The knowledge that you have refused Jared—"

"No, my lady. Jared was right. Mark does not care for me, or at least not sufficiently to make a marriage."

Lord Paxton was with Susan, venting his feelings, when Juliette returned to their suite. She excused herself and went to her room to begin packing. A few minutes later Addie came in, followed by Lord Paxton. To her surprise, they did not bring up the subject of her refusal of the viscount.

"We have been invited to tour the keep before we leave," Addie exclaimed. "Jared just stopped by to say he is taking a few guests through it. Sylvia was with him. I suppose she talked him into it."

"I thought it was unsafe," Julie responded.

"Jared says only the top flight of stairs is shaky. We won't go that far."

Julie shook her head regretfully. "I have wanted to see it, but under the circumstances I think I had best refuse."

"That is just what you will *not* do, my girl," her uncle exclaimed. "You agreed to give Lord Faverill six weeks to court you, and I am going to insist that you not avoid his company."

The smell of musty air and ancient stones assailed Juliette's nostrils as they were ushered into the ancient keep. The 'small group' consisted of some twenty or twenty-five guests. Jared proved surprisingly knowledgeable about the keep, which he explained had been a favorite play area when he was a boy.

When they reached the third floor, Jared reminded his guests that no one was to climb the next flight of stairs, which led to the ancient chapel, the solar, and gave access to the ramparts. Then he directed their attention to the former treasure room.

"There are some interesting showpieces here that were taken from the abbey, though I fear that the jewels are all paste by now, the originals having been sold to support various building projects and mistresses." There was a rumble of masculine chuckles at this, and a sudden fluttering of female hands to rosy cheeks.

Jared had offered Juliette his arm and kept her at his side as he discussed the items on display. As the rest of his guests, the tour over, left the room, he detained her.

"I have a very special treasure to show you, Julie. A rare and authentic jewel. We don't like its presence to be well known."

Curious and yet not a little suspicious, Juliette turned in the direction he pointed her as the others clattered down the stairs.

She heard the door closing behind them. "No!" She broke free and lunged forward, too late. She heard a key turning in the lock. Jared pulled her up and bent to retrieve the key, which had been shoved under the door.

"Oh, yes, my dear Juliette. I told you that you would be willing to marry me eventually. In fact, I should say, within an hour of now."

Jared pocketed the key and then took an ornate watch out of his vest pocket. "Just going on eleven o'clock. I expect we'll be found by twelve or twelve-thirty. My faithful valet will begin to wonder, you see, and the search will eventually lead to the last place we were seen."

Juliette sprang away from the door, out of his reach. "This is despicable. Do you really think your grandparents will permit such a thing?"

"Permit? I should say they'd insist. A wicked man like me, compromising an innocent like you. Ah, Julie, what I do for your sake. I cringe at the thought of the peal my grandfather is going to ring over my head!"

"And your grandmother? What will this villainy to do her?"

Jared had the grace to look a little troubled. "Ah, I am sorry for it, but in the end she'll forgive me, when you put my first chubby son into her arms! Come, Juliette. It's cold in here. These old stone walls drink all warmth from the body. Let's make one another comfortable while we wait, shall we? I've brought a flask of grandfather's finest brandy, to make the situation more tolerable."

"Nothing could make the situation more tolerable. Nothing could make me marry you! Compromise me, and you only cast further soil on your own name. I'd rather be a spinster than marry you!"

Jared was advancing on her as she spoke. She ran lightly around the display cases. She really thought she might keep ahead of him until she wore him out, but he surprised her by his agility and determination. As she began to tire, she stumbled and hit one of the cases, cutting her arm. Pain stabbed her and blood welled from the cut. Before she could recover, he was upon her.

Appearing to be genuinely worried, Jared examined the cut while she struggled, grunting in satisfaction when he decided it was superficial. "Here, you cat. Stop wiggling. Let me bind that up. Good job you didn't really injure yourself."

At the concern in his voice she stopped struggling and let him bind her arm with his handkerchief. "Perhaps now you realize how reprehensible your actions are! Jared, open that door and let us return before we are missed."

He lifted troubled hazel eyes as he finished tying the kerchief. "But the ghost chose you—I must wed you, or I shall die young."

"The ghost didn't chose me. Not for you. I explained to you—"

"It is clear enough that you are to be the next countess!

Well, Mark shan't have you. I've no intention of dying young and leaving him the title!"

Juliette sighed. Jared's lip was protruding stubbornly. Clearly his determination was unshaken.

"Jared, don't you understand? The prophecy concerns the heir finding a woman he can care for, who will care about him, and who is of sufficient strength of character to bring out what is best in him. You do not care for me, nor I for you."

Jared's high forehead wrinkled in thought. Sensing that she was gaining ground, Juliette hurried on. "Don't you see? Marriage is not a magic potion that will save you. You can save yourself."

"But you certainly have strength of character, Juliette. Like my grandmother, who succeeded in making a stuffy pillar of society of my grandfather."

"She succeeded because he loved her and would do what he knew he should, to please her. Would you do anything to please me, Jared?"

He nodded his head vigorously. "Anything, my angel."

"Then open that door and let us leave before we are missed."

"Not now. After we are married."

"Will you give up drinking after we are married? And gaming? Gluttony? No more rich French sauces and cream-filled pastries!"

Jared began to scowl.

"Will you spend hours on the magistrate's bench, and spend your own fortune to see that your tenants have comfortable, modern housing? Study the latest farming methods, and see that your people have the tools and livestock to take advantage of them? Will you attend church each and every Sunday?"

Jared groaned. He had not put in an appearance in the chapel on the three Sundays she had been at Hammerswold.

"You must, you know, as an example to your children and servants. You must cease gaming, and . . . and if you are wed to me there certainly must be no more high-flyers in your keeping!"

Jared held up his hand. "Enough," he exclaimed, his voice filled with disgust. "Egad, Julie, if a man must live so, why would he wish to live a long life?"

In spite of her predicament, Juliette felt the urge to laugh. "These are the things I would insist you do, to save yourself from an early grave and an impoverished earldom."

"Oh, very well," he surprised her by saying, though with no good grace. "I'll do 'em. At least some of 'em. At least . . ." He turned and paced away, toward an arrow slot in the thick stone walls. He drew the brandy flask out of his inside coat pocket once more. "May as well enjoy myself now. Seems like once I wed you I'll truly be leg-shackled." So saying, he tilted his head back and drank deeply.

"You won't wed me!"

He took his watch out of its pocket once again. "Oh, yes, I will. Any time now my valet will have begun to raise the alarm. Too late to stop the thing now." There was some regret in his voice.

"No, it isn't, Jared. Open the door, and we'll be gone our separate ways before the search can lead them here!" She crossed to where he stood peering morosely into the courtyard below. "Please, Jared!" She touched his arm. "I am persuaded we will not suit. I believe instead of bringing out the best in you, I'll make you miserable, and vice versa."

"You may as well relax and enjoy yourself, Julie, for I won't change my mind." Abruptly he threw a beefy arm around her. "Here, have a swig of this. It'll warm your bones and maybe your heart a little, too." He shoved the flask at her, and she began to struggle with him.

"Don't, Jared, don't." The more she struggled, though, the tighter the viscount pressed her against his body.

"You're a pleasant armful, at least there's that. Give me a kiss, Julie. A betrothal kiss." Eyes slightly crossed, Jared bent down, intent on claiming her lips. Disgusted, alarmed, furious, Juliette twisted toward the arrow slot and began to scream.

# Chapter Twenty-one

Mark galloped away from Hammerswold in the height of the storm, not even caring about the danger posed by the lightning. But the storm blew over quickly, and he rode on in the moonlight. Mark had little interest in the beauty of the scene. Though he changed horses at the first stage on the road to Faverill and continued riding, the simple fact was that every mile that he put between himself and Hammerswold castle felt like a leaden weight hung upon his shoulders, until he felt he might sink into the ground with the burden.

After he had been riding about four hours, he found that he was unable to force himself to go on. *I need to stop and think.* He decided to rack up in a little hedge tavern. After a cold collation that he could hardly eat, he stood in the open windows of his room, facing east, facing Hammerswold.

The inn was on a small hill. With a set of binoculars he might have been able to catch a faint glimpse of Hammerswold's ancient tower keep, high on the plateau across the valley. But he had no field glasses, so he stood and stared, seeing neither the towers of Hammerswold nor the ruins of St. Mildryth, but Juliette.

He saw her smiling at some joke, widening her eyes in amazement at some vulgarity, bending tenderly over the countess, scowling sternly at the earl's hoax. He saw her face just after he had kissed her, with joy being replaced by dismay as he stammered his way out of the situation. Suddenly the words she had spoken to him earlier blazed into his conscience: *A girl's first kiss should be given to her by the man who will be her husband.*

*She gave that kiss to me.* He groaned. *What did I do? I tossed it into the dirt. I thrust her into Jared's arms and watched him court her.*

Suddenly he realized that he could not, must not let Juliette marry Jared. No matter what that stupid ghost had decided, Jared would make her miserable. *Jared doesn't even like her!* Selfish or not, Mark loved her and he believed she loved him. If so, it would be a sacrilege for her to marry another. *I never even gave her a choice,* he castigated himself. *I abandoned her to Jared's deceptive wooing and her ambitious uncle's pressure.*

"Promise be damned! Ghost be damned! He shall not have her," Mark declared out loud to the four walls of the room.

The moon had not yet set, but he knew it soon would. He would go on tonight to the next stage where he kept horses stabled on the road to Faverill Springs. There he would get a good, fresh horse. Hurriedly packing his saddlebags, he rode away, no longer leaden with misery, but buoyed up by his new determination.

The moon was approaching the horizon, glowing orange as a summer sunset, when in the road ahead he saw someone walking toward him. As he drew closer it became clear that whoever it was moved slowly and painfully, with a cane for support. Swathed in a gray cape, head lowered, the figure could not be distinguished as male or female. Mark was surprised that this person did not look up in fear at finding a rider approaching.

He drew alongside and spoke gently. "A good evening to you."

There was no response, not even a lifting of the head, so he started to ride on by, when his eye fell upon the cane. Abruptly he reined his horse and dismounted.

"Is it you, then? But what do you here?"

The figure halted. "You are still on your way to Faverill

Springs? Then I am wasting my time. I have done with Hammerswold." Shuffling forward, the figure passed him.

Mark turned and walked alongside. "I am only going to the next stage to get a fresh horse for the return trip, though I should have thought you'd prefer me to stay away."

The hooded head lifted, revealing a gray countenance that was the very image of the portrait of the first Lord Hammerswold. The pained gray eyes lifted to meet his. "You are going back? Why?"

"I expect you will find it reprehensible and try to talk me out of it, but I love Miss Berceau. Jared will just have to find himself another bride."

A relieved smile lit the man's gray features. "I knew you had bottom."

"I am surprised you approve. I thought—"

"I know what you thought. I told that naughty puss to tell you not to worry about Jared, that he was responsible for his own fate, but she wouldn't, of course."

Mark was indignant. "Why not? If I had known that . . . Since you appeared to her in the maze, I have been fearing that if I courted her—"

"You were convinced she was meant to be the heir's bride. Hammerswold would fall to you by Jared's untimely death, something you did not want on your conscience. I know. Your sentiments are dutiful, but did not strike her as sufficiently devoted to her interests."

"Nor were they," Mark admitted. "I am heartily ashamed. I hope it is not too late. After that miracle tonight, she may well accept Jared."

"That is why I came. I—"

"If my marrying Juliette has no impact on Jared or Hammerswold, why have you bothered with us, sir? Why have you not concerned yourself with finding the heir a bride, now he is in a mood to take your advice?"

"Modest or foolish or both," the gray man snapped. "Jared may or may not be the earl one day. I am not allowed a perfect knowledge of the future. But I know him, and thus I know that the future of Hammerswold and all its

dependents rests on your shoulders. Should you depart
from it—"

"As I must if he marries Juliette—"

"Which he intends to do, by fair means or foul. Enough!
I grow weary and time grows short." His voice began to
sound labored. "I came to warn you, assuming you cared,
that Juliette is in danger."

"Danger? What sort of danger?"

"I'm not sure, but I can feel it menacing her. I see a great
staircase ... Only ... love ... can ... save ... her."

As he spoke, the bent man began to shimmer, and then to
fade. His last words, so faint they seemed a mere whisper
on the wind, were "Go quickly!"

Mark shook his head and looked all around. The man
had disappeared in the middle of a clear, wide, moon-
drenched road. Never once questioning the authenticity of
his experience, Mark remounted and touched his spurs to
his horse's heels. He would begin the ride back to Hammerswold immediately.

Mark burst into the castle and quizzed Hopewell about
Juliette's whereabouts. A thrown shoe on one of the horses
he had ridden so hard on the way back had delayed him for
over two hours, and he was frantic with worry. Hopewell
informed him of the expedition to tour the keep.

*The keep! That was what the ghost meant by a great
staircase, and danger. Those top stairs might give way
under her feet!* Mark ran to the ancient tower. His heart
pounding, he jerked open the heavy doors and hastened to
enter.

Momentarily blinded by the gloom, he could just make
out a woman struggling with a man at the foot of the stairs.
He strode over to separate them and was astonished to find
that the woman he had rescued was Sylvia Patchfield. She
was trying to get past Walters, Jared's valet, who was
blocking the stairs.

"What is going on here? Where is Juliette?"

Sylvia grabbed his hand and began pulling him up the

steps. "You must hurry. Help me save him from his own folly."

"Him? I am looking for—"

"I know. Jared shut himself into a room with her."

Without waiting for her to finish, Mark raced up the stairway. Sylvia was on his heels, closely followed by the protesting valet.

They were almost to the landing when Juliette's screams, muffled but unmistakable, began. Mark took the remaining stairs two at a time and arrived to find the door locked. He banged on it with his fist, but the struggle within continued.

Thanking his stars that it was a modern door and lock he had to contend with, Mark backed up and kicked the door. On the third try the lock gave way and he was able to shove his way into the treasure room. Hastening around the cases, he saw Jared struggling with Juliette under the arrow slot. He was cursing; she was screaming. Mark grabbed Jared and dragged him away from her, then hit him with all of his might on the jaw. Jared fell back against the wall and slumped down, half-conscious from the force of the blow.

"Julie, my darling." Mark gathered Juliette into his arms. She huddled there, trembling and crying.

"Oh, Mark, he was going to . . . going to . . ."

"No, I wasn't!" Jared moaned and attempted to rise. "Just wanted a kiss. Never meant anything more. Such a fuss over a kiss! Betrothal kiss, what?"

"Vile beast!" Juliette peeked out from her sanctuary in Mark's arms to hiss at Jared.

"This is nothing to the point," Sylvia said. "Jared, you great looby. She'll make you miserable, and your name will be muddied forever if this gets out!"

"It cannot fail to get out," Jared growled. "My servant has his orders. He knows we've been closeted together. Doubtless he's raising the alarm now."

"He's right here!" Mark stirred from his absorption in Julie's trembling body pressed against his. "I just may see that he hangs for his part in this disgusting plot, if I let him live that long, that is!"

"Please, sir, I only did as my master—"

"Shut up!" Jared snarled. "You can't wiggle out of this, Mark. I know you hope to see me below ground at an early age so you can usurp my title. Preventing me from marrying the ghost's choice is the only way, and you've been undermining me with her since she arrived! Well, she'll have to marry me now. Been shut up with her alone, what?"

Mark set Julie to one side gently, then advanced on his cousin. "No, Jared, I never coveted your title, but it seems I shall have it, for I intend to see you answer for this insult on the field of honor."

Jared tried to look unconcerned, but his pallor suggested his true feelings. "You wouldn't do that. Think of the scandal."

"Imagine the scandal if it becomes known you tried to force yourself on your guest." Mark grabbed Jared's tie and twisted it, shaking his cousin violently.

"Pah!" Jared shoved him away defiantly. "You won't challenge me. NiNi would never get over it."

Sylvia thrust herself between them. "Think, Jared. If you expose Miss Berceau to disgrace in order to force her to wed you, your grandmother would already be devastated by the scandal. What reason would Mark have to keep things quiet?"

Jared had no wish to duel with his cousin. He had spent his life pursuing foxes and shooting grouse with a shotgun. He had never been a good shot with a pistol, and was a clumsy swordsman at best. The look in Mark's eyes clearly said blood—Jared's blood—would be shed.

He turned to Juliette. "This is my final offer, Juliette. Will you or will you not be my wife?"

"I'd rather die first." Juliette didn't bother to suppress the shudder that went through her.

"Will you explain to your lover here that I wasn't trying to force myself on you?"

Juliette's face flamed. "I really don't think he had any such intention, Mark. He did try to kiss me, and I began to scream. When you came in, he was trying to get me to be quiet."

Mark looked only marginally less fierce at this explanation.

"Walters, we will not speak of this incident, is that understood?" Jared put a firm hand on his slender valet's shoulders, almost forcing the man to his knees.

"You have my assurances that I never will." The servant was not looking at Jared, but at Mark, for he felt his very life depended upon convincing the younger man of his willingness to cooperate.

"Well, Mark?"

"If Juliette can come out of this encounter with her reputation intact, I will not call you out."

"Then all is settled." Sylvia stepped forward and took Julie's hand. "Come, Juliette. I will help you tidy yourself a bit, and then we four must leave the keep together, laughing and on good terms, with a servant in attendance."

Juliette lifted her eyes to Mark. "That would serve, don't you think?" Mark nodded solemnly to her. "Very well," she said briskly. "I will need some water to clean away this blood." She held up her bandaged arm.

As the two women started out the room with the valet to find some water, Mark turned on his heel and confronted his cousin. "What did you do to her, you bastard?"

"She did it to herself. Cut it on a case, running from me. Brought it all on herself, you know, by refusing me."

"If you ever bother her again, I will kill you. Is that clear, cousin?"

"Very clear," Jared snarled. "Proud of yourself, ain't you, stealing my bride!"

"As to that, I should tell you, Jared, that the ghost appeared to me on the way to Faverill. It was he that warned me that you were up to no good."

"Damn him, why does he appear to you?"

"Because unlike you, I am necessary to the welfare of Hammerswold."

"To hell with Hammerswold. I want to live a long,

healthy life, as prophesied. But how can I do it if the ghost never appears to me, never selects a bride for me?"

"He told me you were responsible for your own fate. Face it, Jared. Our ancestor, having the deep respect he has for the worth of a good woman, would never condemn such to a life with you!"

Sinking to the ground at his cousin's feet, Jared groaned in despair. "The same thing he told Juliette. Then I am doomed!"

"No, Jared. You could truly change your ways, instead of merely pretending to. You could make of yourself the kind of decent, upright person who would appeal to someone like Juliette or Adelaide. Then you would deserve to wed a good woman. If not, you may as well wed Sylvia Patchfield!"

"At least she cares something for me."

"Or for your title. Pah! I have done with you!"

Mark followed Jared down the stairs and watched as Julie and Sylvia cleaned her arm with water the valet had brought.

Just then there was a loud clap like thunder from above them. Several stones clattered to the floor of the keep. "Look out!" Mark pulled Juliette under the stairs.

A loud voice directed their eyes to the highest gallery, the one from which the battlements could be reached. They saw boiling smoke pouring over the railing. From out of the smoke a figure draped in gray from head to toe stepped forward, arms outstretched.

"The devil," Mark exclaimed. "It's the Ghost of Hammerswold."

# Chapter Twenty-two

A deep voice proclaimed, "Jared Camden, Lord Faverill, step forward."

Jared peered from beneath the stairway. "Eh?"

"I am the ghost of your ancestor. Step forward. I have something to say to you."

Slowly Jared stepped out into the great hall.

"Miss Sylvia Patchfield, step forward," the impressive deep voice intoned.

Sylvia did not hesitate, but went to Jared's side.

Julie drew in a sharp breath. "That's not—"

"Shhhh, love!" Mark gently put his hand over Julie's mouth. She started to object, then subsided, thrilled to be held so close by the man she loved.

She whispered in his ear, "So *that's* why she was so insistent on a tour of the keep!"

Mark took another look at the figure on the gallery above them and then began to chuckle. "Ah, yes. Sylvia! She fair took me apart when I refused her."

The voice boomed again. "Jared! You have been a disappointment to me thus far!"

"This ghost sounds amazingly like Sylvia's gypsy groom," Mark whispered in Juliette's ear, then kissed it in a way that made her bones melt.

The sweating viscount replied, "I . . . I know, sir. I mean to do better."

"Behold the woman who will help you to do it!"

"You mean *Sylvia?*" Astonishment overcame awe.

"Miss Patchfield has deep feelings for you. She will be a good influence. Will you have her?"

Jared looked down at the blonde who waited tensely beside him. "Indeed I will, sir, and thank you!"

"Very well, then. See that you value her as you ought. Farewell!" The figure disappeared back into the cloud of smoke. After a minute or two the smoke itself ceased. A loud clank and a creak or two, and then the keep was silent.

"My Gawd. He appeared. He really appeared!" Jared turned and swept Sylvia into his arms. "You will have me, won't you Sylvia?"

"Oh, yes, Jared," she replied breathlessly. "Let's go tell Mother!"

"We can't let him be deceived this way," Julie said, pulling away from Mark's strong arms.

Nodding, he stepped out from under the stairs to intercept his cousin. "Jared, before you accept this phenomenon as real—"

"Step aside, Mark. I know what I saw. Come, Sylvia." Angrily shouldering Mark aside, Jared swept his new fiancée out the door, followed immediately by the frightened groom.

Mark shrugged his shoulders. "Fool! Let him go. I have more important matters to attend to." He turned to take Julie in his arms. "I was so afraid you might have accepted him."

"Never! But what made you come back?"

"I couldn't let Jared have you! I love you, Julie. Will you marry me?"

"Oh, yes, dearest!" She luxuriated in the long, deep kiss he gave her. *He chose me! He set his loyalty to Jared and Hammerswold aside to choose me!* Like a love song the thought hummed through her consciousness.

"I will speak to your uncle right away."

"I hope he will listen. He is on the verge of disowning me if I don't wed Jared."

Mark frowned. "If I can't get his permission, will you . . . ?"

"As soon as may be! But I would like to know what my uncle will say, first."

What her uncle said to Mark was "No!"

"I have given Lord Faverill permission to wed my niece. It is a distinguished match. You are a very fine young man, Camden, but you haven't much to offer, I fancy."

"She dislikes him, and he returns the favor. I have it on very good authority that he has proposed to Sylvia Patchfield."

"Nonsense. When I saw him last, he was loudly declaring his intention of reforming and winning Juliette's hand. His grandfather assures me he will do as he ought."

"I think, sir, you are about to have your first lesson in Jared Camden's character. He never does what he ought, unless it is also what he wants to do."

Mark didn't want to antagonize Juliette's uncle, so he urged his suit no more at that time. *After Jared has made his intentions clear I will offer again,* he thought. He bowed respectfully to Lord Paxton and withdrew.

While Mark was involved in his unsuccessful interview with Lord Paxton, a loud debate was going on upstairs between the earl and his older grandson. The countess was a distressed but silent onlooker.

"It is quite impossible! You've offered for Juliette Berceau, a formal offer to her guardian, formally accepted."

"Which she refused."

"You said you would still try to persuade her."

"I want to marry Sylvia Patchfield. Don't you understand? The ghost told me—"

"Rot! It is my misfortune to have a fool for a grandson! A child playing at Halloween tricks could have created that illusion. Tell him, Regina."

The countess remained silent, not that Jared gave her time to speak. "Tricks! Tricks indeed. You would know all about tricks, wouldn't you? Well, it ain't a trick, I say! Besides, Mark is speaking to Juliette's uncle right now. Think you he will let me marry her, even if her uncle tries to force her? You think I want a bride who loathes me, and for whom I don't care so very much myself, if you must know the truth?"

"Winton." The countess's voice was soft but persuasive. "Winton. Listen to the boy."

"Thank you, NiNi." Jared turned and knelt by his grandmother's chair, taking her hand. "You see how it must be. I've some fences to mend with Mark, but I think I'll manage to keep him on at Hammerswold if I make the effort. But if I marry the woman he loves—"

"I know, dear." Regina stroked Jared's cheek gently. "I could wish you would wait to find another young lady, though, more suited—"

He shook his head. "Thing you don't understand is, I like Sylvia. We'll deal well together. Won't be a bore being married to her. Our old boy knows I must have a wife to my own taste if I am to have any chance of success."

"Winton?" The countess lifted her eyes to the earl who stood frowning at them. "I think he is right. I think if we try to force a match with Juliette we'll never see Mark again. This way, within a twelve-month we could have, not one, but two great-grandchildren!"

The earl stroked his chin. "I expect you are right as usual, NiNi. We must accept matters as they are and hope for the best. But I leave you, sir, to explain the withdrawal of your proposal to Lord Paxton."

"Done!" Jared offered his hand to his grandfather, kissed his grandmother's cheek, and hastened from the room to inform an anxious Sylvia Patchfield of the outcome.

Juliette entered her uncle's room in a desperate frame of mind. "Uncle Ronald, I must talk to you."

"I was expecting you. Most peculiar. That young man pawing you last night, offering for you today, yet you've never spoken a word of him. Of course I sent him away."

"No!" Julie put her fist to her mouth to stifle a scream.

"What is this? Had you some sort of understanding? If so, why did you not mention him before?"

"I . . . he left without saying anything. I thought he didn't care. But he came back for me."

"Ah! Well, he came back too late. I have promised you to Lord Faverill, and his grandfather is as determined as I for the match."

Before she could frame a reply, someone scratched at the door. She opened it to find Jared standing there, looking quite like the cat that ate the cream.

"Come in, Faverill, come in," her uncle boomed cordially.

Jared bowed to him and winked at Juliette. "Lord Paxton, I am in somewhat of an embarrassing position. No time for anything but plain speaking. I offered for your niece thinking she was the one our ancestor wanted me to marry, the bride of ancient prophecy, as it were. But it turns out the ghost appeared to Mark and told him she was his intended bride."

Juliette gasped and clutched her throat. "No!"

Ignoring her, Jared continued, "Then a few minutes ago the shade appeared to me and ordered me to wed another."

Lord Paxton stared. "Do you mean to say you are withdrawing a formal offer of marriage because of a so-called ghost?"

"Not just for that reason, sir. You see, Juliette don't suit me. Always theologizing or quoting Shakespeare or primming her mouth at me. Sets my back up. Doubtless I'd beat her if I wed her. She don't like me by half, neither! At any rate, thing is done. Offered for Miss Patchfield; she did me the honor of accepting. Witnesses, too. Sure you must see I have to cry off. No one knows about me and Juliette, or at least none who will tell! And it ain't like Julie accepted my offer, you know."

"Get out of here!" Juliette's uncle was trembling with fury. "You are a wastrel and a villain. Get out! And you, Missy. You've lost your chance at a brilliant match. You get out, too! I'm quite out of patience with you!"

\*　　　\*　　　\*

In response to her summons, Mark met Juliette in the middle of the maze. Instead of going into his arms, she stood awkwardly, warily, several feet away.

"Mark, I can't marry you."

"Why, Julie? What has happened?"

Juliette unhappily studied the handsome man before her. *He looks so strong. He seems so reliable.* But appearances could be deceiving, she knew. Her heart ached at the thought that he had only offered for her because of the ghost's command. Could she, should she, marry a man who passively awaited orders, offering for her only at the command of another, even if that other was a ghost?

"Jared told my uncle the ghost appeared to you."

Was he going to lose her after all? Panic stirred in Mark. He wanted to take her in her arms and kiss away her worries. But his dear little rationalist would not settle for that. He thrust his hand through his hair, completing the havoc the breeze had wrought.

"Don't look so unhappy, Juliette. I haven't taken leave of my senses. There really is a ghost!"

"I know that now, but . . . oh, Mark! Did he order you to marry me?"

"Actually, told me he was done with the Hammerswolds forever. That was when he thought I was abandoning you."

"Which you were!" She felt like weeping.

"I tried to make myself do the noble thing, Julie. I feared that I'd have Jared's early demise on my conscience if I didn't. But the farther I got from you the more miserable I became."

"Still, you wouldn't have offered for me unless the ghost told you to." A tear trickled down her cheeks. "You would have let me marry Jared."

"I don't blame you for thinking that, but it's not true. Yes, I had left. But the farther I got from you the more I knew I couldn't stay away. I made up my mind to return and do my best to prevent you from marrying Jared. When I saw the ghost limping down the road, I expected he was there to try to talk me out of returning. But to the contrary, he was quite disgusted with me for leaving you to Jared. When I explained my plans to him, he told me to hurry, that you were in danger. I started back immediately."

"Then . . . then you haven't just offered for me because the ghost told you to?" A lightness began to invade Juliette's heart.

"I've offered for you because I love you. If the ghost had told me you were intended for Jared, I would have advised the old gentleman that his luck was out, and he should return from whence he came!"

"Oh, Mark!" Juliette lifted tear-filled eyes to her beloved's worried countenance. "I feel guilty. The ghost told me I should tell you Jared was responsible for his own fate but I—"

"You wanted me to chose you over everything. I had no idea how demanding you were going to be. What a wife I am taking on!" His deep, happy chuckle deprived his words of any sting. This time when he held out his arms, she went into them joyfully.

"Well, it seems I must reconsider your proposal." Julie's uncle contemplatively filled his pipe while she and Mark confronted him in his sitting room.

"I hope that you will, Lord Paxton."

"What provision can you make for her, young man?"

"My means are limited, as I think you know. I own a small estate near Pemberton. I can dismiss my tenant and run it myself. We will never be rich, but our children will have the necessities."

"And this is your wish, Juliette?"

"Yes, uncle, with all my heart. With Mark as my husband a cottage will be better than a palace."

"Hmmmmm. Would you be interested to know that Lord Hammerswold came to me shortly after you left, and made certain I knew that he would be generous with Mark? He can't leave him much land, because of the entail, but he means to do handsomely in the manner of a marriage settlement. And of course, he hopes Mark will stay on as his estate manager. He says you may make your home here at Hammerswold."

Mark looked down at Julie thoughtfully. "I doubt I will do that, sir. There are reasons why I cannot—"

Julie put her hand on his arm. "Perhaps you and Jared can learn to work together. I do not think he relishes the responsibility of Hammerswold. And at any rate, your grandfather is a hale and hearty man who may live for many years yet."

"You would agree to this after what happened in the keep?"

"There was no passion in it. Jared will never trouble me again, I am sure. I know how much you love Hammerswold, and indeed, I feel as if I belong here."

Mark smiled, a slow smile that broadened into a grin. He took her by her waist and lifted her up, whirling her around. When they were both quite breathless, he set her down. "I adore you! Sir, please give your permission, for I feel I really must kiss her!"

Lord Paxton looked at Julie, standing there breathless beside Mark. "I suppose if I said no, you'd run away like your mother before you. Thought you was the practical one, but you've a deal of your mother in you!"

Julie sobered. "I would, sir, if you refused Mark's suit. But I hope not to have to do so. I love you and Aunt Lydia and Adelaide. I do not want to become estranged from you."

He stood and embraced her, saying gruffly, "Nor I from you! I am somewhat ashamed of myself, Juliette, for pressuring you to accept the viscount. The man's a hereandthereian. That young miss he's marrying will do well to get him to stay home long enough to get himself an heir."

Her uncle turned to Mark, rubbing his hands together. "Well, then, sir, shall we speak of settlements?"

"Settlements?" Mark looked puzzled. "It was my understanding Juliette had no fortune."

"You don't think I mean to let my much-loved niece go

into marriage penniless, do you? Run along, Julie, this young man and I have things to discuss."

Julie waited for Mark in the center of the maze. Evening was drawing near, and it was chilly. Last night's rain had drenched everything and left behind crisp weather. The lingering summer had at last been routed by autumn.

The gardeners had not yet reached the maze with their busy brooms to sweep up the branches and leaves that had been blown off in the storm. The sky was gray and looked as if it could dump more rain any second. Yet she needed to be outdoors. She needed to be here.

"My lord Ghost? Are you here, sir?" She looked around, peering behind the topiary animals and the fountain statues. "I want to speak to you. I want to thank you."

There was no answer. *I suppose ghosts don't appear upon command,* she thought. *I do wish I could apologize to him.* Since hearing her mother's voice she had regretted being so rude to the Ghost of Hammerswold.

Juliette gave up the search and sat on the bench, hugging her happiness to her. Oh, fortunate female! She would make her home here, with Mark! She tilted her head back to look up at the magnificent building looming over her, and saw the countess, peering down at her from the window of her room. She lifted her hand hesitantly. The countess eagerly waved back. By her side the earl, too, waved. No, it wasn't the earl. The caped figure was too short for the earl. It must be Uncle Ramsey. But he was leaning on a cane. He looked so gray. He must be ill. He must be . . .

Julie raised her hand again, and was satisfied to see that her salute was returned just before the figure shimmered and disappeared.

# Epilogue

"Here we are at last!" Mark leaned forward, his eyes seeking the fine Palladian mansion eagerly as they rounded the curving drive. "You've been quite good on this trip, little man!" He smiled down at the two-month-old babe in his arms.

"Yes, and on such a long journey as it is from Hammerswold to Faverill Springs," Juliette laughed. Pierre Winton Ramsey Camden had been born in April. In spite of repeated urging from the earl and countess, Mark had declined to risk his wife and son to the rigors of the road until the warm, sunny days of June were upon them.

Her husband made no return to her teasing sally. The smile had faded from his face. He handed the baby to her and opened the carriage before it quite came to a halt.

Before she could frame a question, Juliette caught a glimpse of the reason for her husband's odd behavior. She began to tremble. The windows and doors of the house were being draped in black by an army of servants. Someone had died. She started to interrogate the footman who ran out to assist them from the carriage, but thought better of it. Mark would not want to learn of his grandfather or grandmother's death from a third footman.

They hurried into the marble entryway to find the indoor servants draping the hall in black crepe. Harley, the longtime Faverill Springs butler, approached them in dignified haste. "Sir, if you would step into the King James drawing room?"

Juliette gave her child into the keeping of the nurse who

had arrived minutes after them in the second carriage, and followed Mark, icy fingers of dread in her heart. Was it the earl? Oh, please let it not be NiNi, who had hung on for two years, determined to live to see her first great-grand-child. That this long-awaited baby might not be in time for her! Juliette's heart broke at the thought of it.

"Sir, Lord Hammerswold asked me to make all plain to you right away. Lady Hammerswold is taking it very well; he thought if I told you and gave you time to compose yourself before you went up, it would make matters easier."

"Speak without further delay or roundaboutation," Mark commanded, though he and Juliette were already feeling re-lief. Whomever the mourning was for, it wasn't the earl or countess.

"It's Master Jared, sir. Lord Faverill, that is."

Juliette put her hands to her mouth.

"I see." Mark remained calm. "What happened, then?"

"Sir, I . . ." The butler paused, coughed, seemed to strug-gle for self-command. Juliette had the mad idea that he was intensely embarrassed.

Finally he straightened himself, assumed his most digni-fied and remote pose, and intoned, "We received word yes-terday evening that Lord Faverill was enjoying a convivial evening with his friends when a wager was made about how many oysters he could eat within five minutes. They were very fresh, it seemed. In fact, the servants were shuck-ing them at table for him, and he, ah, got ahead of them, as it were."

There was a long silence.

"Are you telling me my cousin tried to swallow an un-shelled oyster?"

"Yes, sir."

Mark's expression was blank. Juliette held her breath, dreading the feelings of guilt this untimely demise might engender in her husband, in spite of the Ghost of Hammers-wold's reassurance that Jared would be responsible for his own fate.

"Very good, Harley. Mrs. Camden and I will sit here for a few moments before joining my grandparents."

After he had left, Juliette spoke hesitantly, not liking her husband's frozen attitude. "Mark, you mustn't blame yourself. You had nothing to do with this. *I* had nothing to do with this! Indeed, I think Sylvia would have not have left him for her groom if he had stayed at home. That he has no heir is due entirely to his own negligence."

"I know." Still Mark sat unmoving, an unreadable stillness about him.

Juliette looked at her husband with tender pity. He had never sought it, had in truth never wanted it, but in all likelihood he would one day be the Earl of Hammerswold. Uncle Ramsey had gone to his eternal reward shortly after she and Mark were married. Mark's grandfather, while remarkably healthy, had celebrated his eightieth birthday almost a year ago. In the normal order of things he would depart this earth before Mark.

She said nothing of this inescapable fact to her husband, to whom the realization could only bring pain.

Suddenly Mark startled her with an oath such as she had never before heard from her husband's lips.

"Mark!"

"I am sorry, Julie, but damn him and his disgusting gluttony, his drunken excesses—"

Juliette slid next to her husband and put her arms around him. "Try to remember the good things about him, not the bad." She breathed a silent prayer of thanks that Jared and Mark had been on reasonably good terms since Jared's handsome apology to herself and to Mark two years ago, followed by his urgent request that Mark plan to stay on at Hammerswold permanently. Jared had not wanted to shoulder the responsibilities of his future inheritance.

"I will. But Lord, we'll never hear the end of it. Imagine dying from such a cause. No one but Jared could manage it."

Mark gave a watery chuckle. "I suppose you could say that he died as he lived, enjoying life to the fullest."

Juliette put her forehead to her husband's, smiling through tears of her own. "Yes, it was a very Jared thing to do." She lay her hand along his clenched jaw and stroked it comfortingly. Gradually she felt the tension leave his frame, and he hugged her to him briefly before standing.

"Come," he said. "Let us go upstairs and introduce grandfather and NiNi to the heir to Hammerswold."